A Legacy of Spies

A Legacy of Spies

JOHN LE CARRÉ

VIKING

VIKING

an imprint of Penguin Canada, a division of Penguin Random House Canada Limited

Canada • USA • UK • Ireland • Australia • New Zealand • India • South Africa • China

Published in Viking hardcover by Penguin Canada, 2017
Simultaneously published in the United States by Viking, an imprint of Penguin Random House LLC

LIBRARY AND ARCHIVES CANADA CATALOGUING IN PUBLICATION

Le Carré, John, 1931-, author
A legacy of spies / John le Carré.

Issued in print and electronic formats.
ISBN 978-0-7352-3452-9 (hardcover).—ISBN 978-0-7352-3453-6 (electronic)

I. Title.

PR6062.E42L44 2017   823'.914   C2017-902391-8
                                              C2017-902392-6

Cover design: Paul Buckley
Cover illustration: Matthew Taylor

Printed and bound in the United States of America

10 9 8 7 6 5 4 3 2 1

Every man is born as many men
and dies as a single one.

Heidegger (attrib.)

I

What follows is a truthful account, as best I am able to provide it, of my role in the British deception operation, codenamed Windfall, that was mounted against the East German Intelligence Service (Stasi) in the late nineteen fifties and early sixties, and resulted in the death of the best British secret agent I ever worked with, and of the innocent woman for whom he gave his life.

A professional intelligence officer is no more immune to human feelings than the rest of mankind. What matters to him is the extent to which he is able to suppress them, whether in real time or, in my case, fifty years on. Until a couple of months ago, lying in bed at night in the remote farmstead in Brittany that is my home, listening to the honk of cattle and the bickering of hens, I resolutely fought off the accusing voices that from time to time attempted to disrupt my sleep. I was too young, I protested, I was too innocent, too naive, too junior. If you're looking for scalps, I told them, go to those grand masters of deception, George Smiley and his master, Control. It was their refined cunning, I insisted, their devious, scholarly intellects, not mine, that delivered the triumph and the anguish that was Windfall. It is only now, having been held to account by the Service to which I devoted the best years of my life, that I am driven in age and bewilderment to set down, at whatever cost, the light and dark sides of my involvement in the affair.

How I came to be recruited to the Secret Intelligence Service in the first place – the 'Circus' as we Young Turks called it in those supposedly halcyon days when we were quartered, not in a grotesque fortress beside the River Thames, but in a fustian Victorian pile of red brick, built on the curve of Cambridge Circus – remains as much of a mystery to me as do the circumstances of my birth; and the more so since the two events are inseparable.

My father, whose acquaintance I barely remember, was according to my mother the wastrel son of a wealthy Anglo-French family from the English midlands, a man of rash appetites, fast-diminishing inheritance and a redeeming love of France. In the summer of 1930, he was taking the waters in the spa town of Saint-Malo on Brittany's north coast, frequenting the casinos and *maisons closes* and generally cutting a dash. My mother, sole offspring of a long line of Breton farmers, at that time aged twenty, also happened to be in town, performing the duties of a bridesmaid at the wedding of the daughter of a wealthy cattle auctioneer. Or so she claimed. However, she is a single source, not above a little decoration when the facts were against her, and it would not at all surprise me if she came into town for less upright purposes.

After the ceremony, so her story goes, she and a fellow bridesmaid, the better for a glass or two of champagne, played truant from the reception and, still in their finery, took an evening stroll along the crowded promenade, where my father was also strolling with intent. My mother was pretty and flighty, her friend less so. A whirlwind romance followed. My mother was understandably coy about the pace of it. A second wedding was hastily arranged. I was the product. My father, it appears, was not naturally connubial, and even in the early years of marriage contrived to be more absent than present.

But now the story takes an heroic turn. War, as we know,

changes everything, and in a trice it had changed my father. Scarcely had it been declared than he was hammering on the doors of the British War Office, volunteering his services to whoever would have him. His mission, according to my mother, was to save France single-handed. If it was also to escape the ties of family, that is a heresy I was never permitted to utter in my mother's presence. The British had a newly formed Special Operations Executive, famously tasked by Winston Churchill himself with 'setting Europe ablaze'. The coastal towns of south-west Brittany were a hotbed of German submarine activity and our local town of Lorient, a former French naval base, the hottest bed of all. Five times parachuted into the Breton flatlands, my father allied himself with whatever Resistance groups he could find, caused his share of mayhem and died a gruesome death in Rennes prison at the hands of the Gestapo, leaving behind him an example of selfless dedication impossible for any son to match. His other legacy was a misplaced faith in the British public school system, which notwithstanding his dismal performance at his own British public school condemned me to the same fate.

The earliest years of my life had been passed in paradise. My mother cooked and prattled, my grandfather was severe but kindly, the farm prospered. At home we spoke Breton. At the Catholic primary school in our village, a beautiful young nun who had spent six months in Huddersfield as an au pair taught me the rudiments of the English language and, by national decree, French. In the school holidays I ran barefoot in the fields and cliffs around our farmstead, harvested buckwheat for my mother's crêpes, tended an old sow called Fadette and played wild games with the children of the village.

The future meant nothing to me until it struck.

At Dover, a plump lady called Murphy, cousin to my late father, detached me from my mother's hand and took me to her house in Ealing. I was eight years old. Through the train window I saw my first barrage balloons. Over supper, Mr Murphy said it would all be over in months and Mrs Murphy said it wouldn't, both of them speaking slowly and repeating themselves for my benefit. The next day Mrs Murphy took me to Selfridges and bought me a school uniform, taking care to keep the receipts. The day after that, she stood on the platform at Paddington station, and wept while I waved goodbye to her with my new school cap.

The Anglicization wished on me by my father needs little elaboration. There was a war on. Schools must put up with what they got. I was no longer Pierre but Peter. My poor English was ridiculed by my comrades, my Breton-accented French by my beleaguered teachers. Our little village of Les Deux Eglises, I was informed almost casually, had been overrun by Germans. My mother's letters arrived, if at all, in brown envelopes with British stamps and London postmarks. It was only years later that I was able to imagine through whose brave hands they must have passed. Holidays were a blur of boys' camps and proxy parents. Redbrick preparatory schools turned into granite-grey public schools, but the curriculum stayed the same: the same margarine, the same homilies on patriotism and Empire, the same random violence, careless cruelty and unappeased, unaddressed sexual desire. One spring evening in 1944, shortly before the D-Day landings, the headmaster called me to his study and told me that my father had died a soldier's death, and that I should be proud of him. For security reasons, no further explanation was available.

I was sixteen when, at the end of a particularly tedious summer term, I returned to peacetime Brittany a half-grown English misfit. My grandfather had died. A new companion named Monsieur Emile was sharing my mother's bed. I did not care for Monsieur Emile. One half of Fadette had been given to the

Germans, the other to the Resistance. In flight from the contradictions of my childhood and fuelled by a sense of filial obligation, I stowed away on a train to Marseilles and, adding a year to my age, attempted to enlist in the French Foreign Legion. My quixotic venture came to a summary end when the Legion, making a rare concession to my mother's entreaties on the grounds that I was not foreign but French, released me back into captivity, this time to the London suburb of Shoreditch, where my father's unlikely stepbrother Markus ran a trading company importing precious furs and carpets from the Soviet Union – except he always called it Russia – and had offered to teach me the trade.

Uncle Markus remains another unsolved mystery in my life. I do not know to this day whether his offer of employment was in some way inspired by my later masters. When I asked him how my father had died, he shook his head in disapproval – not of my father, but of the crassness of my question. Sometimes I wonder whether it is possible to be born secret, in the way people are born rich, or tall, or musical. Markus was not mean, or tight, or unkind. He was just secret. He was middle-European, his name was Collins. I never learned what it was before that. He spoke accented English very fast, but I never learned what his mother tongue was. He called me Pierre. He had a lady friend named Dolly who ran a hat shop in Wapping and collected him from the door of the warehouse on Friday afternoons. But I never knew where they went for their weekends, whether they were married to each other, or to other people. Dolly had a Bernie in her life, but I never knew whether Bernie was her husband, her son or her brother, because Dolly was born secret too.

And I don't know even in retrospect whether the Collins Trans-Siberian Fur & Fine Carpet Company was a bona fide trading house, or a cover company set up for the purpose of intelligence gathering. Later, when I tried to find out, I met a blank wall.

I knew that every time Uncle Markus was preparing to visit a trade fair, whether in Kiev, Perm or Irkutsk, he trembled a lot; and that when he came back, he drank a lot. And that in the days leading up to a trade fair, a well-spoken Englishman called Jack would swing by, charm the secretaries, pop his head round the door to the sorting room and call 'hullo, Peter, all well with you?' – never Pierre – then take Markus out to a good lunch somewhere. And after lunch, Markus would come back to his office and lock the door.

Jack claimed to be a broker in fine sable, but I know now that what he really dealt in was intelligence, because when Markus announced that his doctor wouldn't allow him to do fairs any more, Jack suggested I come to lunch with him instead, and took me to the Travellers Club in Pall Mall, and asked me whether I would have preferred life in the Legion, and if I was serious about any of my girlfriends, and why I had fled my public school considering I'd been captain of boxing, and whether I had ever thought of doing something useful for my country, by which he meant England, because if I felt I'd missed out on the war on account of my age, this was my chance to catch up. He mentioned my father once only, over lunch, in terms so casual that I might have supposed the topic could equally well have slipped his memory altogether:

'Oh, and concerning your much revered late papa. Strictly off the record, and I never said this. All right by you?'

'Yes.'

'He was a very brave chap indeed, and did a bloody good job for his country. Both his countries. Enough said?'

'If you say so.'

'So here's to him.'

Here's to him, I agreed, and we drank a silent toast.

At an elegant country house in Hampshire, Jack and his colleague Sandy, and an efficient girl called Emily, whom I immediately fell in love with, gave me the short course in clearing a dead letter box in mid-town Kiev – actually a chunk of loose masonry in the wall of an old tobacco kiosk – of which they had a replica set up in the orangery. And how to read the safety signal that would tell me it was all right to clear it – in this case a piece of tattered green ribbon tied to a railing. And how afterwards to indicate that I had cleared the letter box, by tossing an empty Russian cigarette packet into a litter bin next to a bus shelter.

'And maybe, Peter, when you apply for your Russian visa, better to use your French passport rather than your Brit version,' he suggested breezily, and reminded me that Uncle Markus had an affiliate company in Paris. 'And Emily's off-limits, by the way,' he added, in case I was thinking otherwise, which I was.

★

And that was my first run, my first ever assignment for what I later came to know as the Circus, and my first vision of myself as a secret warrior in my dead father's image. I can no longer enumerate the other runs I made over the next couple of years, a good half-dozen at least, to Leningrad, Gdansk and Sofia, then to Leipzig and Dresden, and all of them, so far as I ever knew, uneventful, if you took away the business of gearing yourself up, then gearing yourself down again afterwards.

Over long weekends in another country house with another beautiful garden, I added other tricks to my repertoire, such as counter-surveillance and brushing up against strangers in a crowd to make a furtive hand-over. Somewhere in the middle of these antics, in a coy ceremony conducted in a safe flat in South Audley Street, I was allowed to take possession of my father's gallantry medals, one French, one English, and the citations that explained them. Why the delay? I might have asked. But by then I had learned not to.

7

It was not until I started visiting East Germany that tubby, bespectacled, permanently worried George Smiley wandered into my life one Sunday afternoon in West Sussex, where I was being debriefed, not by Jack any more but by a rugged fellow called Jim, of Czech extraction and around my age, whose surname, when he was finally allowed to have one, turned out to be Prideaux. I mention him because later he too played a substantial part in my career.

Smiley didn't say much at my debriefing, just sat and listened and occasionally peered owlishly at me through his thick-rimmed spectacles. But when it was over he suggested we take a turn in the garden, which seemed endless and had a park attached to it. We talked, we sat on a bench, strolled, sat again, kept talking. My dear mother – was she alive and well? She's fine, thank you, George. A bit dotty, but fine. Then my father – had I kept his medals? I said my mother polished them every Sunday, which was true. I didn't mention that she sometimes hung them on me and wept. But, unlike Jack, he never asked me about my girls. He must have thought there was safety in numbers.

And when I recall that conversation now, I can't help thinking that, consciously or not, he was offering himself as the father figure he later became. But perhaps the feeling was in me, and not in him. The fact remains that, when he finally popped the question, I had a feeling of coming home, even though my home was across the Channel in Brittany.

'We were wondering, you see,' he said in a faraway voice, 'whether you'd ever considered signing up with us on a more regular basis? People who have worked on the outside for us don't always fit well on the inside. But in your case, we think you might. We don't pay a lot, and careers tend to be interrupted. But we do feel it's an important job, as long as one cares about the end, and not too much about the means.'

2

My farmstead at Les Deux Eglises consists of one straight-backed nineteenth-century granite *manoir* of no distinction, one tumble-down barn with a stone cross on its gable, remnants of fortifications from forgotten wars, an ancient stone well, now unused but formerly requisitioned by Resistance fighters to hide their weapons from the Nazi occupier, an equally ancient out-door baking oven, a cider press, obsolete, and fifty hectares of indifferent pasture descending to cliff land and the sea's edge. The place has been in the family's possession for four generations. I am the fifth. It is neither a noble nor a profitable acquisition. To my right, as I look out of my living-room window, I have the knobbly spire of a nineteenth-century church; and to my left, a white stand-alone chapel, thatched. Between them, they have endowed the village with its name. In Les Deux Eglises, as in all of Brittany, we are Catholic or we are nothing. I am nothing.

To reach our farmstead from the town of Lorient, you first drive for half an hour or so along the southern coast road, which in winter is lined with skinny poplar trees, passing on your way west chunks of Hitler's Atlantic Wall which, being unremovable, are fast acquiring the status of a latter-day Stonehenge. After thirty kilometres or so, you start to watch out for a pizza restaurant grandly named Odyssée on your left and soon after it on your right a reeking junkyard where the misnomered Honoré, a drunken vagabond whom my mother always cautioned me to avoid, and known locally as the poison dwarf, peddles bric-à-brac, old car tyres and manure. On reaching a battered sign saying *Delassus*, this being my mother's family name, you turn up a pitted track, braking hard as you go over the potholes or, if you are Monsieur Denis the postman, weaving deftly between them at full speed: which was what he was doing this sunny morning in early autumn, to the indignation of the chickens in the courtyard and the sublime indifference of Amoureuse, my beloved Irish setter, who was far too occupied grooming her latest litter to give her attention to mere human affairs.

As for me, from the moment Monsieur Denis – alias le Général, thanks to his great height and supposed resemblance to President de Gaulle – had unwound himself from his yellow van and started towards the front steps, I knew at one glance that the letter he was grasping in his spindly hand was from the Circus.

★

I wasn't alarmed at first, just quietly amused. Some things about a British secret service never change. One of them is an obsessive anxiety about what sort of stationery to use for its overt correspondence. Not too official or formal looking: that would be bad for cover. The envelope not see-through, so preferably lined. Stark white is too visible: go for a tint, just nothing amorous. A dull blue, a hint of grey, both are acceptable. This one was pale grey.

Next question: do we type the address, do we handwrite it? For answer, consider as always the needs of the man in the field, in this case, me: Peter Guillam, ex-member, out to grass and grateful for it. Long-time resident in rural France. Attends no veterans' reunions. No listed significant others. Draws full pension and therefore torturable. Conclusion: in a remote Breton hamlet where foreigners are a rarity, a typed, semi-formal-looking grey envelope with a British stamp could raise local eyebrows, so go for handwritten. Now for the hard bit. The Office, or whatever the Circus calls itself these days, can't resist a security classification, even if it's only *Private*. Maybe add a *Personal* for extra force? *Private & Personal, addressee only*? Too heavy. Stick to *Private*. Or better, as in this case, *Personnel*.

1 Artillery Buildings
London, SE14

My dear Guillam,

We haven't met, but allow me to introduce myself. I am business affairs manager at your old firm, with responsibility for both current and historical cases. A matter in which you appear to have played a significant role some years back has unexpectedly raised its head, and I have no option but to ask you to make yourself available in London as soon as possible to assist us in preparing a response.

I am authorized to offer you reimbursement for your travel arrangements (economy class) and a London-weighted *per diem* of £130 for as long as your presence is required.

Since we appear to have no telephone number for you, kindly feel free to call Tania at the number above and reverse the charges, or if you have email, at the email address below. Without wishing to inconvenience you, I have to stress that the matter is of some urgency. Allow me in closing to draw your attention to Paragraph 14 of your termination agreement.

Yours sincerely,
A. Butterfield
(LA to CS)

For 'LA to CS' read *Legal Adviser to Chief of Service*. For 'Paragraph 14' read *lifelong duty to attend, should Circus needs dictate*. And for 'allow me to remind you' read *just remember who pays your pension*. And I don't have email. And why doesn't he date his letter: security?

Catherine is down in the orchard with her nine-year-old daughter Isabelle, playing with a pair of vicious young goats we recently had wished on us. She is a slight woman with a broad Breton face and slow brown eyes that measure you without expression. If she stretches out her arms, the goats leap into them and little Isabelle, who pleases herself in her own ways, puts her hands together and spins round on her heel in private delight. But Catherine, muscular though she is, must be careful to catch her goats one at a time, because if they're allowed to jump at her together they can knock her flat. Isabelle ignores me. Eye contact bothers her.

In the field behind them, deaf Yves the occasional labourer is bent double cutting cabbages. With his right hand he slices the stems, with his left he tosses them into a cart, but the angle of his arched back never changes. He is watched by an old grey horse called Artemis, another of Catherine's foundlings. A couple of years back we took in a stray ostrich who had broken loose from a neighbouring farm. When Catherine alerted the farmer, he said keep him, he's too old. The ostrich expired gracefully and we gave him a state funeral.

'You wish something, Pierre?' Catherine demands.

'Got to go away for a few days, I'm afraid,' I reply.

'To Paris?' Catherine does not approve of me going to Paris.

'To London,' I reply. And because even in retirement I need a cover story: 'Someone's died.'

'Someone you love?'

'Not any more,' I reply, with a firmness that takes me by surprise.

'Then it is not important. You leave tonight?'

'Tomorrow. I'll take the early flight from Rennes.'

Time was, the Circus had only to whistle and I would race to Rennes for a plane. Not today.

*

You have to have grown to spy's estate in the old Circus to understand the aversion that came over me as, at four o'clock the following afternoon, I paid off my cab and started up the concrete catwalk to the Service's shockingly ostentatious new headquarters. You had to be me in the prime of my spying life, returning dog-weary from some godforsaken outpost of empire – the Soviet empire most likely, or some member of it. You've come straight from London airport by bus, then by tube to Cambridge Circus. The Production team is waiting to debrief you. You climb five scruffy steps to the doorway of the Victorian eyesore that we variously call HO, the Office or just the Circus. And you're home.

Forget the fights you've been having with Production or Requirements or Admin. They're just family quarrels between field and base. The janitor in his box wishes you good morning with a knowing 'welcome back, Mr Guillam' and asks you whether you'd like to check your suitcase. And you say thanks Mac, or Bill, or whoever's on duty that day, and never mind showing him your pass. You're smiling and you're not sure why. In front of you stand the three cranky old lifts that you've hated since the day you joined – except that two of them are stuck upstairs, and the third is Control's own, so don't even think about it. And anyway you'd rather lose yourself in the labyrinth of corridors and dead ends that is the physical embodiment of the world you've chosen to live in, with its worm-eaten wooden staircases, chipped fire extinguishers, fish-eye mirrors and the stinks of stale fag smoke, Nescafé and deodorant.

And now this monstrosity. This Welcome to Spyland Beside the Thames.

Under the scrutiny of dour men and women in tracksuits, I present myself at the armoured-glass welcome desk and watch my British passport being snapped up by a sliding metal tray. The face behind the glass is a woman's. The absurd emphases and electronic voice are Essex Man's:

'Kindly place *all* keys, mobile phones, cash, *wrist* watches, writing instruments and any *other* metal objects you may have about you *in* the box on the table *to* your left, retain the *white* tag identifying your box, then duly proceed *shoes* in hand *through* the door marked Visitors.'

My passport returns. Duly proceeding, I am frisked with a ping-pong bat by a merry girl of about fourteen, then radiated in an upended glass coffin. Having returned the shoes to my feet and tied the laces – somehow a far more humiliating procedure than taking them off – I am escorted to an unmarked lift by the merry girl, who asks me if I've had a nice day. I haven't. Or a nice night either, if she wants to know, which she doesn't. Thanks to A. Butterfield's letter I had slept worse than I have slept in a decade, but I can't tell her that either. I'm a field animal, or was. My natural habitat was spying's open spaces. What I'm discovering in my so-called mature years is that a Dear John letter coming out of the blue from the Circus in its new incarnation demanding my immediate presence in London sets me off on a night-time journey of the soul.

We have reached what feels like the top floor, but nothing says so. In the world I once inhabited, its biggest secrets were always on the top floor. My youthful escort has a bunch of ribbons round her neck with electronic tabs on them. She opens an unmarked door, I enter, she closes it on me. I try the handle. It doesn't budge. I've been locked up a few times in my life, but always by the opposition. There are no windows, just childish paintings of flowers and houses. The work of A. Butterfield's offspring? Or the graffiti of former inmates?

And where has all the noise gone? The silence gets worse the longer I listen. No jolly chatter of typewriters, no unanswered telephones ringing off the hook, no clapped-out file trolley rattling its way like a milkman's float over the bare-board corridors, no furious male roar of *stop that bloody whistling!* Somewhere along the road between Cambridge Circus and the Embankment, something has died, and it isn't just the squeak of trolleys.

I perch my backside on a steel and leather chair. I thumb a grimy copy of *Private Eye* and wonder which of us has lost our sense of humour. I get up, try the door again and sit down on a different chair. By now I have decided that A. Butterfield is making an in-depth study of my body language. Well, if he is, good luck to him, because by the time the door flies open and a short-haired, agile woman of forty-odd wearing a business suit sweeps in and says in a class-free sanitized accent, 'Oh. Hi, Peter, great. I'm Laura, want to come in now?' I must have relived in quick order every misfire and disaster I'd been involved in over a lifetime of licensed skulduggery.

We troop across an empty corridor and enter a white, hygienic office with sealed windows. A fresh-faced, bespectacled, English public schoolboy of indefinable age in shirt and braces bounces out from behind a table and seizes my hand.

'*Peter!* Gosh! You look positively *jaunty!* And half your age! You travelled well? Coffee? Tea? *Honestly* not? Really, really good of you to come. A *huge* help. You've met Laura? Of course you have. *So* sorry to have kept you waiting in there. A call from on high. All well now. Have a pew.'

All this to confiding squeezes of the eyes for extra intimacy as he guides me to an upright naughty chair with arms for a long stay. Then sits himself back the other side of the table, which is stacked with old-looking Circus files flagged in the colours of all nations. Then sets his shirt-sleeved elbows between them where I can't see, and links his hands in a cat's cradle under his chin.

'I'm *Bunny*, by the by,' he announces. 'Bloody silly name, but it's followed me around since infancy and I can't get rid of it. Probably the reason I ended up in *this* place, come to think of it. You can't very well strut your stuff in the High Court of Justice with everyone running after you yelling "Bunny, Bunny", can you?'

Is this his usual patter? Is this how your average middle-aged Secret Service lawyer speaks these days? Now racy, now one foot in the past? My ear for contemporary English is shaky, but judging by Laura's expression as she takes her place next to him, yes, it is. Seated, she is feral, ready to pounce. Signet ring on middle finger of right hand. Her daddy's? Or a coded signal about sexual preference? I'd been out of England too long.

Meaningless small talk, led by Bunny. His children adore Brittany, both are girls. Laura has been to Normandy, but not Brittany. She doesn't say who with.

'But you're Brittany born, Peter!' Bunny protests suddenly, out of nowhere. 'We should be calling you Pierre!'

Peter's fine, I say.

'So what we *have*, Peter, bluntly, is a bit of a serious *legal porridge* to sort out,' Bunny resumes at a slower, louder pace, having spotted my new hearing aids peeking out of my white locks. 'Not a *crisis* yet, but active, and I'm afraid rather *volatile*. And we very much need your help.'

To which I reply that I'm only too happy to oblige in any way I can, Bunny, and it's nice to think one can still be of use after all these years.

'Obviously I'm here to protect the *Service*. That's my job,' Bunny goes on, as if I haven't spoken. 'And *you're* here as a private individual, an ex-member admittedly, long and happily retired, I am sure, but what I *can't* guarantee is that *your* interests and *our* interests are going to coincide at every turn.' Eyes to slits. Rictal grin. 'So what I'm saying to you *is*, Peter: for all that we respect you enormously for all the splendid things you have done for the Office in days of yore, this *is* the *Office*. And you are *you*, and *I* am a lethal lawyer. How's Catherine?'

'Fine, thank you. Why do you ask?'

Because I haven't listed her. To put the wind up me. To tell me the gloves are off. And what big eyes the Service has.

'We wondered whether she should be added to the rather long list of your significant others,' Bunny explains. 'Service regulations and so forth.'

'Catherine is my tenant. She's the daughter and granddaughter of previous tenants. I choose to live on the premises, and insofar as it's your business, I've never slept with her and I don't intend to. Does that cover it?'

'Admirably, thank you.'

My first lie, ably told. Now go for the swift deflection: 'Sounds to me as if I need a lawyer of my own,' I suggest.

'Premature, and you can't afford one. Not at today's prices. We have you down as married, then unmarried. Are both correct?'

'They are.'

'All within the one calendar year. I'm impressed.'

'Thank you.'

Are we joking? Or provoking? I'm suspecting the second.

'A youthful folly?' Bunny suggests, in the same courteous tone of enquiry.

'A misunderstanding,' I reply. 'Any more questions?'

But Bunny does not give way easily, and wishes me to know it. 'I mean, so who by – the child? Whose was it? The father?' – still in the same glossy voice.

I affect to ponder. 'Do you know, I don't think I ever thought to ask her,' I reply. And while he's still meditating on this: 'Since we're talking about who does what to whom, maybe you'll tell me what Laura's doing here,' I suggest.

'Laura is *History*,' Bunny replies sonorously.

History as an expressionless woman with short hair, brown eyes and no make-up. And nobody smiling any more, except me.

'So what's on the charge sheet, Bunny?' I ask cheerfully, now that we're getting to close quarters. 'Setting fire to the Queen's dockyards?'

'Oh come, *charge sheet* is going it a bit, Peter!' Bunny protests, just as cheerfully. 'Things to resolve, that's all. Let me ask you just *one* question ahead of the rest of the field. May I?' – squeeze of the eyes. 'Operation *Windfall*. How was it mounted, who drove it, where did it go so wrong, and what was your part in it?'

Does an easing of the soul take place when you realize your worst expectations have been fulfilled? Not in my case.

'Windfall, Bunny, did you say?'

'Windfall' – louder, in case he hasn't reached my deaf aids.

Keep it slow. Remember you're of an age. Memory not your strong point these days. Take your time.

'Now Windfall was *what* exactly, Bunny? Give me a pointer. What sort of date are we looking at?'

'Early sixties, broadly. Today.'

'An operation, you say?'

'Covert. Called Windfall.'

'Against what target?'

Laura, coming in from the blind side: 'Soviet & Satellite. Directed against East German Intelligence. Otherwise known as the *Stasi*' – bellowing for my benefit.

Stasi? Stasi? Give me a moment. Ah yes, the Stasi.

'With what aim, Laura?' I ask, having got it all together.

'Mount a deception, mislead the enemy, protect a vital source.

18

Penetrate Moscow Centre with the purpose of identifying the perceived traitor or traitors inside Circus ranks.' And changing gear to downright plaintive: 'Only we have absolutely *zilch* files on it any more. Just a bunch of cross-references to files that have vanished into thin air. Like missing, believed stolen.'

'Windfall, Windfall,' I repeat, shaking my head and smiling the way old men do, even if they're not quite as old as other people may think they are. 'Sorry, Laura. Just doesn't ring a bell, I'm afraid.'

'Not even a distant chime?' – Bunny.

'Not a one, alas. Total blank' – fighting off images of my youthful self in the garb of a pizza-delivery boy, bent over the handlebars of my learner's motorbike as I rush a special order of late-night files from Circus headquarters to Somewhere in London.

'And just in case I didn't mention it, or you didn't hear it,' Bunny is saying, in his blandest voice. 'It's our understanding that Operation Windfall involved your friend and colleague Alec Leamas, who you may *just* remember got himself shot dead at the Berlin Wall while hastening to the assistance of his girlfriend Elizabeth Gold, who'd been shot dead at the Berlin Wall already. But perhaps you've forgotten that too?'

'Of course I bloody haven't,' I snap. And only then, by way of explanation: 'You were asking me about Windfall, not about Alec. And the answer's no. I don't remember it. Never heard of it. Sorry.'

★

In any interrogation, denial is the tipping point. Never mind the courtesies that went before. From the moment of denial, things are never going to be the same. At the secret-policeman level, denial is likely to provoke instant reprisal, not least because the average secret policeman is more stupid than his subject. The sophisticated interrogator, on the other hand, finding the door slammed in his face, does not immediately try to kick it in. He prefers to regroup and advance on his target from a different angle. And to judge by Bunny's contented smile, that's what he is sizing up to do now.

'So, Peter.' His voice for the hard of hearing, despite my assurances: 'Setting the issue of Operation Windfall aside for a moment, would you mind awfully if Laura and I asked you a few *background questions* regarding the more general issue?'

'Which is what?'

'Individual accountability. The old problem of where *obedience* to superior orders *stops*, and responsibility for one's individual actions begins. Follow me?'

'Barely.'

'You're in the field. Head Office has given you the green light, but not everything goes to plan. Innocent blood is shed. You, or a colleague close to you, are perceived to have exceeded orders. Have you ever thought of a situation like that?'

'No.'

Either he's forgotten I can't hear, or he's decided that I can.

'And you can't think, you personally, purely in the abstract, of how such a stressful situation might arise? Looking back over the many tight corners you must have found yourself in during a long operational career?'

'No. I can't. Sorry about that.'

'Not one single moment where you felt you'd exceeded Head Office orders, started something you couldn't stop? Put your own feelings, needs – *appetites* even – above the call of duty, perhaps? With dire consequences that you might not have intended or foreseen?'

'Well, that would get me a reprimand from Head Office,

wouldn't it? Or a recall to London. Or in a really severe case, the door,' I suggest, giving him my disciplinary frown.

'Try going a bit wider than that, Peter. I'm suggesting there could be aggrieved third parties out there. Ordinary people from the outside world who – in consequence of something you've done – in error, in the heat of the moment or when the flesh is a bit weak, let's say – suffered collateral damage. People who might decide, *years later*, maybe a generation later, that they've got a pretty juicy legal case against this Service. Either by way of damages or, if that doesn't stick, a private prosecution for manslaughter or worse. Against the Service at large, or' – eyebrows shooting up in fake surprise – 'a named former member of it. You've never considered *that* as a possibility?' – sounding less like a lawyer than a doctor softening you up for really bad news.

Give it time. Scratch the old head. No good.

'Too busy making trouble for the opposition, I suppose' – with a veteran's weary smile. 'Enemy out in front of you, Head Office on your tail, not a great deal of time for philosophizing.'

'Their *easiest* course being to kick off with a *parliamentary procedure*, and pave the way for *legal proceedings* by way of a *letter before action*, but not go the whole hog.'

Still thinking, I'm afraid, Bunny.

'Then of course once *legal proceedings* are initiated, any *parliamentary inquiry* would step aside. Leaving the courts a free hand.' He waits, in vain, comes in harder:

'And Windfall still no bells whatever? A covert operation spread over two years in which you played a considerable – some would say heroic – role? And it doesn't ring a single bell?'

And Laura asking me the same question with her nun's unblinking brown eyes, while I affect yet again to delve in my old man's memory and – drat it – come up with absolutely nothing, but that's anno Domini for you, I suppose – ruefully shaking my white head in frustration.

'Wasn't some sort of training exercise, was it?' I ask gamely.

'Laura just told you what it was,' Bunny retorts, and I do an 'ah, yes, of course she did,' and try to look embarrassed.

★

We have put Windfall aside, and are back instead to considering the spectre of an ordinary person from the outside world, first hounding a named former member of the Service through Parliament, then having a second bite of them in the law courts. But we haven't yet said *whose* name, or *which* former member, we might be talking about. I say *we* because, if you've ever done a stint of interrogating and find yourself in the hot seat, there's a complicity that puts you and your inquisitors together on one side of the table, and the issues to be thrashed out on the other.

'I mean, just take your own personal file, what's left of it, Peter,' Laura complains. 'It's not that it's just been weeded. It's been filleted. All right, it contained sensitive annexes deemed too secret for the General Archive. Nobody can complain about that, far as it goes. It's what secret annexes are for. But when we go to the *Restricted* Archive, what do we find? A great big blank.'

'Fuck all,' Bunny puts in by way of clarification. 'Your entire Service career, according to your file, is a shitload of destruction certificates.'

'If that,' Laura comments, evidently quite unbothered by this unlawyerly display of foul language.

'Ah, but to be *fair*, Laura' – Bunny now assuming the spurious mantle of prisoner's friend – 'what we might be looking at here could very well be the handiwork of Bill Haydon of evil memory, could it not?' – and then to me: 'But perhaps you've forgotten who Haydon is too.'

Haydon? *Bill* Haydon. Got the fellow: Soviet-owned double agent who, as Head of the Circus's omnipotent Joint Steering Committee, commonly known as Joint, had for three decades diligently betrayed its secrets to Moscow Centre. He's also the man whose name goes through my head most hours of the day, but I am not about to leap into the air and cry 'that bastard, I could break his neck for him' – which in the event was what somebody else I happen to know did for him anyway, to the general satisfaction of the home side.

Laura, meanwhile, is pursuing her conversation with Bunny:

'Oh, I've no doubt of that at all, Bunny. That entire Restricted Archive has the marks of Bill Haydon all over it. And Peter here was one of the very early ones to sniff him out, right, Pete? In your role as George Smiley's personal assistant. His gatekeeper and trusted disciple, were you not?'

Bunny shakes his head in awe. 'George Smiley. The best operator we ever had. The conscience of the Circus. Its Hamlet, as some called him, perhaps not entirely fairly. What a man. All the same, you don't think that in the case of Operation Windfall,' he goes on, still addressing Laura as if I'm not in the room, 'it might not have been *Bill Haydon* who was plundering the Restricted Archive, but George Smiley, for whatever reason? There are some pretty odd signatures on those destruction certificates. Names you and I have never heard of. I'm not saying Smiley *personally*. He'd have used a willing proxy, of course he would. Someone who would blindly obey his orders, whatever their legality. Never one to get his own hands dirty, our George, great man as he was.'

'Got a view about that, Pete?' Laura enquires.

I have indeed got a view, and a vigorous one. I hate *Pete*, and this conversation is getting seriously out of hand:

'Why on earth, Laura, would George Smiley, of all the people in the world, need to go stealing Circus files? Bill Haydon, I grant you. Bill would have stolen a widow's mite and had a bloody good laugh about it.'

And a chuckle, and a shake of the old head to indicate that you young people these days can't possibly know how it really was.

'Oh, I think George could have a reason for stealing them, all right,' Bunny replies, on Laura's behalf. 'He was Head of Covert for the ten coldest years of the Cold War. Waged a bare-knuckle turf war with Joint. No holds barred, whether it was poaching one another's agents or busting into one another's safes. Masterminded the blackest ops this Service put its hand to. Overcame his conscience whenever the greater need dictated. Which it seems to have done pretty often. I think I could see your George sweeping a few files under the carpet quite easily.' To me now, straight into my face: 'And I could see you helping him, too, without a qualm. Some of those funny signatures look remarkably like your handwriting. You didn't even have to steal them. Just sign them out under somebody else's name and bingo. As to the much lamented Alec Leamas who died so tragically at the Berlin Wall – *his* personal file's not even filleted. It's gone AWOL. Not so much as a dog-eared card in the general index. You seem strangely unmoved.'

'I'm shocked if you want to know. And moved, too. Deeply.'

'Why? Simply because I'm suggesting you nicked the Leamas file out of the secret archive and hid it in a hollow tree? You've nicked a few files in your day for your Uncle George. Why not Leamas's? Something to remember him by after he got himself mown down alongside – what was his girl's name again?'

'Gold. Elizabeth Gold.'

'Ah. You remember. And Liz, for short. *Her* file's vanished too. One could wax romantic about the notion of Alec Leamas's and Liz Gold's files fading into the far yonder together. How come you and Leamas became quite such firm buddies, by the way? Brothers-in-arms to the end, from all one hears.'

'We did stuff together.'

'Stuff?'

'Alec was older than I was. And wiser. If he had an op running and needed a sidekick, he'd ask for me. If Personnel and George agreed, we'd be paired.'

Laura is back: 'So give us a couple of examples of this *pairing*' – in a voice that clearly disapproves of pairing, but I am only too happy to digress.

'Oh, Alec and I must have kicked off in Afghanistan in the mid-fifties, I suppose. Our first spell together was infiltrating small groups into the Caucasus, up into Russia. Probably sounds a bit *old hat* to you.' Another chuckle. A shake of the head. 'Wasn't a roaring success, I have to admit. Nine months later they moved him to the Baltic, running joes in and out of Estonia, Latvia and Lithuania. He asked for me again, so up I went as his help.' And for her enlightenment: 'The Baltic States being part of the Soviet bloc in those days, Laura, as I'm sure you know.'

'And *joes* being agents. We say *asset* these days. And Leamas officially based in Travemünde, correct? North Germany?'

'Correct indeed, Laura. Under cover as a member of the International Maritime Survey Group. Fishery protection by day, fast-boat landings by night.'

Bunny interrupts our tête-à-tête: 'Did these night landings have a name at all?'

'Jackknife, if I remember rightly.'

'So not Windfall?'

Ignore him.

'Jackknife. Ran for a couple of years, then got packed in.'

'Ran how?'

'First, rustle up your volunteers. Get 'em trained in Scotland, the Black Forest or wherever. Estonians, Latvians. Then set about putting 'em back where they came from. Wait for no moon. Rubber boat. Softly-softly outboard. Night vision. Reception party on the beach signals the all-clear. In you go. Or your joes do.'

'And when your *joes* have gone in, you and Leamas do what? Apart from open a bottle, obviously, which in Leamas's case was par for the course, one gathers.'

'Well, we're not going to sit around, are we?' I reply, again refusing to rise. 'Get the hell out fast is the message. Leave them to it. Why are you asking me all this, actually?'

'Partly to get the feel of you. Partly because I'm wondering why you remember Jackknife so vividly when you don't remember a damn thing about Windfall.'

Laura again: 'By *leaving them to it*, I presume you mean leave the agents to their fate?'

'If you want to put it that way, Laura.'

'Which was what? Their fate. Or have you forgotten?'

'They died on us.'

'Died literally?'

'Some were grabbed as soon as they landed. Others a couple of days later. Some got turned and played back at us and were only executed later,' I retort, hearing the anger rising in my voice and not particularly wanting to stop it.

'So who do we blame for that, Pete?' Laura still.

'For what?'

'For the deaths.'

A little explosion does no harm. 'Bloody Bill Haydon, our in-house traitor, who d'you think? The poor devils were blown before we ever left the German coast. By our own dear Head of Joint Steering, the same outfit that had planned the op in the first place!'

Bunny dips his head, consults something below the parapet. Laura looks first at me, then at her hands, which she prefers. Short fingernails like a boy's, scrubbed clean.

'Peter' – Bunny's turn, firing in groups now, rather than single shots. 'I am rather concerned, as the Service's chief lawyer – not *your* lawyer, I repeat – by certain aspects of your past. That is to say, an impression could be created around you by skilful counsel down the line – if ever Parliament were to step aside and leave the field open to the courts, secret or other, which heaven forfend – that, in the course of your career, you were associated with a quite exorbitant number of deaths, and were callous about them. That you were assigned – let us say by the impeccable George Smiley – to covert operations where the death of innocent people was considered an acceptable, even necessary outcome. Even, who knows, a desired one.'

'Desired outcome? Death? What are you blabbering about?'

'Windfall,' says Bunny patiently.

3

'Peter?'

'Bunny.'

Laura has assumed a disapproving silence.

'Can we just go back for a moment to 1959, when I believe Jackknife was shelved?'

'Not brilliant on dates, I'm afraid, Bunny.'

'Shelved by Head Office on the grounds that the operation had proved unproductive, and expensive of treasure and life. You and Alec Leamas, on the other hand, suspected there was dirty work on the home front.'

'Joint Steering was crying cock-up. Alec was crying conspiracy. Never mind which bit of the coast we landed on, the opposition was there ahead of us every time. Radio links blown. Everything blown. It had to be someone on the inside. That was Alec's view and from my worm's-eye view I tended to share it.'

'So you decided, the two of you, that you would make a *démarche* to Smiley. Presumably you considered Smiley himself out of contention as a potential traitor.'

'Jackknife was Joint's operation. Under Bill Haydon's command. Haydon, then Alleline, Bland, Esterhase. Bill's Boys, we called 'em. George was nowhere near it.'

'And Joint and Covert at daggers drawn?'

'Joint were forever conspiring to get Covert under their wing. George saw that as a power grab, and resisted. Strenuously.'

'Where was our gallant Chief of Service in all this? *Control*, as we must call him.'

'Playing Covert and Joint off against each other. Dividing and ruling, as usual.'

'Am I right in thinking there were personal issues between Smiley and Haydon?'

'Could have been. There was talk around the bazaars that Bill had had a fling with Ann, George's wife. It blurred George's aim. Sort of move you'd expect from Bill. He was a clever shit.'

'Smiley discussed his private life with you?'

'Wouldn't think of it. Not how you talk to an underling.'

Bunny thinks about this, doesn't believe it, seems to want to pursue it, changes his mind.

'So with the demise of Operation Jackknife, you and Leamas took your troubles to Smiley. Face to face. The three of you. You. Despite your junior position.'

'Alec asked me to come along. Didn't trust himself.'

'Why not?'

'Alec fired up too easily.'

'Where did this meeting *à trois* take place?'

'Why the hell should that matter?'

'Because I'm picturing a safe haven. A place you haven't told me about, but you will in due course. I thought this might be a moment to ask.'

I had lulled myself into believing that with all this tittle-tattle we might be drifting into less perilous waters.

'We could have used a Circus safe house, but safe houses were bugged as a matter of course by Joint. We could have used

George's place in Bywater Street, but Ann was in residence. There was a sort of understanding around that she shouldn't be put in the way of stuff she couldn't handle.'

'She'd go running to Haydon?'

'That's not what I said. There was a feeling around. Nothing more. Do you want me to go on or not?'

'Very much, if you wouldn't mind.'

'We picked George up from Bywater Street and walked him along the South Bank for his health. It was a summer's evening. He was always moaning that he didn't get enough exercise.'

'And out of this evening stroll beside the river, Operation Windfall was born?'

'Oh, for Christ's sake! Grow up!'

'Oh, I'm grown up, don't worry. And you're getting younger by the minute. How did the conversation go? I'm all ears.'

'We talked treachery. In the large, not in detail, there was no point. Anyone who was a present or recent member of Joint was suspect by definition. So fifty, sixty people, all potential traitors within. We talked about who had the right sort of access to blow Jackknife, but we knew that with Bill running Joint, and Percy Alleline eating out of his hand, and Bland and Esterhase getting in on the act any way they could, all that any traitor had to do was show up at Joint's free-for-all planning sessions, or sit around the senior officers' bar and listen to Percy Alleline sounding off. Bill always said compartmentation was a bore, let's have everybody knowing everything. That gave him all the cover he needed.'

'How did Smiley respond to your *démarche*?'

'He'd do some hard thinking and get back to us. Which was as much as anyone ever got out of George. Look here, I think I'll take that coffee you offered me, if you don't mind. Black. No sugar.'

I stretched, shook my head, yawned. I'm of an age, for God's sake. But Bunny wasn't buying, and Laura had given up on me long ago. They were eyeing me like a couple of people who'd had about enough of me, and coffee was off the menu.

★

Bunny had put on his legal face. No more squeezing of the eyes. No more raising the voice for a slow-witted older man who doesn't hear too well.

'I want to go back to where we came in – that all right with you? You and the Rule of Law. The Service and the Rule of Law. Do I have your full attention?'

'I suppose so.'

'I mentioned to you the British public's insatiable interest in historic crime. Something by no means lost on our gallant parliamentarians.'

'Did you? Probably.'

'*Or* the law courts. The historic blame game that is the current rage. Our new national sport. Today's blameless generation versus your guilty one. Who will atone for our fathers' sins, even if they weren't sins at the time? But you're not a father, are you? Whereas your file rather suggests you should be overrun by grandchildren.'

'I thought you said my file had been filleted. Are you now telling me it hasn't?'

'I'm trying to read your emotions. I can't. You either have none, or you have too many. You go lightly over Liz Gold's death. Why? You go lightly over Alec Leamas's death. You pretend total amnesia about Windfall, whereas we know perfectly well that you were Windfall cleared. Significantly, your late friend Alec Leamas was *not* so cleared, despite the fact that he died in harness to an operation he wasn't cleared for. I'm not asking you to interrupt, so kindly don't. However,' he went on, forgiving me my ill manners, 'I do begin to discern the outlines of a deal between us. You admitted that Operation Windfall might ring a distant bell for you. Possibly a training exercise, you said graciously and idiotically. So how's this? In exchange for greater transparency on *our* side, might the distant chimes of that bell get a little clearer on *yours*?'

I ponder, shake my head, try to capture those distant chimes. I have a sense of fighting to the last man, and the last man is me.

'The way I think I *dimly* remember it, Bunny,' I concede, signalling a slight change of direction in his favour, 'Windfall, if it comes back to me at all, wasn't an *operation*, it was a *source*. A dud one. I think that's where we've been misunderstanding each other' – hoping for some sort of easing from the other side of the table and not getting any – 'a *potential* source who fell flat on his back at the first fence. And was promptly, and very sensibly, dumped. File and forget.' I plunge on: 'Source Windfall was a relic from George's past. Another *historic* case, if you like' – deferential nod to Laura – 'an East German professor of Baroque Literature at Weimar University. A pal of George's from the war years who'd done a bit of this and that for us. He got in touch with George through some Swedish academic or other, back in '59 or so' – keep it flowing, keep it imprecise, a golden rule. 'The *Prof*, as we called him, claimed to have red-hot news about a super-secret compact being struck between the two halves of Germany and the Kremlin. Said he'd heard all about it from some like-minded pal in the East German administration.' It's really tripping off the tongue by now, just like old times. 'The two halves of Germany were to be reunited on condition they remained neutral and disarmed. In other words, exactly what the West *didn't* want: a power vacuum bang in the centre of Europe. If the Circus would just spirit the Prof to the West, he would give us chapter and verse.'

Rueful smile, shake of the old white head. And nothing coming back to me across the big divide.

'Turned out all the Prof wanted for himself was a chair at Oxford, a job for life, a knighthood and tea with the Queen' – chuckle. 'And of course he'd made the whole thing up. Pure bollocks. Case closed,' I ended, feeling it was a job well done nonetheless, and Smiley, wherever he was, would be silently applauding.

But Bunny was not applauding. Neither was Laura. Bunny looked insincerely worried, Laura plain incredulous.

'You see, the problem *is*, Peter,' Bunny explained after a while, 'what you've just pitched us is exactly the same tired bullshit that we're getting from the *dummy* files on Windfall in the old central archive. Am I right, Laura?'

Evidently he was, because she came in bang on cue.

'Practically word for word, Bunny. Concocted with the sole purpose of leading any nosy enquirer up the garden path. No such professor ever existed, and the story is total fabrication from start to finish. And I mean all fair and good: if Windfall had to be protected from the prying eyes of the Haydons of this world, a dummy file for smoke in the central archive makes good sense.'

'What *doesn't* make sense however, Peter, is that you sit here at your great age trying to sell us the same shitload of disinformation that you and George Smiley and the rest of Covert were putting out a generation ago,' Bunny said, and managed a half-squeeze of the eyes for friendly.

'We've found the reigning Control's old financial returns, you see, Pete,' Laura explained helpfully, while I'm still considering my reply. 'For his reptile fund. That's the slice of the secret vote that Control gets for his personal pocket money, but it still has to be accounted down to the last penny, right, Peter?' – as to a child. 'Hand-submitted by the man himself to his trusted ally at Treasury. Oliver Lacon his name was, later Sir Oliver, now the late Lord Lacon of Ascot West—'

'Do you mind telling me what all this has got to do with *me*?'

'Everything actually,' Laura said calmly. 'In his financial returns to Treasury, Lacon's eyes only, Control gives the names of two Circus officers who, if requested, will provide full and frank disclosure regarding the costs pertaining to a certain Operation Windfall. That's in case the extra expenditure should ever be challenged by posterity. Control was very high-minded in such regards, whatever else he wasn't. Name One was George Smiley. Name Two was Peter Guillam. You.'

For a while Bunny seemed not to have heard anything of this exchange. He was head down again, eyes below the parapet, and whatever he was reading required his full attention. Eventually he emerged.

'Tell him about the Windfall safe flat you've unearthed, Laura. Covert's shady nook where Peter stashed all the files he stole,' he suggested in a tone to imply he was busy with other matters.

'Yes, well, there's this safe flat that's mentioned in the accounts, like Bunny says,' Laura explained obligingly. '*And* a safe flat housekeeper, what's more' – indignantly – '*and* a mysterious gentleman called Mendel, who isn't even on the Service's books but has been hired by Covert exclusively on an agent basis for Windfall. Two hundred quid a month to his Post Office savings account in Weybridge, plus travel and exes up to another two hundred, accountable, paid out of an unnamed client account run by a chichi City law firm. And one George Smiley with effective power of attorney over the account in its entirety.'

'Mendel being *who*?' Bunny enquired.

'Retired police officer, Special Branch,' I replied, by now on autopilot. 'First name Oliver. Not to be confused with Oliver Lacon.'

'Acquired how and where?'

'George and Mendel went way back. George had worked with him on an earlier case. Liked the cut of his jib. Liked it that he wasn't Circus. My breath of clean air, he called him.'

Bunny was suddenly exhausted by the whole discussion. He had flopped back in his chair and was flapping his wrists around, easing his body on a long flight.

'So let's just get real, for a change, can we?' he suggested, with an implicit yawn. 'Control's reptile fund is at this exact point or moment in time the sole, exclusive piece of credible evidence that provides us with (a) a path to the conduct and purpose of Operation Windfall, and (b) a means to defend ourselves in any frivolous civil action or private prosecution brought against this Service, and against you Peter Guillam personally, by one *Christoph* Leamas, sole heir of the late Alec, and one *Karen* Gold, spinster, sole daughter of the late Elizabeth or Liz. Did you hear any of that? You did. Don't say we've surprised you at last.'

Still slumped in his chair, he emitted a low *'Jesus'* while he waited for my reaction. And probably it was a long time coming because I also have a memory of him bellowing an imperious *'Well?'* at me.

*

'Liz Gold had a *child*?' I hear myself ask.

'A feisty edition of herself, on present showing. She had just turned fifteen when she was knocked up by some oaf at her local grammar. On her parents' insistence she gave the baby into adoption. Somebody christened it Karen. Or maybe not christened. She's Jewish. Having grown to woman's estate, the said Karen exercised her legal right to know the identity of her natural parent, and became understandably curious about the place and manner of her mother's death.'

35

He paused in case I had a question. Belatedly, I had: where the hell did Christoph and Karen get our names from? He ignored it.

'Karen was much encouraged in her quest for truth and reconciliation by Christoph, son of Alec, who ever since the Wall came down had, unknown to her, been busting a gut to find out how and why his father had died – not, I have to say, with the enthusiastic assistance of this Service, which has gone out of its way to put every fucking obstacle in their path that we could think of, and then some. Unfortunately, our best efforts have proved counter-productive, despite the fact that the said Christoph Leamas has a German police record as long as your arm.'

Another pause. And still no question from me.

'The two plaintiffs have now bonded. They have convinced themselves, not without reason, that their respective parents died as a consequence of what appears to have been a five-star cock-up by this Service, and by you and George Smiley personally. They are seeking full disclosure, punitive damages and a public apology that will name names. Yours for one. Were you aware that Alec Leamas had engendered a son?'

'Yes. Where's Smiley? Why isn't he here instead of me?'

'So do you happen to know who was the fortunate mother?'

'A German woman he met in the war when he was operating behind the lines. She later married a Düsseldorf lawyer called Eberhardt. Eberhardt adopted the boy. His name isn't Leamas, it's Eberhardt. I asked you where George is.'

'Later. And thank you for your excellent powers of recall. Were other people aware of the boy's existence? Your friend Leamas's *other* colleagues? We'd know, except his file's been stolen, you see.' And already sick of waiting for my answer: 'Was it, or was it not, generally known in and around this Service that Alec Leamas had sired a German bastard named Christoph, resident in Düsseldorf? Yes or no?'

'No.'

'How the fuck not?'

'Alec didn't talk a lot about himself.'

'Except to you apparently. Did you meet him?'

'Who?'

'Christoph. Not Alec. Christoph. I think you're back to being deliberately obtuse.'

'I'm being nothing of the kind, and the answer's *no*, I did not meet Christoph Leamas,' I retorted, because why spoil him with the truth? And while he is still digesting this: 'I asked you where Smiley is.'

'And I ignored the question, as you may have noticed.'

A pause while we both waited to collect ourselves and Laura stared moodily out of the window.

'*Christoph*, as we may call him,' Bunny resumed in a lethargic tone, 'is not without his talents, Peter, criminal or semi-criminal though they may be. Perhaps the genes help. Having confirmed that his natural father died at the Berlin Wall on the Eastern side, he wangled his way, by what means we know not but respect, into a stash of supposedly sealed Stasi archives, and came up with three significant names. Yours, the late Elizabeth Gold's and George Smiley's. Within weeks he was on the scent of Elizabeth, thence by way of public records to her daughter. A tryst was arranged. The unlikely pair bonded – to what extent, not ours to pry. Together they consulted one of those admirably high-minded civil rights lawyers with open-toed sandals who are the bane of this Service. We in response are considering offering the plaintiffs a fortune of public money in exchange for their silence, but are only too aware that, in doing so, we confirm to them that they have a decent case, and thus encourage them to become even more strident than they are at present. "To hell with your money, you men of evil. History must be allowed to speak. The canker must be cut out. Heads must roll." Yours for one, I fear.'

'And George's too, presumably.'

'We are therefore faced with the ludicrous Shakespearean premise whereby the ghosts of two victims of a fiendish Circus plot rise up to accuse us in the form of their offspring. Thus far, we have managed to contain the media by implying – not entirely truthfully, but who's counting? – that, in the event of Parliament stepping aside to make way for the legal process, the case will be heard in the decent seclusion of a *secret* court, and we alone will decide who gets the tickets. The plaintiffs in response, egged on as ever by their thoroughly annoying lawyers, are saying "screw that, we want openness, we want full disclosure." You asked, somewhat ingenuously, where the Stasi could have got your names from. Why, from Moscow Centre, of course, who duly passed them on to the Stasi. Where did Moscow Centre get your names from? From this Service, of course, thanks yet again to the ever-diligent Bill Haydon, at that time very much at large, and destined to remain so for another six years, until St George rode up on his white horse and smoked him out. Are you still in touch?'

'With George?'

'With George.'

'No. Where is he?'

'And have not been over recent years?'

'No.'

'So your last communication with him was when?'

'Eight years ago. Ten.'

'Describe.'

'I was in London. I looked him up.'

'Where?'

'In Bywater Street.'

'How was he?'

'Fine, thank you.'

'We seek him here, we seek him there. The wayward Lady

Ann? You're not in touch with her either? *Touch* strictly in the metaphorical sense, naturally.'

'No. And I don't need the innuendo either.'

'Well, I need your passport.'

'What for?'

'The same one that you presented at reception downstairs, please. Your UK passport' – hand outstretched above the parapet.

'Why on earth?'

I gave it to him anyway. What else was I supposed to do? Fight him for it?

'Is this all of them?' – mulling thoughtfully through the pages. 'You've had a scad of passports in your time, under various guises. Where are they all now?'

'Turned in. Shredded.'

'You have dual nationality. Where's your French passport?'

'I was born to a British father, I served as a Brit, Brit's good enough for me. Now can I have my passport back, please?'

But it had already disappeared beneath the parapet.

'So, Laura. *You* again,' said Bunny, rediscovering her. 'Can we now go a little deeper into that Windfall safe flat, please?'

It's over. I've fought to the last lie. I'm dead and I'm out of ammunition.

★

Laura once more examines papers below my eye-line, and I do my best to ignore the beads of sweat rolling down my ribcage.

'Yes, well, safe flat *and how*, Bunny,' she agrees as her head comes up again in relish. 'A dedicated safe flat for sole use of Windfall, and that's just about the entire job description. To be situate within the purlieus of Inner London, plus a statement that the said flat will be known for cover purposes as the Stables, and a permanent housekeeper to be assigned at Smiley's discretion. And that's about our lot.'

'Ring a bell after all?' Bunny enquires.

They wait. So do I. Laura resumes her private conversation with Bunny.

'It's like Control didn't want even Lacon to know where the place was, or who looked after it, Bunny. Which, given Lacon's seat of power at the Treasury and his comprehensive knowledge of other areas of Circus business, strikes me as a touch paranoid on Control's part, but who are we to criticize?'

'Who indeed? Stables as in sweep them clean?' Bunny asks, all curiosity.

'I assume so,' she says.

'Smiley's choice?'

'Ask Pete,' she suggests helpfully.

But Pete, which I detest, has gone even more deaf than he pretends to be.

'And the *good* news is' – Bunny to Laura again – 'there still *is* a Windfall safe flat! Because either by design or sheer neglect, I *suspect* the latter, the Stables has remained on the private imprest of no fewer than four *successive* Controls. And it's there *now*. And our very own top floor doesn't even know it exists, let alone where it is. Funnier still, in these times of austerity, its existence hasn't been questioned by the dear old Treasury. They've nodded it through, bless them, year after year.' He affects a homophobe lisp: '*Too secret to ask, darlings. Sign along the dotted line, and not a word to Mummy.* It's leasehold, and we have not the faintest idea when the lease expires, who holds it or what generous arsehole pays the bills.' And to me on the same savage note: 'Peter. Pierre. Pete. You're very quiet. Enlighten us, please. Who *is* that generous arsehole?'

When you're cornered, when you've tried all the tricks in

your locker and they haven't worked, there aren't many ways left to wriggle. You can spin the story within the story. I'd done that, and it hadn't worked. You can try a partial hangout and hope it ends there. I'd done that too, but it hadn't ended there. So you accept that you've reached the end of the road, and the only option left to you is be bold, tell the truth, or as little as you can get away with, and earn a few Brownie points for being a good boy – none of which struck me as a very likely outcome, but it might at least get me my passport back.

*

'George had a tame lawyer,' I said, as the sinful relief of confession rose in me despite myself. 'The one you call chichi. A distant relative of Ann's. He or she agreed to play cut-out. It's not a safe flat, it's a safe house three floors high, and it was leased by an offshore trust registered in the Dutch Antilles.'

'Spoken like a hero' – Bunny's approval – 'and the safe house keeper?'

'Millie McCraig. A former agent of George's. She'd kept for him before. Had all the skills. When Windfall started up, she was keeping a Circus safe house for Joint in the New Forest. Place called Camp 4. George told her to resign, then reapply to Covert. He transferred her to the reptile fund and set her up in the Stables.'

'Which is situate where, may we now know?' – still Bunny.

So I told them that too, complete with the Stables phone number, which tripped off my tongue as lightly as if it had been straining to come out all along. Then there was stage business while Bunny and Laura made themselves a gully through the files on the table between us, and Bunny plonked a broad-bottomed telephone of a complexity that was totally beyond me in the gap and, having touched a succession of keys at lightning speed, handed me the receiver.

At a tenth of Bunny's speed, I touched in the Stables phone number and was startled to hear the dialling tone blaring out all over the room, which wasn't just grossly insecure to my guilty ear, but an act of outright betrayal, as if I'd been blown, captured and turned in a single move. The phone bawled out its ringing tone. We waited. Still no answer. And I was thinking, either Millie's at church, because she used to do a lot of that, or she's out bicycling, or she's a sight less agile than she used to be, like the rest of us. But more likely she's dead and buried because, beautiful and unattainable though she was, she had a good five years on me.

The ringing stopped. There was a rustle and I assumed the call was going over to answerphone. Then, to my astonishment and disbelief, I heard Millie's voice, the same voice, the same saw-edge of puritanical Scottish disapproval that I would mimic to make George laugh when he was feeling low:

'Yes? Hullo?' – and when I hesitated – 'Who *is* that, please?' – indignantly, as if it was midnight rather than seven in the evening.

'It's me, Peter Weston, Millie,' I said. And throwing in Smiley's cover name for good measure: 'Friend of Mr Barraclough's, if you remember.'

I was expecting, even hoping, that for once in her life Millie McCraig would need time to collect herself, but she came back so sharply that it was I, not she, who was disconcerted.

'Mr *Weston?*'

'Himself, Millie, not his shadow.'

'Kindly identify yourself, Mr Weston.'

Identify myself? Hadn't I just given her two cover names? Then I realized: she wants my *pinpoint*, which was a form of obscure coded communication more often used over Moscow's telephone system than London's, but Smiley in our darkest days had insisted on it. So I grabbed a brown wooden pencil that was lying on the desk in front of me and, feeling a total idiot, stooped over Bunny's super-elaborate telephone and tapped my thousand-year-old pinpoint code on to the speaker, hoping it would have the same effect as if I'd tapped it on to the mouthpiece, three taps, pause, one tap, pause, two taps. And evidently it did, because no sooner had I delivered the last tap than Millie was back, all sweet and accommodating, saying it was nice to hear my voice after all these years, Mr Weston, and what could she be doing to help me at all?

To which I might have replied: Well, since you ask, Millie, could you kindly confirm that these events are playing out in the real world and not in some murky corner of the middle world reserved for unsleeping spies of yesterday?

4

On my arrival from Brittany the previous morning, I had booked myself into a dismal hotel near Charing Cross station and forked out ninety pounds in advance for a room the size of a hearse. On my way there, I had also paid a courtesy call on my old friend and former joe Bernie Lavendar, Gentlemen's Tailor to the Diplomatic Corps, whose cutting rooms were situated in a minuscule semi-basement off Savile Row. But size had never mattered to Bernie. What had mattered to him – and to the Circus – was getting inside the diplomatic parlours of Kensington Palace Gardens and St John's Wood, and doing his bit for England, with a modest tax-free income on the side.

We embraced, he drew the blind and dropped the latch on the door. For old times' sake I tried on a couple of his uncollecteds: jackets and suits made for foreign diplomats who for unknown reasons had failed to collect them. And finally, also in the spirit of old times, I entrusted him with a sealed envelope to pop in his safe until my return. It contained my French passport, but if it had contained the plans for the D-Day landings, Bernie couldn't have treated it with greater reverence.

Now I have come to reclaim it.

'And how's Mr Smiley, then?' he asks, dropping his voice out of reverence, or an exaggerated sense of security. 'Have we heard of him at all, Mister G?'

We haven't. Has Bernie? Alas, Bernie hasn't either, so we make do with a chuckle about George's habit of disappearing for long periods without explaining himself.

But inside, I wasn't chuckling. Was it possible George was *dead*? And that Bunny *knew* he was dead and wasn't telling? But not even George could die in secret. And how about Ann, his ever-faithless wife? Word had reached me a while back that, tiring of her many adventures, she had espoused a fashionable charity. But whether the attachment had endured any longer than its predecessors was anybody's guess.

With my French passport back in my pocket, I took myself to Tottenham Court Road and invested in a couple of disposable mobile phones with ten pounds' worth of phone time apiece. And, as an afterthought, the bottle of Scotch I had neglected to buy at Rennes airport, which probably accounts for the merciful fact that I have no memory of the night that somehow passed.

Rising with the dawn, I walked for an hour through drizzle, and ate a bad breakfast in a sandwich bar. Only then, with a sense of resignation tinged with disbelief, did I pluck up the courage to hail a black cab and give the driver the address that for two years had been the scene of more rejoicing, stress and human anguish than any other place in my life.

*

As I remembered it, No. 13 Disraeli Street, alias the Stables, had been a shabby, unrestored Victorian end-of-terrace house in a Bloomsbury side street. And to my astonishment, that is the house that stands before me now: unchanged, unrepentant, a standing reproach to its shiny, prinked-up neighbours. The time is nine a.m., the appointed hour, but the doorstep has been commandeered by a slender woman in jeans, sneakers and leather jacket who is talking vituperatively into her mobile phone.

I'm about to begin another circuit when I realize she is Laura-who-is-History in modern dress.

'Sleep well, Pete?'

'Like an angel.'

'Which bell do I press without catching gangrene?'

'Try Ethics.'

Ethics being Smiley's own choice for the least alluring doorbell he could think of. The front door swung open and there in the half-darkness stood the ghost of Millie McCraig, her once jet-black hair as white as mine, her athlete's body bent with age, but the same zealous light burning in the moist blue eyes as she allowed me one air kiss on each frugal Celtic cheek.

Laura brushed past us into the hall. The two women squared up to each other like boxers before the fight, while I underwent such turbulent feelings of recognition and remorse that my one desire was to steal back into the street, close the door after me and pretend I'd never been here. What I was seeing around me would have surpassed the dreams of the most demanding archaeologist: a scrupulously preserved burial chamber, its seals unbroken, dedicated to Operation Windfall and all who had sailed in her, complete with every original artefact, from my pizza-delivery gear hanging from its hook to Millie McCraig's upright ladies' bicycle, a vintage model even in its day, with wicker basket, ting-a-ling bell and Rexine carrier bag, parked on its stand in the hallway.

'Will you be wishing to look around at all?' Millie is saying to Laura, as indifferently as if she is talking to a potential purchaser.

'There's a back door,' says Laura to Millie, producing an architect's plan of the building; and where in God's name had she got *that* from?

We stand at the glazed kitchen door. Below us, a handkerchief-sized garden, and at its centre, Millie's vegetable patch. Oliver

Mendel and I gave it its first dig. The washing line bare, but Millie was expecting us. The birdhouse, the same one. Mendel and I had cobbled it together one midnight out of bits of spare timber. Mendel, under my slightly drunken guidance, had embellished it with a pokerwork plaque declaring *No bird turned away*. And there it stood, as proud and upright as on the birthday it had celebrated. A stone path weaves between the vegetable beds to the kissing gate that leads to the private car park that leads to the side street. No safe house George countenanced was complete without a rear entrance.

'Anybody ever come in that way?' Laura enquires.

'Control,' I reply, sparing Millie the need to answer. 'Wouldn't have come in by the front to save his life.'

'And the rest of you?'

'Used the front door. Once Control had decided the back way was his, it became his private lift.'

Be generous in small things, I am advising myself. Keep the rest in your memory locked, and throw away the key. Next on her itinerary is the winding wooden staircase, a miniature replica of every dingy staircase at the Circus. We are about to ascend it when, to the tinkle of a small bell, a cat appears: a large, black, long-haired, malign-looking animal with a red collar. It sits, yawns and stares at us. Laura stares back at it, then turns to Millie.

'Is she on the budget too?'

'She's a he, and I pay for him myself, thank you.'

'Does he have a name?'

'Yes.'

'But it's classified?'

'Yes.'

With Laura striding ahead and the cat cautiously following, we ascend to the half-landing and come to a halt before the green-baize door with its combination lock. Beyond it lies the cypher room. When George first took the place, the door was glazed, but Ben the cypher clerk wouldn't allow his fingers to be watched, hence the baize.

'*Right.* Who's got the combination?' – Laura in scout-mistress mode.

Since Millie again says nothing, I reluctantly recite the combination: 21 10 05, the date of the Battle of Trafalgar.

'Ben was Royal Navy,' I explain, but if Laura understands the reference, she gives no sign of it.

Parking herself in the swivel chair, she glowers at the array of dials and switches. Flips a switch. Nothing. Turns a dial. Nothing.

'Power's been off ever since,' Millie murmurs to me, not to Laura.

Swinging round in Ben's chair, Laura jabs a finger at a green Chubb wall safe.

'*Right.* Has that thing got a key?'

The *rights* are getting on my nerves. They're like Pete. From a bunch at her side, Millie selects a key. The lock turns, the safe door swings open, Laura peers in and with a scything movement of her arm sweeps the contents on to the coconut matting: codebooks blazoned Top Secret and Beyond, pencils, reinforced envelopes, faded one-time pads in cellophane packs of twelve.

'We leave everything as it is, right?' she announces, swinging back to us. 'Nobody touches anything anywhere. Got that? Pete? Millie?'

She is midway up the next flight of stairs when Millie with an 'Excuse *me!*' stops her in her tracks.

'Would that be my personal quarters you're proposing to enter at all?'

'And if I am?'

'You are welcome to make an inspection of my apartment

and personal possessions provided I have advance notice in writing and in good time signed by the appropriate authority at Head Office,' Millie pronounces in a single unmodulated sentence, which I suspect she has been rehearsing. 'In the meantime, I'll trouble you to respect my personal privacy as becomes my age and station.'

To which Laura comes back with a heresy that not even Oliver Mendel would have risked on a good day:

'Why's that, Mill? You got someone tucked away up there?'

★

The classified cat has removed itself. We stand in the Middle Room, so called from the day Mendel and I cleared away the old hardboard partitions. Look at it from the street, all you got was another dingy net-curtained ground-floor window. But on the inside there was no window, because one snow-swept Saturday afternoon in February we bricked it up, consigning the room to eternal darkness until you switched on the green-shaded gamblers' lights we bought from a shop in Soho.

Two cumbersome Victorian desks filled the centre, the one Smiley's, the other – but only occasionally – Control's. Their origin had remained a mystery until an evening when Smiley revealed to us over a Scotch that a cousin of Ann's was selling off a country pile in Devon to pay death duties.

'What in the name of all that's holy is *that* hideous thing when it's at home?'

Laura's eye has lighted, not to my surprise, on the garish three-foot-by-two-foot wall chart hanging behind Control's desk. Hideous? Not to my eyes. But life-threatening, yes indeed. Before I knew it, I had grabbed the ash walking stick hanging over the back of Control's chair and embarked on an explanation designed not to enlighten, but divert.

49

'This section *here*, Laura' – waving the stick at a maze of coloured lines and cover names resembling a crazy London Underground map – 'is a homemade representation of the Circus's East European network, codenamed Mayflower, as it stood before Operation Windfall was conceived. Here we have the great man himself, source Mayflower, the network's inspiration, founder, cut-out and hub, here his sub-sources, and here, in descending order, *their* sub-sources, conscious or otherwise, together with a capsule description of their product, its rating in the Whitehall market place, and our own in-house assessment of the sources' and sub-sources' reliability on a scale of one to ten.'

With which I hung the stick back on its chair. But Laura didn't appear quite as diverted or confused as I would have wished. She was examining the chart's cover names one by one, checking them off. Behind me, Millie is sidling from the room.

'Well, now we do know a *couple* of things about Operation Mayflower, as it happens,' Laura remarked in a superior tone. 'From the odd file you were kind enough to leave behind in the General Archive. Plus a couple of other sources of our own.' And having let this sink in: 'What's with naming everybody after garden plants, anyway?'

'Ah well, that's from the days when we used *themes*, Laura,' I replied, maintaining as best I could the lofty tone. 'Mayflower, so flowers, not the ship.'

But again I had lost her.

'What the hell are these *stars* for?'

'Sparks, Laura. Not stars. Figurative sparks. In cases where field agents have been issued with radio sets. Red for active, yellow for cached.'

'*Cached?*'

'Buried. In oilskins usually.'

'If I *hide* something, I *hide* it, right?' she informs me, still

50

hunting among the cover names. 'I don't *cache*. I don't do spy-speak and I'm not a boys' club. What are these *plus signs* anyway?' – stabbing her fingertip at the bubble around a sub-source and keeping it there.

'They're not *plus signs*, actually, Laura. They're *crosses.*'

'You mean they're doubles? They've been *double-crossed*?'

'I mean they're extinct.'

'How?'

'Blown. Resigned. A raft of reasons.'

'What happened to this man?'

'Codename Violet?'

'Yeah. What happened to Violet?'

Was she closing in on me? I was beginning to suspect she was.

'Missing, believed interrogated. Based East Berlin 1956 to 1961. Ran a team of train-watchers. It's all in the bubble' – meaning, read it for yourself.

'And this fellow? Tulip?'

'Tulip's a woman.'

'And the hashtag?'

Has she been waiting all this time for her fingertip to land where it is now?

'The hashtag, as you call it, is a *symbol.*'

'I think I got that. What of?'

'Tulip was a Russian Orthodox convert, so they gave her a Russian Orthodox cross.' My voice steady as she goes.

'Who did?'

'The women. The two senior secretaries who worked here.'

'Did every agent who had religion get a cross?'

'Tulip's Orthodoxy was part of her motivation to work for us. The cross marked that.'

'What happened to her?'

'Disappeared from our screens, alas.'

'You didn't have screens.'

'Our assumption was that she had decided to call it a day. Some joes do that. Break off contact and disappear.'

'Her actual name was *Gamp*, right? Like umbrella. Doris Gamp?'

This is absolutely not a wave of nausea I am feeling. That was not any kind of lurch of the stomach.

'Probably. Gamp. Yes, I think it was. I'm surprised you know.'

'Maybe you didn't steal enough files. Was it a big loss?'

'Was what?'

'Her decision to call it a day.'

'I'm not sure she *announced* her decision. Just ceased to operate. Still, yes, over time it *was* a loss. Tulip was a major source. Substantial. Yes.'

Too much? Too little? Too light? She's thinking about it. For too long.

'I thought it was Windfall you were interested in,' I remind her.

'Oh, we're interested in all of it. Windfall's just an excuse. What happened to Millie?'

Millie? Ah, Millie. Not Tulip. Millie.

'When?' I say stupidly.

'Just now. Where did she go?'

'Upstairs to her flat, probably.'

'Would you mind whistling for her, please? She hates me.'

But when I open the door, there's Millie waiting with her keys. Pushing past her, Laura strides ahead down the corridor, map in hand. I hang back.

'Where's George?' I murmur to Millie.

She shakes her head. Don't know? Or don't ask?

'Keys, Millie?'

Millie dutifully unlocks the double doors to the library. Laura takes a pace forward, then slapstick-style two back as she emits the mandatory cry of *Holy shit!* – so shrill it must have awakened the dead in the British Museum. Incredulously, she advances on the ranks of tattered tomes that cram the book-shelves from floor to ceiling. Gingerly she makes her first selection, volume 18 of a broken thirty-book set of the *Encyclopaedia Britannica*, published 1878. She opens it, flips a couple of pages in disbelief, dumps it on a side table and treats herself instead to *Treks Through Araby and Beyond*, published 1908, also part of a broken set, and priced, as I unaccountably remember, at five shillings and sixpence a volume, a pound for the lot, after Mendel had beaten down the dealer.

'Do you mind telling me who reads this crap? Or did?' – to me again.

'Anyone who was Windfall cleared and had good reason.'

'Meaning *what*?'

'Meaning,' I reply with as much dignity as I can muster, 'that George Smiley was of the opinion that, since we were not blessed with an armed fortress beside the Thames, natural concealment was better than physical protection. And that, while barred windows and a steel safe would act as an open invitation to any local footpad to break and enter, the thief had yet to be born whose ideal heist was a skipload of—'

'Just show me, okay? Whatever you stole. Whatever's here.'

Placing a set of library steps in front of a fireplace filled with Millie's dried flowers, I fish from the top shelf a copy of *A Layman's Guide to the Science of Phrenology* by Henry J. Ramken, MA (Cantab.), and from its gouged cavity a buff folder. Passing the folder down to Laura, I restore Dr Ramken to his shelf and descend to firm ground to find her perched on the arm of a library chair scrutinizing her bounty; and Millie again nowhere to be seen.

'I have a *Paul* here,' Laura says accusingly. 'Who's Paul when he's at home?'

This time I am not quite so successful at controlling my tonal responses:

'He's not *at home*, Laura. He's dead. *Paul*, pronounced the German way, was one of several cover names that Alec Leamas used in Berlin for his joes.' Belatedly, I managed the casual: 'He alternated. Didn't trust the world much. Well, didn't trust Joint Steering, let's say.'

She's interested but doesn't want me to know it. 'And these are *all* the files, right? The whole caboose. Everything you stole is right here, hidden in these old books? Yes?'

I am only too pleased to enlighten her: 'Not *all* by any means, Laura, I'm afraid. George's policy was to keep as little as possible. Whatever could be dispensed with was shredded. We shredded, then we burned the shreds. George's law.'

'Where's the shredder?'

'Right over there in the corner.'

She'd missed it.

'Where did you burn them?'

'In that fireplace.'

'Did you keep destruction certificates?'

'Then we'd have had to destroy the destruction certificates, wouldn't we?'

While I am still relishing my little victory, her gaze shifts to the darkest and most distant corner of the room, where two long photographs of standing men hang side by side. And this time she emits no cry of 'Holy shit' or any other exclamation, but advances on them in slow steps, as if afraid they'll fly away.

'And these beauties?'

'Josef Fiedler and Hans-Dieter Mundt. Respectively Head and deputy Head of the Stasi's operational directorate.'

'I'll take the one on the left.'

'That's Fiedler.'

'Description?'

'German Jewish, sole surviving son of academic parents who

died in the camps. Studied humanities in Moscow and Leipzig. Late entrant to the Stasi. Fast-streamed, smart, hates the guts of the man standing next to him.'

'Mundt.'

'By a process of elimination, yes, Mundt,' I agree. 'First name Hans-Dieter.'

Hans-Dieter Mundt in a double-breasted suit with all his jacket buttons done up. Hans-Dieter Mundt with his murderer's arms pressed to his sides, thumbs downward, staring contemptuously into camera. He's attending an execution. His own. Someone else's. Either way, his expression will never change, the knife slash down the side of his face will never heal.

'He was your mark, right? The man your pal Alec Leamas was sent to eliminate, right? Except Mundt eliminated Leamas instead. Right?' She returns to Fiedler. 'And Fiedler was your super-source? Right? The ultimate secret volunteer. The walk-in who never walked in. Just dumped a pile of red-hot intelligence on your doorstep, pressed the bell and ran away without leaving his name. Over and over. And you still don't know for sure he was your joe, as you call him. That right?'

I take a breath: 'All the unsolicited Windfall material that we received pointed in Fiedler's direction,' I reply, picking my words with precision. 'We even asked ourselves whether Fiedler was positioning himself to defect and, so to speak, casting his bread on the waters in advance.'

'Because he hated Mundt so much? Mundt the ex-Nazi who never quite reformed?'

'That would have been a motive. Combined, we assumed, with a disillusionment about the democracy or lack of it as practised by the German Democratic Republic, the GDR. The feeling that his Communist god might have failed him, turning to certainty. There'd been an unsuccessful counter-revolution in Hungary, which the Soviets had repressed rather brutally.'

'Thank you. I think I knew that.'

Of course she did. She's History.

Two dishevelled youths were standing in the doorway, one male, one female. My first thought was that they must have come in by the back entrance, which had no bell; and my second – a wild one, I admit – that they were Karen, daughter to Elizabeth, and her fellow plaintiff Christoph, son to Alec, come to make a citizen's arrest. Laura gives herself a lift-up on the stepladder for extra authority.

'Nelson. Pepsi. Say hullo to Pete,' she commands.

Hi, Pete.

Hi, Pete.

Hi.

'Okay. Listen up, everyone. The premises where you are standing will henceforth be treated as a crime scene. They are also *Circus* premises. That includes the garden. Every bit of paper, file, piece of detritus, whatever's on the walls by way of charts, pegboards, whatever's in the drawers and bookshelves, is Circus property and potentially a court exhibit, to be copied, photographed and listed accordingly. Right?'

Nobody says it isn't right.

'*Pete* here is our *reader*. For his reading *Pete* will be accommodated here in the library. Pete will read, he will be briefed and debriefed by Head of Legal and myself. *Only.*' Back to the dishevelled youths: 'Your conversations with Pete will be social, right? They will be courteous. They will not at any point touch on the material he is reading, or the reasons why he's reading it. All of which you both know, but I'm repeating it for Pete's information. Should either one of you have cause to suppose that Pete or Millie, by mistake or deliberately, is attempting to remove documents or exhibits from Circus premises, you will immediately notify Legal. Millie.'

No answer, but she's still in the doorway.

'Was your area – your apartment – ever used – is it *now* used – for any kind of Service business?'

'Not that I'm aware of.'

'Does your area contain Service equipment? Cameras? Listening devices? Secret writing materials? Files? Papers? Official correspondence?'

'It does not.'

'Typewriter?'

'My own. Purchased by myself, out of my personal money.'

'Electronic?'

'Remington manual.'

'Radio?'

'A wireless. My own. Purchased by myself.'

'Tape recorder?'

'For the wireless. Purchased by myself.'

'Computer? iPad? Smartphone?'

'Just a normal telephone, thank you.'

'Millie, you just had your advance notice. Written confirmation is in the post. Pepsi. You will please accompany Millie to her apartment *now*, right? Millie, please provide whatever assistance Pepsi requires. I want the place picked into small pieces. Pete.'

'Laura.'

'How do I identify the active volumes in these shelves?'

'All quarto books on the top shelf with authors' surnames beginning A to R should contain papers, if they haven't been destroyed.'

'Nelson. You remain here in the library till the team arrives. Millie.'

'What now?'

'The bicycle in the hallway. Kindly move it. It's in the way.'

★

Seated in the Middle Room, Laura and I are alone for the first time. She has offered me Control's chair. I prefer Smiley's. She appropriates Control's for herself, lounging on her flank, either for her relaxation or for my benefit.

'I'm a lawyer. Right? A pretty fucking good one. First I went private, then I went corporate. Then I got pissed off and applied to join your crowd. I was young and beautiful so they gave me History. I've been History ever since. Whenever the past threatens to bite the Service in the arse, it's *get Laura*. And Windfall, believe me, is looking like quite some bite.'

'You must be very pleased.'

If she notices the irony in my voice, she ignores it.

'And what we want from *you*, corny as it may sound, is the whole truth and nothing but, and screw your loyalty to Smiley or anybody else. Right?'

Not right at all, so why bother to say it?

'Once we have the truth, we'll know how to doctor it. Maybe in your favour too, where our interests coincide. My job is to head off the shit before it hits the fan. That's what you want too, right? No scandals, however historic. They're a distraction, they raise unpleasant comparisons with our own times. A Service marches on its reputation and its good looks. Rendition, torture, playing footsie in the woodshed with murderous psychopaths: it's bad for the public image, bad for trade. So we're on the same side, right?'

Again I manage to say nothing.

'So here's the bad news. It's not just the offspring of the Windfall victims who are after our blood. Bunny was soft-pedalling out of kindness. There's a bunch of attention-hungry MPs who want to use Windfall as an example of what happens when the surveillance society is allowed to run amok. They can't get their hands on the real stuff, so give them history.' And growing

58

impatient at my silence: 'I'm telling you, Pete. If we don't have your total cooperation, this thing could—'

She waits for me to complete the sentence. I let her do the waiting instead.

'And you really haven't heard from him, right?' she says finally.

It takes me a moment to realize I am sitting in his chair.

'No, Laura. Once again, I have not heard from George Smiley.'

She leans back and hauls an envelope from her back pocket. For a mad moment I think it's going to be from George. Electronically printed. No watermark. No human hand.

Temporary accommodation has been obtained for you effective today's date at apartment 110B, Hood House, Dolphin Square, London SW. Following conditions apply.

I am to keep no pets. No unauthorized third party to be admitted to the premises. I am to be present and available in the premises between 2200 and 0700 hours, or supply Legal Department with notification in advance. In view of my position (unstated) a concessionary rental of £50 per night will be set against my pension. There will be no charge for heat, light or electricity, but I will be held accountable for any loss or damage to property.

The dishevelled youth called Nelson is poking his head round the door.

'Van's up, Laura.'

The sacking of the Stables is about to begin.

5

Dusk was falling. An autumn evening, but by English standards warm as summer. Somehow my first day in the Stables had ended. I walked for a while, had a Scotch in a pub full of deafening young, took a bus to Pimlico, hopped out a few stops early and walked again. Soon the lighted hulk of Dolphin Square was rising at me out of the haze. Ever since I had rallied to the secret flag, the place had given me the shivers. Dolphin Square in my day had more safe flats to the cubic foot than any building on the planet, and there wasn't one of them where I hadn't briefed or debriefed some luckless joe. It was also the place where Alec Leamas had spent his last night in England as a guest of Moscow's recruiter before setting out on the journey that killed him.

Flat 110B Hood House did nothing to dispel his ghost. Circus safe flats had always been models of planned discomfort. This one was a classic of the breed: one industrial-sized fire extinguisher, red; two lumpy armchairs with springs gone; one reproduction watercolour of Lake Windermere; one minibar, locked; one printed warning not to smoke EVEN WITH WINDOW OPEN; one very large television set that I automatically assumed was two-way; and one mossy black telephone with no number on it, to be used, as far as I was concerned, for disinformation purposes only. And in the tiny bedroom, one iron-hard school bed, single, to discourage venery.

Closing the bedroom door on the television set, I unpacked my overnight bag and cast round for somewhere to cache my French passport. A framed INSTRUCTIONS IN CASE OF FIRE was badly screwed to the bathroom door. Easing the screws, I slid the passport into the cavity, tightened them again, went downstairs and devoured a hamburger. Back in the flat, I treated myself to a liberal shot of Scotch and tried to recline in an austerity armchair. But barely had I drifted off than I was awake again and cold sober, this time in West Berlin in the year of Our Lord nineteen fifty-seven.

★

It's a Friday, end of day.

I've been in the divided city a week, and I'm looking forward to a couple of carnal days and nights in the company of a Swedish journalist called Dagmar, with whom I have fallen passionately in love in the space of three minutes at a cocktail party given by our British High Commissioner, who doubles as British Ambassador to the eternally provisional West German Government in Bonn. I'm due to meet her in a couple of hours, but before doing so I've decided to drop in on our Berlin Station and say my hullos and goodbyes to my old pal Alec.

Down at Berlin's Olympic Stadium, in an echoing redbrick barracks built for Hitler's glory and once known as the House of German Sports, the Station is packing up for the weekend. I find Alec standing in the queue at the barred window of the Registry, waiting his turn to hand in a tray full of classified papers. He isn't expecting me, but nothing much surprises him any more, so I say hullo, Alec, great to see you, and Alec says oh, hullo, Peter, it's you, what the hell are you doing here? Then, after some uncharacteristic hesitation, he asks me whether I'm tied up for the weekend. And I say, I am actually. To which he says, oh, pity,

I thought you might come with me to Düsseldorf. And I say, why on earth Düsseldorf? And he does some more hesitation.

'I just need to get out of bloody Berlin for once,' he says, with an unconvincing shrug of indifference. And because he seems to accept that I could never, in my wildest dreams, imagine him as a casual tourist: 'Got to see a man about a dog,' he explains, from which I take it that he wishes me to understand he has a joe he's got to take care of, and I might in that case be useful to him as a foil or a back-up or whatever. But that's no reason to stand up Dagmar:

'Can't do, I'm afraid, Alec. A Scandinavian lady needs my undivided attention. And I need hers.'

He thinks about this for a while, but not in a way that I associate with Alec. It's as if he feels hurt, or puzzled. A registry clerk is gesturing impatiently the other side of the grille. Alec hands over his papers. The clerk signs them in.

'A woman would be good,' he says, without looking at me.

'Even a woman who thinks I'm from the Ministry of Labour, scouting for German scientific talent? Come off it!'

'Bring her. She'll be fine,' he says.

And if you knew Alec as well as I did, that was as close to a cry for help as you would ever hear from him. In all the years we had hunted together, amid all the ups and downs, I had never once seen him at a loss, till now. Dagmar is game, so the same evening the three of us fly the corridor to Helmstedt, pick up a car, drive to Düsseldorf and book into a hotel Alec knows. Over dinner he barely speaks, but Dagmar, who is turning out to be a real trouper, more than holds her own, and we slip off to bed early and have our carnal night, both parties thoroughly pleased with themselves. Saturday morning we all meet for late breakfast and Alec says he's got tickets for a football match. I'd never in my life heard Alec express the smallest interest in football. Then it turns out he's got *four* tickets.

'Who's the fourth?' I ask him, fantasizing that he's got a secret love tucked away who's only available on Saturdays.

'Kid I know,' he says.

We get into the car, Dagmar and self in the back, and off we go. Alec pulls up at a street corner. A tall, rigid-faced boy in his teens is standing under a Coca–Cola sign, waiting for him. Alec shoves open the door, the boy jumps into the front seat and Alec says, 'This is Christoph,' so we say, 'Hullo, Christoph,' and off we drive to the stadium. Alec speaks German as well as he speaks English, probably better, and he speaks it to the boy in undertones. The boy grunts, nods or shakes his head. How old is he? Fourteen? Eighteen? Whatever age he is, he is the eternal German adolescent of the authoritarian class: sullen, spotty and resentfully obedient. He's blond, pallid and square-shouldered, and for a kid he doesn't smile a lot. On a rise, set back from the touchline, he and Alec stand side by side and exchange the odd word I can't hear, but the boy doesn't cheer, he stares, and at half-time the two of them disappear, I'm assuming for a pee or a hot dog. But only Alec returns.

'Where's Christoph?' I ask.

'Had to head back home,' he replies gruffly. 'Mum's orders.'

And for the rest of the weekend that was that. Dagmar and I spent more happy times in bed, and what Alec got up to I've no idea. I just assumed that Christoph was the son of one of his joes and needed an outing, because with joes it's welfare first and everything else second. It wasn't till I was about to return to London and Dagmar was safely back in Stockholm with her husband, and Alec and I were having a farewell drink together in one of his many favourite Berlin watering holes, that I asked him casually 'How's Christoph?' because it had crossed my mind that the boy had seemed a bit astray, a bit hard to please, and probably I even said something to this effect.

At first I thought I was going to get another of those odd silences, because he had turned away from me so that I couldn't see his face.

'I'm his bloody *father*, for Christ's sake,' he said.

Then in short, reluctant bursts, mostly without verbs, and not even bothering to tell me to keep it to myself because he knew I would, the story, or as much of it as he was willing to tell: German woman courier he'd used when he was based in Bern and she lived in Düsseldorf: good girl, good pals, had a fling with her. Wanted me to marry her. Wouldn't, so she married a local lawyer. Lawyer adopted the boy, only decent thing he ever did. She lets me see him now and then. Can't tell her bloody husband or the bastard would beat her up.

And the final image that I'm seeing now, as I rouse myself from my austerity chair: Alec and the boy Christoph, standing shoulder to shoulder, staring rigidly at the match. And the same set expression on their faces, and the same Irish jaw.

★

At some point in the night I must have slept, but had no memory of it. The time in Dolphin Square is six a.m., in Brittany seven. Catherine will be up and about by now. If I was at home, I would be up and about too, because Isabelle starts her singing as soon as Chevalier, our chief cockerel, starts his. Her voice carries straight across the courtyard from Catherine's cottage because Isabelle needs her bedroom window open at all times, never mind the weather. They will have fed the goats their breakfast, and Catherine will be feeding Isabelle hers, probably in a chase game round the courtyard with Isabelle escaping and Catherine coming after her with a spoonful of yoghurt. And the chickens, under the useless command of Chevalier, generally behaving as if the world is ending.

As I pictured this scene it crossed my mind that if I called the main house and Catherine happened to be passing, and had her keys with her, she might hear the ring and answer it. So I gave it a shot on the off-chance, using one of my disposable mobile phones because I was damned if I was going to have Bunny listening. There's no answering system on the farm phone, so I let it ring for a few minutes and was just giving up hope when I heard Catherine's voice, which is Breton, and sometimes a little more severe than perhaps she intends.

'You are well, Pierre?'

'Fine. You too, Catherine?'

'You have said goodbye to your friend who died?'

'Still a couple of days to go.'

'You will make a big speech?'

'Enormous.'

'You are nervous?'

'Terrified. How's Isabelle?'

'Isabelle is well. She has not changed in your absence.' By now I had noticed an undertone of annoyance, or something stronger in her voice. 'A friend came to visit you yesterday. You were expecting a friend, Pierre?'

'No. What sort of a friend?'

But, like every tough questioner, Catherine has her own way with answers: 'I told him: no, Pierre is not here, Pierre is in London, he is being a Good Samaritan, somebody has died, he has gone to comfort those who are grieving.'

'But who *was* he, Catherine?'

'He didn't smile. He was not polite. He was persistent.'

'You mean he made a pass at you?'

'He asked who had died. I said I don't know. He asked why don't I know? I said, because Pierre does not tell me everything. He laughed. He said, maybe at Pierre's age, all friends are dying. He asked, was it sudden? Was it a woman, a man? He asked, do you stay in a hotel in London? Which one? What is the address? What is the name? I say I don't know. I am busy, I have a child and a farm.'

'Was he French?'

'Maybe German. Maybe American.'

'Did he come by car?'

'Taxi. From the station. With Gascon. First you pay me, Gascon told him. Otherwise, I don't drive you.'

'What did he look like?'

'He was not agreeable, Pierre. Farouche. Big like a boxer. Many rings on his fingers.'

'Age?'

'Maybe fifty. Sixty. I did not count his teeth. Maybe more.'

'Did he tell you his name?'

'He said it was not necessary. He said you are old friends. He said you watch football together.'

I lie motionless, barely breathing. I think I should get out of bed, but have a *fuite du courage*. How the devil, Christoph, son of Alec, litigant, purloiner of closed Stasi files, criminal with a record as long as your arm, did you find your way to Brittany?

The farmstead at Les Deux Eglises had come down to me on my mother's side. It still bore her maiden name. There was no Pierre Guillam in the local phone book. Had Bunny for his own arcane reasons slipped Christoph my address? To what conceivable purpose?

Then I remember my motorcycle pilgrimage to a rain-swept cemetery in Berlin on a pitch-dark winter's day in 1989 and everything makes sense.

★

The Berlin Wall has been down a month. Germany is ecstatic, our village in Brittany a little less so. And I seem to be hovering somewhere between the two, one minute rejoicing that peace of a sort has broken out, then lapsing into introspection as I think of the stuff we did and the sacrifices we made, not least of other people's lives, in the long years when we thought the Wall was going to be there for ever.

It was in this uncertain mood that I was wrestling with the farmstead's annual tax returns in the counting room at Les Deux Eglises when our new young postman Denis, not yet dignified by Monsieur, and certainly not le Général, arrived not by yellow van but by pushbike, and handed a letter, not to me but to old Antoine, a one-legged war veteran, who as usual was hanging around the courtyard with a pitchfork in his hands and nothing in particular to do.

Having examined the envelope front and back, and conceded that I might have it after all, Antoine hobbled to the door, presented me with it, then stood back to scrutinize me while I read the contents.

Mürren,
Switzerland

Dear Peter,

I thought you would wish to know that the ashes of our friend Alec have recently been laid to rest in Berlin, close to the spot where he died. It seems that the bodies of those murdered at the Wall were customarily incinerated in secret, and their ashes dispersed. Thanks to meticulous Stasi records, however, it appears that exceptional steps were taken in Alec's case. His remains have come to light and he has been given a decent, if belated, funeral.

As ever,
George

And on a separate sheet of paper – old habits die hard – the address of a small cemetery in the Berlin district of Friedrichshain, officially set aside for victims of war and tyranny.

I was with Diane at the time, another passing fancy nearing its end. I think I told her that a friend was ill. Or maybe that the friend had died. I jumped on my motorbike – it was still those days – drove myself non-stop to Berlin through some of the worst weather I'd ever come across, went straight to the cemetery and asked at the entrance where I would find Alec. Dense, non-stop rain. An old man who was some kind of sacristan gave me an umbrella and a map and pointed me down a long grey avenue of trees. After hunting around, I found what I was looking for: one fresh grave, one marble headstone inscribed ALEC JOHANNES LEAMAS, washed eerily white by the rain. No dates, no job description, and a full-length mound to indicate a body where only ashes lay. For cover? All those years of knowing you, I thought, and you never told me about the Johannes: typical. I hadn't brought flowers; I thought he'd laugh at me. So I stood under my umbrella and had a sort of internal dialogue with him.

As I was getting back on my bike, the old man asked me whether I'd like to sign the condolence book. *Condolence book?* It was his personal duty to maintain one, he explained; not so much a duty, more as a service to the departed. So I said why not? The first entry was signed 'GS', address 'London'. In the tributes column, the one word 'Friend'. So that was George, or as much of him as he was willing to admit to. Below George, a bunch of German names that meant nothing to me, with tributes like 'Never forgotten', until we reach the one name 'Christoph', on its own, no surname after it. And under tributes, the word 'Sohn' – son. And under home address, 'Düsseldorf'.

Was it a passing fit of euphoria about the Wall coming down

and all the world being free again, which I severely doubt – or a gut feeling that I'd done enough secrecy in my life – or simply an urge to stand up in the pouring rain and be counted as another of Alec's *friends*? Whatever it was, I did the lot: wrote down my real name, my real address in Brittany, and in the tributes column, because I couldn't think of anything better, '*Pierrot*', which was what Alec called me on the rare occasions he was feeling affectionate.

And Christoph, my farouche fellow mourner and Alec's son? What did *you* do? On one of your later visits to your father's grave – I am assuming on no particular grounds that you made a few more, if only for research purposes – you happened to take another look in the condolence book, and what did you see? *Peter Guillam* and *Les Deux Eglises* written out for you *en clair*, not an alias, not a cover address or a safe house, just the unprotected me and where I live. And that's what got you all the way to Brittany from Düsseldorf.

So what's your next move, Christoph, son of Alec? I'm hearing Bunny's fruity legal voice from yesterday:

Christoph is not without his talents, Peter. Perhaps the genes help.

6

'Pete here is our *reader*,' Laura had declared to her admiring audience. 'For his reading Pete will be accommodated here in the library.' I see myself in the days that followed, not so much a reader as some sort of senior student forced to sit an examination he should have taken half a lifetime ago. Intermittently, the late developer is hauled out of the examination room and compelled to undergo a viva voce by examiners whose knowledge of his subject is mysteriously uneven, but that doesn't stop them from trying to give him a hard time. Intermittently, he is so appalled by the antics of his earlier self that he is on the verge of denying them, until the evidence condemns him out of his own mouth. Each morning on arrival I am served with a wad of folders, some familiar, some not. Just because you've stolen a file, doesn't mean you've read it.

On the morning of my second day, the library remained closed to all comers. From the thumps that issued from it, and the scurrying of tracksuited young men and women I wasn't introduced to, I assumed an all-night fingertip search. Then, by afternoon, an ominous quiet. My desk was not a desk, but a trestle table set gallows-like at the centre of the library floor. The bookshelves were gone, leaving only a ghostly imprint like the shadow of prison bars on the Anaglypta walls.

'When you hit a rosette, stop,' Laura commands me, and departs.

Rosette? She means the pink-headed paperclips wedged at intervals among the folders. Nelson silently assumes the invigilator's chair and opens a hefty paperback. Henri Troyat's life of Tolstoy.

'Give us a shout if you want a pee break, right? My dad pees like every ten minutes.'

'Poor chap.'

'Just don't take anything with you.'

★

A freak evening when Laura without explanation replaces Nelson on the invigilator's chair and, having surveyed me dourly for half an hour or more, says:

'Fuck it. Want to take me out for a free meal, Pete?'

'Now?' I say.

'Now. Tonight. When do you think?'

Free to whom? I'm wondering as I shrug my cautious acquiescence. Free to her? Me? Or free to both of us because the Office is setting us up? We adjourn to a Greek restaurant up the road. She's booked a table. She's wearing a skirt. It's a corner table, with an unlit candle in a red cage. I don't know why the image of the unlit candle lingers, but it does. And the patron leaning over us, lighting it and telling me I have the best view in the room, meaning Laura.

We have an ouzo, then another. Straight, no ice, her idea. So is she a lush, is she on the make – me at my age, for Christ's sake? – or does she think alcohol is going to loosen the old fart's tongue? And what should I be making of the very ordinary middle-aged couple sitting at the next table and determinedly not looking at us?

She's wearing a sleeveless halter top that sparkles in the candlelight and the neckline has slipped southward. We order the usual starters – tarama, houmous, whitebait – she adores moussaka so we settle for two, and she starts on a different kind of interrogation, the flirtatious kind. So is it really true, Pete, what you told Bunny, that you and Catherine are just good friends?

'Because *frankly*, Pete' – voice softening to intimate – 'what with *your* record, how can you *possibly* be shacked up with a super-attractive French girl you don't even *shag*? Unless of course you're secretly gay, which is what Bunny thinks. Mind you, Bunny thinks everyone's gay. So he's probably gay himself, and won't admit it.'

One half of me wants to tell her to go to hell, the other half wants to know what she thinks she's up to. So I let it go.

'But I mean honestly, Pete, it's *crazy!*' she persists. 'I mean, don't tell me you've *withdrawn your cavalry from the charge*, as my dad used to say: an old stoat like you, you can't *possibly!*'

I ask her, against my better instincts, what makes her think Catherine is so attractive? And she says, oh, a little bird has told her. We're drinking Greek red, black as ink and tastes like it, and she's leaning forward, giving me the full benefit of her neckline.

'So, Pete, tell me true. Scout's honour, okay? Of *all* the women you've bonked over the years – who gets the absolute number-one slot?' – her unfortunate choice of the word *slot* causing her to collapse in a fit of giggles.

'How about you first?' I retort, and the joke's over.

I call for the bill, the couple next door call for theirs. She says she'll take the tube. I say I'll walk a bit. And to this day I have no idea whether she was on a mission to draw me out; or was she just another unattached soul, looking for a bit of human warmth?

*

72

I am the Reader. The buff cover of the folder I am reading is blank except for a handwritten file reference – whose hand escapes me, but probably my own. The leading serial is marked Top Secret and Guard, which means keep it away from the Americans, and it is a report – apologia would be a better word – written by one Stavros de Jong, all six foot three of him, an ungainly Circus trainee of twenty-five. Stas for short is a Cambridge graduate with six months still to go before his confirmation. He's on attachment to Berlin Station's Covert section, which is commanded by my comrade-in-arms in a string of abortive operations, the veteran fieldman Alec Leamas.

As a matter of protocol, Leamas as local commander is also de facto deputy Head of Station. Stas's report is accordingly addressed to Leamas in that capacity, and forwarded to his Head of Covert in London, George Smiley.

Report by S. de Jong to DH / Station Berlin [Leamas], *copy to JS* [Joint Steering].

I am instructed to submit the following report.

New Year's Day being cold but sunny and a public holiday, my wife Pippa and I decided to take our children (Barney, 3 and Lucy, 5) and our Jack Russell (Loftus) to Köpenick, East Berlin, for a lakeside picnic in warm clothes, and a ramble in the adjoining woods.

Our family car is a blue Volvo estate with British military number plates front and rear, entitling us to unrestricted passage between Berlin sectors, Köpenick in East Berlin being one of our regular picnic spots and a favourite with the children.

I parked as per usual beside the perimeter wall of Köpenick's old brewery, now abandoned. There was no other car in sight, and at the waterside only a few seated fishermen who ignored us. From the car, we carried our picnic basket through the woods to our usual grass promontory beside the lake, and afterwards played hide-and-seek with Loftus barking loudly, to the irritation of one of the fishermen who shouted abuse at us over his shoulder, insisting Loftus had disturbed the fish.

The man was gaunt and in his fifties with greying hair, and I would recognize him if I saw him again. He wore a black peak cap and an old Wehrmacht topcoat stripped of its markings.

It being by now around 1530 hours and Barney due for his rest, we packed our picnic things together and let the children run ahead to the car carrying the basket between them, with Loftus following and barking.

On reaching the car, however, they dropped the basket and ran back in alarm, followed by Loftus barking, to report that the driver's door had been forced open by a burglar 'who has completely stolen Daddy's camera!' – Lucy.

The driver's door had indeed been forced, and the handle broken, but the old Kodak camera, which I had inadvertently left in the glove compartment, had not been stolen, nor had my overcoat or the groceries and other provisions that we had picked up at the Naafi, which to our surprise was open on New Year's Day, before crossing into East Berlin.

Far from committing a burglary, it transpired, the intruder had left a Memphis tobacco tin next to my camera. Inside it was a small nickel cartridge, which I immediately identified as a standard Minox container for sub-miniature film.

Since today is a public holiday, and I have recently attended an operational photography course, I decided there were insufficient grounds at this stage to call out the Station duty officer. On arriving home, I therefore immediately developed the film in our bathroom, which is windowless, using my Service-issue equipment.

By 2100 hours, having examined some one hundred frames of developed negative under a magnifying glass, I alerted the deputy Head of Station [Leamas], who instructed me to bring the material forthwith to headquarters and prepare a written report, which I duly did.

I fully accept, in hindsight, that I should have taken the undeveloped film directly to Berlin Station for processing by photographic section, and that it was insecure and potentially disastrous for me as a probationer to undertake the development in my own home. In mitigation I would like to repeat that 1 January was a public holiday and that I was reluctant to rouse the Station with what might have been a false alarm, plus I had passed my operational photography course at Sarratt with straight As. Nevertheless I sincerely regret my decision, and would like to state that I have learned my lesson.

S de J

And along the bottom of the letter, Alec's enraged hand-scrawled note to his Head of Covert, Smiley:

George – the stupid little bugger copied this lot to Joint before anyone had a chance to stop him. That's education for you. Suggest you smooth-talk P. Alleline, B. Haydon, T. Esterhase and Roy bloody Bland and company into believing it was a bum steer: i.e. no further action required, second-rate pedlar material, etc.

Alec

But Alec was never one to sit on his thumbs, least of all when his future career was in the balance. His contract with the Circus was up for renewal, he was way past the age limit for fieldmen, with precious little prospect of a cosy desk job in Head Office, which explains Smiley's somewhat untrusting account of what Alec did next:

H/Covert Marylebone [Smiley] *to Control. Eyes Only. Personal, hand-delivered.*
Subject: AL, H/Covert Berlin.

And handwritten, in George's own immaculate hand:

C: You will be as surprised as I was that AL appeared unannounced on the doorstep of my Chelsea home at ten o'clock last night. Ann being away on a health cure, I was alone in the house. He smelt of drink, not unusual, but was not drunk. He insisted I unplug the phone in the drawing room before we speak, and that, despite the prevailing very cold weather, we sit at the conservatory end overlooking the garden on the grounds that 'you can't bug glass'. He then told me he had flown from Berlin by civilian plane that afternoon in order not to appear on the RAF flight list, which he suspects is routinely monitored by Joint Steering. For the same reason he no longer trusts Circus couriers.

He first needed to know, had I put Joint off the scent, as he had asked, regarding the Köpenick material? I replied that I believed I had been able to achieve this, since it was well known that Berlin Station was besieged with offers of worthless pedlar intelligence.

He then produced the attached folded sheet of paper from his pocket, explaining that it was a summary, prepared by himself alone, of the material contained in the Köpenick cassettes, but without benefit of collateral from any other covert or overt source.

I have two visions simultaneously: the one of George and Alec huddled head to head in the chilly conservatory in Bywater Street; the second of Alec alone the night before, crouched over his ancient Olivetti and a bottle of Scotch in his smoke-filled basement office in the Olympic Stadium in West Berlin. The result of his labours lies before me: one grimy typewritten page, blotched by Tipp-Ex and encased in cellophane, text as follows:

1. Minutes KGB conference East Bloc intelligence services, Prague, 21 Dec 1957.
2. Name and rank home-based KGB officers on attachment to Stasi directorates, as of 5 July 1956.
3. Identity of current Stasi head agents in Sub-Saharan Africa.
4. Names, rank and worknames of all Stasi officers undergoing KGB training in USSR.
5. Location of six new covert Soviet signals installations in GDR and Poland, as of 5 July 1956.

Turn a page and I am back to Smiley's handwritten minute to Control, not a crossing-out:

The rest of Alec's story runs as follows. Regularly each week, after de Jong's scoop, if such it was, Alec commandeered the de Jongs' family Volvo and dog, put $500 in the glove compartment together with a children's colouring book with the number of his direct line to Berlin Station scrawled in it, threw his fishing gear into the back (I did not till now know that Alec fished and am inclined to doubt it), drove to Köpenick and parked where de Jong had parked at the same hour. With the dog beside him, he went fishing and waited. On the third attempt, he struck lucky.

The $500 had been replaced by two cassettes. The children's colouring book with the phone number had gone.

Two nights later, back in West Berlin, he received a call on the direct line from a man who refused to give his name, but said he fished in Köpenick. Alec instructed him to present himself outside a given house number on the Kurfürstendamm at seven-twenty the next evening carrying the previous week's edition of *Der Spiegel* in his left hand.

The resulting treff [i.e. covert meeting, as borrowed by Berlin hands from German espionage vernacular] took place in a Volkswagen people-carrier driven by de Jong, and lasted eighteen minutes. MAYFLOWER, as Alec has arbitrarily christened him, at first refused to reveal his name, insisting the cassettes came not from himself but from a 'friend inside the Stasi', whom he must protect. His own role was merely that of voluntary intermediary, he insisted, his motive not mercenary but ideological.

But Alec wasn't having this. Unsourced material delivered by an anonymous intermediary was a drug on the market, he said. So no deal. Finally – and only in response to Alec's entreaties, we are asked to believe – Mayflower produced a card from his pocket with the name Dr med. Karl Riemeck and the address of the Charité Hospital in East Berlin on one side, and on the back, an address in Köpenick, handwritten.

It is Alec's conviction that Riemeck had only been waiting to get the measure of his man before revealing himself, and that after ten minutes he abandoned his reservations. But we should never forget the Irishman in Alec.

So to the obvious questions:

Even if Dr Riemeck is who he says he is, who is his magic sub-source?

Are we dealing with yet another elaborate Stasi set-up?

Or – though it pains me to suggest it – are we dealing with something a little more home-brewed by Alec himself?

In conclusion:

Alec is asking with some passion, I have to say, to be allowed to develop Mayflower to the next stage *without* subjecting him to any of the usual searches and background checks which as things stand could not be conducted without the knowledge and assistance of Joint Steering. His reservations are well known to us both, and I venture to suggest we cautiously share them.

Alec however exhibits no such restraint regarding his suspicions. Last night after the third Scotch it was Connie Sachs he had cast as Moscow Centre's double agent within the Circus, with Toby Esterhase running a close second. His theory, based on nothing but his own whisky-fuelled intuition, was that the pair of them had got themselves caught up in a sex-driven *folie à deux*, the Russians had found out and were blackmailing them. I finally got him to bed around 2.00 a.m., only to find him in the kitchen at 6.00 a.m., cooking himself bacon and eggs.

The question is what to do. On balance, I am inclined to let him have one more run with his Mayflower (which means, effectively, with his mysterious alleged sub-source in the Stasi) on his own terms. As we both know, his days in the field are numbered, and he has every reason to extend them. But we also know that the hardest part of our work is to invest trust. Based on little more than instinct, Alec declares himself solidly convinced of Mayflower's bona fides. This can be either the inspired hunch of a veteran, or the special pleading of an ageing field officer facing the natural end of his career.

79

I respectfully recommend that we allow him to go forward in that knowledge.

GS

But Control is not so easily won over: see following exchange.

Control to GS: Seriously concerned that Leamas is paddling his own canoe. Where are the other indicators? Surely we may test the intelligence in areas that in Leamas's vision of things are not contaminated?

GS to Control: Have separately consulted FO and Defence under a pretext. Both speak well of material, do not believe it is fabrication. Chickenfeed as a prelude to a major deception always a possibility.

Control to GS: Puzzled why Leamas does not consult his Berlin Head of Station. Backstage manoeuvrings of this sort do Service no good.

GS to Control: Unfortunately Alec regards his H/Stn as anti-Covert and pro-Joint.

Control to GS: I cannot divest myself of a *galère* of top-notch officers on the unproven supposition that one of them is a bad apple.

GS to Control: I'm afraid Alec sees Joint as a bad orchard.

Control to GS: Then perhaps it's he who should be pruned.

Alec's next written offering is of a different order altogether: immaculately typed and in a prose style far superior to his own. My immediate suspect as Alec's amanuensis is Stas de Jong, first-class honours in modern languages. So this time it's the six-foot-three Stas I see crouched at the Olivetti in the smoke-filled basement in Berlin Station while Alec prowls the room, puffing at one of his vile Russian cigarettes and dictating raucous Irish obscenities that de Jong discreetly omits.

Encounter Report, 2 February 1959. Location: Berlin Safe House K2. Present: DH/Station Berlin Alec Leamas (PAUL) and Karl Riemeck (MAYFLOWER).
Source MAYFLOWER. Second Treff. Beyond Secret, Personal & Private from AL to H/Covert Marylebone.

Source Mayflower, known to the GDR's elite as 'The Doctor of Köpenick' after Carl Zuckmayer's play of similar title, is physician of choice to a select coterie of ranking SED [Socialist Unity (i.e. Communist) Party] and Stasi *prominenz* and their families, several of whom reside in Köpenick's lakeside villas and apartments. His leftist credentials are impeccable. His father Manfred, a Communist since the early thirties, fought with Thälmann in the Spanish Civil War and later joined the Red Orchestra network against Hitler. During 1939–45 war Mayflower smuggled messages for his father, who was hanged by the Gestapo at Buchenwald concentration camp in 1944. Manfred did not therefore live to see the coming of the revolution to East Germany, but his son Karl, for love of his father, was determined to be its devoted comrade. After excelling at high school, he studied medicine in Jena and Prague. Qualified *magna cum laude*. Not content with working long hours at East Berlin's one teaching hospital, he opened up his family house in Köpenick, which he shares with ageing mother Helga, as an informal surgery for selected patients.

As a natural-born member of the GDR's elite, Mayflower is also tasked with medical missions of a sensitive nature. A ranking SED official contracts VD while on a visit to distant parts and doesn't wish his superiors to know. Mayflower obliges with a false diagnosis. A Stasi prisoner has died of heart failure under interrogation, but the death certificate must tell a different story. A high-value Stasi prisoner is about to be subjected to harsh treatment. Mayflower is required to check the prisoner's psychological and physical condition and assess tolerance.

In view of these responsibilities, Mayflower has been awarded the status of *Geheime Mitarbeiter* (secret collaborator) or GM for short, which requires him to report monthly to his Stasi controller, one Urs ALBRECHT, a 'functionary of no great imagination'. Mayflower says his reports to Albrecht are 'selective, mostly invented, of no possible consequence'. Albrecht in return has told him that he is 'a good doctor but a lousy spy'.

Exceptionally, Mayflower has also been granted a pass to the 'Little City', otherwise the Majakowskiring in East Berlin, where many of the GDR's elite are accommodated, while being rigorously protected from the general public by the Dzerzhinsky Brigade, a specially trained unit. Although the 'Little City' boasts its own medical centre – not to mention privilege shop, kindergarten, etc. – Mayflower is permitted to enter the hallowed area for the purpose of attending his illustrious 'private' patients. Once inside the cordon, he reports, rules of discretion are relaxed, gossip and intrigue are rife, tongues loosened.

Motivation:
Mayflower's claimed motivation is disgust with GDR regime, father's Communist dream seen as betrayed.

Offer of service:
Mayflower claims that sub-source TULIP, a female patient and Stasi employee, not only provided the catalyst for his

self-recruitment, but is the source of the original sub-miniature cassettes that he deposited on her behalf in de Jong's Volvo. He describes Tulip as neurotic but extremely controlled, and highly vulnerable. He insists that she is his patient, and nothing more. He reiterates that neither he nor Tulip requires financial reward.

Resettlement in the West in the event of compromise not yet discussed. See below.

But we don't see below. Next day Smiley himself flies to Berlin to take a look at this Riemeck for himself, and orders me to accompany him. Yet source Mayflower is not the primary reason for our journey. Of much greater interest to him is the identity, access and motivation of the neurotic but extremely controlled female sub-source, codename Tulip.

*

Dead of night in an unsleeping West Berlin swept by freezing winds of sleet and snow. Alec Leamas and George Smiley sit cloistered with their new prospect Karl Riemeck aka Mayflower over a bottle of Talisker, Alec's favourite, and for Riemeck a first. I sit at Smiley's right shoulder. Berlin safe house K2 lies in the Fasanenstrasse, at No. 28, and is a stately and unlikely survivor of Allied bombing. It is built in the Biedermeier style with a pillared doorway, a bay window and a good back exit leading on to the Uhlandstrasse. Whoever chose it had a taste for imperial nostalgia and an operational eye.

Some faces, try as they may, cannot conceal the good heart of their owners, and Riemeck's is such a face. He is balding, bespectacled – and sweet. The word is simply not to be denied. Never mind the medic's studious frown: humanity breathes out of him.

Recalling now that first encounter, I have to remind myself that in 1959 there was no great drama to an East Berlin doctor coming across to West Berlin. Many did, and a lot never went back, which was why the Wall was built.

The file's opening serial is typed and unsigned. It is not a formal report, and I can only assume that the author is Smiley; and that, since no addressee is indicated, he is writing for the file – in other words, to himself.

Asked to identify the process by which he entered what he describes as the 'chrysalis' stage of his opposition to the GDR regime, Mayflower points to the moment when the Stasi's interrogators ordered him to prepare a woman for 'investigative confinement'. The woman was a GDR citizen in her fifties allegedly working for the CIA. She suffered from acute claustrophobia. Solitary confinement had already driven her half mad. 'Her screams as they nailed her into a box are with me still' – Mayflower.

In the wake of this experience, Mayflower, who claims he is not given to rash decisions, says he 'reappraised his situation from every angle'. He had heard the Party's lies at first hand, observed its corruption, hypocrisies and abuse of power. He had 'diagnosed the symptoms of a totalitarian state posing as its opposite'. Far from the democracy his father had dreamed of, East Germany was 'a Soviet vassal run as a police state'. With this perception made, he says, only one course was open to the son of Manfred: resistance.

His first thought was to establish an underground cell. He would select one or other elite patient who from time to time had given signs of dissatisfaction with the regime, and proposition him or her. But to do what? And for how long? Mayflower's father Manfred had been betrayed by his comrades. In that regard at least, the son did not propose to follow in the father's footsteps. So whom did he trust enough, in all circumstances and all weathers? Answer, not even his mother Helga, an avowed Communist come what may.

Very well, he reasoned, he would remain what he already was: 'a terrorist cell of one'. He would emulate, not his father but a boyhood hero, Georg Elser, the man who in 1939, without benefit of accomplice or confidant, had made, planted and detonated a bomb in the Munich beer cellar where minutes before the Führer had been addressing his faithful. 'Only infernal luck had saved him' – Mayflower.

But the GDR, he reasoned, was not a regime that could be blown away with a single blast, any more than Hitler's was. Mayflower was first and last a doctor. A rotten system must be treated from within. How to do that would reveal itself in due course. Meanwhile, he would confide in no one, trust in no one. He would be himself alone, sufficient to himself, answerable to himself. He would be *a secret army of one*.

The 'chrysalis' burst open, he maintains, when at 2200 hours on 18 October 1958, a distraught young woman who was unknown to him rode her bicycle to Köpenick in the eastern suburbs of Berlin and presented herself at Mayflower's surgery, demanding an abortion.

At which point Smiley's account breaks off, and it is Dr Riemeck who is speaking to us directly. George must have felt that his account, for all its length, was too precious to compress:

Comrade [deleted] is a highly intelligent woman of undoubted attraction, outwardly abrupt in the approved Party manner, highly resourceful, but in the privacy of a medical consultation intermittently childlike and defenceless. Though I am not given to off-the-cuff diagnoses of a patient's mental condition, I would tentatively suggest a form of selective schizophrenia, rigidly controlled. That she is also a woman of personal courage and high principle should not be perceived as a paradox.

I inform Comrade [deleted] that she is not pregnant and therefore requires no abortion. She tells me she is surprised to hear this considering she has slept with two equally repugnant men in the same cycle. She asks if I have any alcohol. She says she is not an alcoholic but both her men drink heavily and she has acquired the habit. I offer her a glass of the French cognac given me by a Congolese minister of agriculture in gratitude for my medical services. Having swallowed it at one gulp, she interrogates me:

'Friends told me you are a decent man and discreet. Are they right?' she demands.

'Which friends?' I ask.

'Secret friends.'

'Why do your friends have to be secret?'

'Because they are from the Organs.'

'Which organs?'

I have annoyed her. She snaps at me. 'The *Stasi*, Comrade Doctor. What do you think?'

I caution her. I may be a doctor but I have my responsibilities to the State. She prefers not to hear me. She has a right to choose, she says. In a democracy where all comrades are equal, she can choose between a sadistic shit of a husband who beats her up and refuses to admit that he's homosexual, and a fat fifty-year-old swine of a boss who regards it as his good right to screw her in the back of his Volga staff car any time he feels like it.

She has twice in this conversation let fall the name Dr Emmanuel Rapp. She calls him the Rappschwein. I ask her whether this Rapp is any relation of Comrade Brigitte Rapp, who insists on consulting me for a range of illusory ailments. Yes, she confirms, Brigitte is the name of the swine's wife. The connection is made. Frau Brigitte Rapp has already confided to me that she is married to a senior Stasi functionary who does as he pleases. I am therefore in the presence of Dr Emmanuel Rapp's very angry personal assistant and – according to her – secret mistress. She says she has considered putting arsenic into Rapp's coffee. She says she keeps a knife under the bed for the next time her homosexual husband assaults her. I advise her that these are dangerous fantasies and she should abandon them.

I ask her whether she speaks in these seditious terms to her husband or in the workplace. She laughs and assures me she does not. She has three faces, she says. In this she is lucky because in the GDR most people have five or six: 'In the workplace, I am a devoted and diligent comrade, I am well dressed and have orderly hair at all times and especially at meetings, and I am also the sex-slave of an illustrious swine. At home, I am the hate-object of a sadistic warm brother (homosexual) more than ten years my senior for whom the sole aim of life is to become a member of the Majakowskiring elite and sleep with pretty young men.' Her third identity is the one I see before me now: a woman who detests every aspect of life in the GDR except her son, and has found secret solace in God the Father and His saints. I ask her who else she has confided this third identity to apart from myself. Nobody. I ask her whether she hears voices. She is not aware of doing so, but if she heard anyone's voice it would be God's. I ask her whether she is indeed tempted to do herself harm, as she suggested to me earlier. She replies that she was recently minded to throw herself off a bridge, but was restrained by love of her son Gustav.

I ask her whether she has been tempted to commit other

demonstrative or vengeful acts, and she replies that on one recent occasion, when Dr Emmanuel Rapp left his pullover on his chair one evening, she took a pair of scissors and hacked it to pieces, then gathered the pieces into a burn-bag for secret waste. When Rapp returned next morning and complained that he had mislaid his pullover, she helped him look for it. When he decided that someone had stolen it, she suggested culprits.

I ask her whether her vengeful feelings towards Comrade Dr Rapp have since abated. She retorts that they are stronger than ever, and the only thing she hates more than Rapp is the system that elevates swine like him to positions of power. Her hidden hatreds are alarming and it is something of a miracle to me that she contrives to conceal them from the ever-vigilant eye of her work comrades.

I ask her where she lives. She replies that she and her husband lived till recently in a Soviet-style apartment in the Stalinallee, where there was no special protection and she had only a ten-minute cycle ride to Stasi headquarters in the Magdalenenstrasse. Recently – whether through homo-sexual influence or money she doesn't know, since her husband is secretive about the money that was left him by his father – they moved into a protected area in Berlin Hohenschönhausen set aside for government officials and higher civil servants. There are lakes and forest, which she loves, a playground for her son Gustav, and even a small private garden with a barbecue. In any other circumstances the house would be an idyll, but sharing it with her odious husband makes it a mockery. She is a passionate cyclist, still rides her bicycle to work, and reckons half an hour from door to door.

It is one a.m. I ask her what she will tell her husband Lothar when she gets home. She replies that she will tell him nothing and adds the following words:

88

'When my darling Lothar is not raping me or getting drunk, he sits on the edge of the bed with GDR Foreign Office papers on his lap, growling and writing like a man who hates the whole world, not only his wife.'

I ask her whether these are secret papers that her husband brings home. She replies that they are extremely secret, and that he brings them home illegally because in addition to being a sexual pervert he is obsessively ambitious. She asks me whether, on the next occasion that she visits me, I will make love to her on the grounds that she has yet to make love to a man who is not a pig or a rapist. I believe she is joking but I am not certain. In any event I decline, explaining that I have made it a principle not to sleep with my patients. I leave her with the possible consolation of knowing that if I were not her doctor I would sleep with her. As she mounts her bicycle to depart, she informs me that she has placed her life in my hands. I reply that, as a doctor, I shall respect her confidences. She asks me for a second appointment. I offer her next Thursday at six in the evening.

Overcome by a wave of inner revulsion, I rise involuntarily to my feet.

'Know where it is?' Nelson enquires, without lifting his eyes from his book.

I lock myself in the toilet, remain there as long as I dare. When I resume my place at the table, Doris Gamp, alias Tulip, has arrived punctually for her second appointment, having cycled all the way to Köpenick with her son Gustav riding in a basket.

Riemeck again:

The mood of mother and son is merry and relaxed. The weather is beautiful, her husband Lothar has been summoned to a conference in Warsaw at short notice, he will not be back for two days, they are in high spirits. Tomorrow she and Gustav will bicycle to her sister Lotte, 'the only other person in the world I love', she informs me gaily. Entrusting the child to my dear mother, who wishes only that he were mine, I escort Comrade [deleted] to my attic surgery and play Bach loudly on the gramophone. Ceremoniously – I would say skittishly – she presents me with a box of chocolates which she says was given her by Emmanuel Rapp, and advises me not to eat them all at once. On opening the box I see that it contains, instead of Belgian chocolates, two cassettes of sub-miniature film. I sit on a stool beside her, her mouth close to my ear. I ask her what is in the sub-miniature film. She replies Stasi secret documents. I ask her how she obtained them and she replies that she photographed them this very afternoon with the aid of Emmanuel Rapp's own Minox camera in the wake of a particularly degrading sexual encounter. The act was barely consummated than the Rappschwein had scurried away to a meeting in House 2 for which he was already late. She was feeling vengeful and bold. The documents were strewn over his desk. His Minox camera lay in the drawer where he keeps it during the day.

'Stasi officers are supposed to be secure in their habits at all times,' she tells me, adopting the tone of a Stasi apparatchik. 'The Rappschwein is so arrogant that he believes he is superior to Service regulations.'

'And the cassettes?' I ask her. How will she account for them?

The Rappschwein is infantile, therefore his whims must be gratified instantly, she says. It is totally forbidden even for officers of rank to keep special equipment such as secret cameras or recording devices in their personal safes, but Rapp ignores this edict, as others. Furthermore, on leaving the room in such haste he actually left the safe door ajar, another flagrant breach of security, enabling her to bypass the wax-lock.

I ask her: what is a wax-lock? She explains that on Stasi safes there is an elaborate lock which is capped by a coating of soft wax. On closing the safe, the rightful owner makes his own imprint in the wax, using the Stasi-issued key and its attached signet [*Petschaft*] that he keeps on his person at all times. Each *Petschaft* is numbered, individually crafted and unique to itself. As to cassettes, he has cardboard boxes full of them, a dozen at a time. He keeps no count of them, and uses his Minox like a toy for many unofficial and dissolute purposes. For instance he has tried many times to persuade her to pose naked for him, but she has always refused. He also keeps bottles of vodka and slivovitz in his safe, since like many Stasi bigwigs he drinks heavily, and when drunk speaks indiscreetly. I ask her how she succeeded in smuggling the sub-miniature film out of Stasi headquarters and she giggled and replied that a doctor like me should know.

However she insists that, despite the Stasi's obsession with internal security, those with the correct passes are not subject to physical searches. For instance, Comrade [deleted] has a pass entitling her to move at will between Houses 1 and 3 of the Stasi complex. I ask her what she expects me to do with the cassettes now that she has compromised me with them, and she replies that I should kindly pass them to British Intelligence. I ask why not American, and she is shocked. She is a Communist, she says. Imperialist America is her enemy. We return downstairs. Gustav is playing dominoes with my dear mother. She reports that he is a delightful child, and very good at dominoes, and she would like to steal him.

Covert's technical arm, always on the lookout for an excuse to join the feast, chimes in:

Berlin Covertech to H/Covert Berlin [Leamas].
Re your Head Agent MAYFLOWER:

1. You report his attic surgery in Köpenick contains old-style radio. Tech Ops to adapt as recording device?
2. You report that Mayflower owns an Exakta single-lens reflex camera that is Stasi-approved for recreational use. He also owns a sunlamp for therapeutic use and, from his student days, a microscope. Since he already has the basic components, should he be instructed in the manufacture of microdots?
3. Köpenick is a rural, densely wooded area, ideal for cachement of W/T and other operational equipment. Stay-behind team to reconnoitre and report?
4. Wax-locks. In the course of Tulip's dalliances with Emmanuel Rapp, might she have occasion to take an impression of his personal safe key and attached signet [*Petschaft*]? Technical stores have a wide variety of CDs [concealment devices] for containing suitable plasticine-type substances.

The inner revulsion returns. *In the course of her dalliances?* They weren't *Tulip's* bloody dalliances, they were the Rappschwein's, damn you! Tulip submitted to them because she knew if she didn't she'd be out on her ear on trumped-up disciplinary charges, and Gustav would never get to that elite school she dreamed of. And all right, she was a passionate woman and easily aroused. That does *not* mean she enjoyed herself *either* with the Rappschwein *or* with her husband!

But in Berlin, Alec Leamas has no such concerns:

H/Covert Berlin [Leamas] *to H/Covert Marylebone* [Smiley].
DO letter, copy to file.

Dear George,

   A perfect pour!

Happy to report that the impression of Emmanuel
Rapp's *Petschaft* and key, covertly taken by sub-source
Tulip, has produced a clean facsimile with sharp lettering
and numerals. The cowboys in Tech have advised that,
for safety's sake, she should apply a slight twist as she
withdraws the *Petschaft* from the wax. So doubles all round!

   Yours in the faith,

Alec

P.S. Attached: Tulip's PP, as per HO regs, for COVERT'S
EYES ONLY!!   AL

PP for Personal Particulars. PP for the shorthand of any human
life in which the Service has a passing interest. PP for penance.
PP for pain.

Full name of sub-agent: Doris Carlotta Gamp.
Date and place of birth: Leipzig 21.x.'29.
Education: Graduated Jena and Dresden universities in
Political and Social Sciences.
One sister: Lotte, elementary school teacher in Potsdam,
unmarried.
CV and other personal particulars: Age 23, recruited as junior
filing clerk, Stasi HQ, East Berlin. Access restricted to
Confidential and below. After six-month probationary period,
access raised to Secret. Assigned section J3, responsible for
processing and evaluating reports from overseas stations.
   One year into employment, forms relationship with

forty-one-year-old Lothar Quinz, held to be a rising star of GDR Foreign Service. Pregnancy and civil marriage follow.

Six months into marriage, Quinz née Gamp gives birth to a son, names him Gustav after father. Unknown to her husband, she has boy christened by eighty-seven-year-old retired Russian Orthodox priest and *starets* (holy wanderer), a self-styled Rasputin attached to Red Army barracks in Karlshorst. How the supposed conversion to Russian Orthodoxy occurred is not otherwise known. To escape Quinz's notice, Gamp told him she was visiting her sister in Potsdam, and made the journey to Rasputin by bicycle with Gustav in the basket.

10 June 1957, at end of her fifth year of employment, again promoted, this time to assistant to Emmanuel Rapp, KGB-trained director of overseas operations.

To retain Rapp's patronage, also obliged to provide him with sexual favours. When she complains of this to her husband, he tells her the wishes of a comrade of Rapp's importance should not be denied. She believes that this is an attitude shared by her Stasi colleagues. According to Tulip, they are aware of the affair, and aware that it constitutes a gross infringement of Stasi discipline. But they also fear that, given the extent of Rapp's power, if they report it they will suffer the consequences.

Operational experience to date:
On joining Stasi, attended indoctrination course for all junior staff. Unlike most of her colleagues, has good spoken and written Russian. Selected for additional training in conspiratorial methods, covert meetings, recruitment and deception. Also instructed in secret writing (carbon and fluids), clandestine photography (sub-miniature, microdot), surveillance, counter-surveillance, basic W / T. Aptitude rated 'good to excellent'.

As Emmanuel Rapp's PA and 'golden girl' (Rapp's description), regularly accompanies him to Prague, Budapest and Gdansk where he attends KGB-organized intelligence conferences of East Bloc liaison services. Twice employed at such conferences as stenographer of record. Despite her antipathy to him, dreams of accompanying Rapp to Moscow to see Red Square at night.

Concluding Comments by Case Officer:
H/Covert Berlin to H/Covert Marylebone [no doubt with the assistance of Stas de Jong]
Sub-source Tulip's relationship with this Service is conducted exclusively through Mayflower. He is her medical doctor, handler, confidant, personal confessor and best pal in that order. So what we've got is a one-dog girl in thrall to our head agent, and for my money that's how things should stay. As you know, we recently supplied her with her own Minox, built into the fastener of her shoulder bag, and cassettes in the base of a talc tin. She is also as of now the proud possessor of a duplicate key and *Petschaft* for the wax-lock on Rapp's safe.

It is gratifying therefore that Mayflower reports that Tulip shows no disturbing signs of strain. To the contrary, he says her morale has never been higher, she appears to relish danger, and his only concern is that she will become over-confident and take needless risks. For as long as the two of them are able to meet naturally in Berlin under medical cover, he is not greatly concerned.

However, an entirely different operational problem arises when she is escorting Rapp to conferences outside the GDR. Since dead letter boxes are no answer to ad hoc requirements, can Covert consider putting a blind courier on standby to service Tulip at short notice in non-German Bloc cities?

I turn a page. My hand is steady. Under stress it always is. This is normal operational discourse between Covert headquarters and Berlin.

George Smiley to Alec Leamas in Berlin, personal, handwritten note, copy to file:

Alec. In anticipation of Emmanuel Rapp's forthcoming visit to Budapest, please arrange for the attached photograph of Peter Guillam, who will be acting as her blind courier, to be shown to sub-source Tulip asap.

Best, G

George Smiley to Peter Guillam, handwritten note, copy to file:

Peter. This will be your lady in Budapest. Study her well!

Bon voyage, G

'Say something?' Nelson asked sharply, looking up from his book.

'Nothing. Why?'

'Must have been out in the street.'

*

When you're examining the features of an unknown woman for operational purposes, carnal thoughts are on hold. You're not looking for charm. You're wondering whether she'll be wearing her hair short or long, tinted, under a hat or free, and what her face has to offer in the way of distinguishing features: broad brow, high cheekbones, small or large eyes, whether they are round or naturally attenuated. After the face, you'll be looking at the shape and size of the body and trying to work out how it would look if it was wearing something more recognizable than the standard Party trouser suit and clunky lace-up shoes. You're not looking for its sex appeal, except insofar as it may draw the eye of an impressionable watcher. My sole concern at this stage was how the owner of this face and this body was going to perform opposite a blind courier on a hot summer's day in the closely watched streets of Budapest.

And the short answer turned out to be: immaculately. Skilled, deft, anonymous, purposeful. And I, as her blind courier, no less. A sunny day, a bustling street, two strangers, we advance on each other, are about to collide, I veer left, she right, there is momentary entanglement. I grunt an apology, she ignores it and sweeps on. I am richer by two cassettes of microfilm.

A second brush in Warsaw Old Town four weeks later, although more demanding, also passes off without mishap, as witness my handwritten report to George, copy to Alec:

PG to H/Covert Marylebone, copy to AL, Berlin.
Subject: Sub-source TULIP blind treff.

___

As on previous occasions we achieved early mutual recognition. Interbody contact was undetectable and swift. I do not believe that even close surveillance could have caught the moment of transfer.

It was clear that Tulip had been excellently briefed by Mayflower. My subsequent offload to H/Stn Warsaw presented no difficulties.

PG

And Smiley's handwritten response:

Deftly done again, Peter! Bravo!   GS

97

But maybe not quite as deftly as Smiley thinks, or quite as un-eventfully as my handwritten minute was so keen to suggest.

*

I am a French tourist from Brittany travelling with a Swiss tour group. My passport describes me as a company director but questioned by my fellow travellers I reveal myself to be a humble traveller in agricultural fertilizer. Together with my group, I am enjoying the sights of Warsaw's splendidly restored Old Town. A well-grown young woman in baggy jeans and tartan waistcoat is striding towards us. Her hair, last seen hidden by a beret, is today flowing free and auburn. With each step it bounces in the sunshine. She wears a green neck scarf. No scarf means no handover. I am wearing a Party cloth cap with a red star, bought at a street stall. Shove the cap in my pocket, no handover. The Old Town is milling with other tour groups. Ours is less manageable than our Polish guide would wish. Three or four of us are already lost to her, chatting among ourselves instead of being lectured about the city's miraculous rebirth after the Nazi bombing. A bronze statue has caught my eye. It has caught Tulip's too because this is how our encounter has been choreographed. There will be no slowing down as we meet. Nonchalance is all, just not too much of it. No eye contact, but nothing too studied about the way we ignore each other. Warsaw is a very wired town. Tourist attractions head the watch list.

So what's this jaunty swinging of the hips she's doing suddenly, what's with the light of explicit welcome in the big, almond eyes? For a fleeting second – but less fleeting than I am prepared for – our right hands curl into each other. But instead of instantly parting, her fingers, having deposited their tiny contents, nestle in my palm, and would have gone on nestling there for longer if I hadn't prised them free. Is she mad? Am I? And what's with that flash of welcoming smile I caught? – or am I deluding myself?

We go our separate ways: she to her conference of Warsaw Pact espiocrats, I with my group to a cellar bar, where the Cultural Secretary from the British Embassy and his wife happen to be regaling themselves at a corner table. I order a beer and adjourn to the men's lavatory. The Cultural Secretary, known to me in another life as a fellow trainee at Sarratt, follows me. The offload is swift and wordless. I rejoin my group. But the flutter of Tulip's fingers hasn't gone away.

And it hasn't gone away now, as I read Stas de Jong's hymn of praise to sub-source Tulip, brightest star of the Mayflower network:

Tulip has been made fully conscious that she is reporting to this Service and that Mayflower is our unofficial assistant as well as her cut-out. She has decided she loves England unconditionally. She is particularly impressed by the high quality of our tradecraft, and singled out her most recent treff in Warsaw as an example of British excellence.

Tulip's terms of resettlement on termination of work, whenever that should occur, will be £1,000 per month of service completed, plus a one-time ex gratia payment of £10,000, as approved by H/Covert [GS]. But her greatest wish is that, when the time comes, whenever that is, she and her son Gustav will become British citizens.

Her own covert gifts are perhaps even more impressive. Her success in installing a sub-miniature camera in the base of the shower platform in the women's toilet in her corridor relieves her of the stress of taking it in and out of House 3 in her handbag. Her Office-built *Petschaft* and key enable her to enter and leave Rapp's safe whenever the coast is clear and she feels inclined. Last Saturday she confided to Mayflower that her most recurrent dream was of one day marrying a beautiful Englishman!

'Something wrong then?' Nelson demands, this time with intent.

'I've hit a rosette,' I reply, which happens to be true.

★

Bunny has brought a briefcase with him and wears a dark suit. He has come straight from a meeting at the Treasury, who with or why he doesn't say. Laura lounges in Control's chair with her legs crossed. Bunny takes a bottle of warm Sancerre from his briefcase and pours us all a glass. Then opens a packet of salted cashews, saying we're to help ourselves.

'Heavy going, Peter?' he enquires genially.

'What do you expect?' I reply in the aggrieved tone I have decided to adopt. 'Not exactly a happy walk down memory lane, is it?'

'But helpful, I hope. Not too stressful, revisiting old times and faces?'

I let this go. The interrogation begins, at first languidly:

'Can I ask you first about *Riemeck*, an unusually attractive character for an agent, I would have thought?'

Nod.

'And a doctor. A pretty good one.'

Nod again.

'So why do Mayflower reports of the day, as distributed to lucky Whitehall customers, describe the source as – and I quote – *a well-placed official employed in the mid-levels of the East German Socialist Unity Party with regular access to highly classified Stasi material?*'

'Disinformation,' I reply.

'Planted by?'

'George, Control, Lacon in Treasury. They all knew the Mayflower material was going to cause a stir the moment it hit the stands. The first thing customers would be asking was who's the source. So they cooked up a fictional source of equal weight.'

'And your Tulip?'

'What about Tulip?'

Too fast. I should have waited. Is he goading me? Why else is he giving me that knowing, mirthless smirk that makes me want to hit him? And why is Laura smirking too? Is she getting her own back after our misfired Greek dinner?

Bunny is reading from something on his lap, and his subject is still Tulip: '*Sub-source is a senior secretary in the Interior Ministry with access to the highest circles.* Isn't that going it a bit?'

'Going it how?'

'Doesn't it give her a bit more – well, *respectability* than she deserves? I mean, what about *promiscuous* senior secretary, for starters? *Office nympho* might be a better fit, if we're looking for some sort of equivalence in the real world. Or *holy whore*, per-haps, in deference to her religious preferences?'

He is watching me, waiting for my outburst of fury, indigna-tion, denial. Somehow I manage to deny him the satisfaction.

'Still, I suppose you should know your Tulip,' he goes on. 'You who serviced her so diligently.'

'I did *not* service her, and she is not *my* Tulip,' I reply with measured deliberation. 'The entire time she was in the field, Tulip and I did not exchange a single word.'

'Not one?'

'Not in all our treffs. We brush-passed, we never spoke.'

'So how come she knew your name?' he enquires with his most charming, boyish smile.

'She did *not* know my bloody name! How the hell could she, when we never said so much as *hullo* to each other?'

'*One* of your names, put it that way,' he persists, unruffled.

Laura's cue: 'Try *Jean-François Gamay* for size, Pete,' she suggests, in the same jocular vein. 'Partner in a French electronics company based in Metz, enjoying a package holiday beside the Black Sea with the Bulgarian State travel company. That's a bit more than *hullo*.'

My outburst of merry laughter is unconfined, and so it should be, since it's the product of spontaneous and genuine relief.

'Oh for Christ's sake!' I exclaim, joining in the fun. 'That's not what I told *Tulip*. That's what I told *Gustav*!'

★

So here you are, Bunny and Laura, and I hope you're sitting comfortably for this cautionary tale about how the most secretive and best-laid plans can founder on a child's innocence.

My workname is indeed Jean-François Gamay, and yes, I'm a member of a large, closely observed travel group enjoying low-cost sea and sun in a not very salubrious Bulgarian beach resort on the Black Sea.

Across the bay from our dismal hotel sits the Party Workers' Hostel, a brutalist hulk of Soviet-style concrete covered in Communist flags and we can hear its martial music booming at us over the water, punctuated with uplifting messages of peace and goodwill from a battery of loudspeakers. Somewhere within its walls, Tulip and her five-year-old son Gustav are taking a workers' collective holiday, thanks to the influential connections of the odious Comrade Lothar, Tulip's husband, who has mysteriously overcome the Stasi's reluctance to allow its members to romp on foreign sands. She is accompanied by her sister, Lotte, the schoolteacher from Potsdam.

On the beach, between four and four-fifteen, Tulip and I will undertake a brush pass, and this time it will include her son Gustav.

Lotte will be safely confined to the hostel, attending a workers' council. The initiative lies with the agent in the field, in this case Tulip. My job will be to respond to her creatively. And here she is now, coming towards me through the surf, clad in a Mother Hubbard beach robe with a rope shoulder bag. As she advances she directs Gustav's eye to a seashell or precious stone for his bucket. She has the same skittish swing of the hips that I had refused to acknowledge in Warsaw Old Town – except that I am careful not to mention her hips to Bunny and Laura, who are following my every light-hearted word with undisguised scepticism.

Drawing closer, she forages in her rope shoulder bag. Other sun-worshippers, other children, are splashing, sunbathing, eating sausage sandwiches and playing chess, and Tulip on stage is not beyond a smile or a word for this or that comrade. I don't know by what ruse she persuades Gustav to approach me, or what she says to him that makes him laugh out loud and scamper towards me in a dare, and thrust into my hand a chunk of blue, white and pink coconut fudge.

But I know that I must be charming, I must express delight. I must pretend to eat some of the fudge, I must drop the rest in my pocket, sink into a crouch, discover magically in the surf the seashell that was already secreted in my hand and offer it to Gustav as payment in return.

To all of which Tulip laughs gaily – rather too gaily, but I don't tell Laura and Bunny that bit either – and beckons him, come back now, darling, and leave the nice comrade alone.

But Gustav doesn't want to leave the nice comrade alone, which is the whole point of my witty story to Bunny and Laura. Gustav, who's a sassy kid by anybody's standards, has gone way off script. He reckons he has cut a deal with the nice comrade, fudge for shell, and he needs to get to know his new trading partner socially and commercially.

'What's your name?' he demands.

'Jean-François. What's yours?'

'Gustav. Jean-François who?'

'Gamay.'

'And your age?'

'A hundred-and-twenty-eight. What's yours?'

'Five. Where does the comrade come from?'

'Metz, France. What about you?'

'Berlin, Democratic Germany. Would you like to hear a song?'

'Very much.'

So Gustav stands himself to attention in the surf and sticks his chest out and gives me the benefit of a school song thanking our beloved Soviet soldiers for shedding their blood for a Socialist Germany. Meanwhile his mother, who is standing behind him, coolly unfastens the girdle of her beach robe and, with her gaze fixed on me, displays her naked body in its undoubted glory before languidly retying the girdle and joining me in my lavish applause for her son's performance; then looks on like the proud mother she is as I shake Gustav's hand, take a smart pace back and, right fist raised, return his Communist salute.

But the glory of Tulip's naked body is also something I keep to myself, while I ponder a question that has been burning in me before I ever embarked on my amusing story: *how the devil did you know that Tulip knew my name?*

7

I don't know what particular variety of fugue swept over me as, released early from my labours, I stepped out of the gloom of the Stables into the afternoon bustle of Bloomsbury and, on no impulse I was aware of, headed south-west towards Chelsea. Humiliation, certainly. Frustration, bewilderment, no question. Outrage at having my past dug up and thrown in my face. Guilt, shame, apprehension, any amount. And all directed in a single blast of pain and incomprehension at George Smiley for making himself unfindable.

Or was he? Was Bunny lying to me, as I was lying to him, and was George not quite as unfindable as he protested? Had they already found him and wrung him dry, as if that were ever possible? If Millie McCraig knew the answer – and I suspected she did – she was also bound to silence by her own version of the Official Secrets Act which laid down that, alive or dead, George Smiley was undiscussable.

Approaching Bywater Street, once a quiet cul-de-sac for the not-so-well-off and now just another of London's millionaires' ghettos, I refuse to acknowledge the wave of nostalgia sweeping over me, or make the obligatory mental note of parked cars, scan them for occupants or run a careless eye over doors and windows of the houses opposite. When was the last occasion I had come here? My memory stops at the night I circumvented

George's little wiles with wooden wedges in the front door and lay in wait to whisk him off to Oliver Lacon's sprawling red castle in Ascot on the first leg of his anguished journey to his dear old friend Bill Haydon, arch-traitor and his wife's lover.

But on this late, idle, autumnal afternoon, No. 9 Bywater Street knows nothing and has seen nothing of these things. Blinds drawn, front garden overgrown with weeds, occupants gone away or dead. I climb the four steps to the front door, press the bell, hear no familiar ring, no footstep light or heavy. No George, blinking his pleasure as he polishes his spectacles on the inside lining of his tie – 'hullo, Peter, you look as though you need a drink, come on in.' No Ann in a flurry with only half her make-up on – '*just* about to go out, Peter darling – kiss, kiss – but *do* come in and sort the world out with poor George.'

I return at military pace to the King's Road, hail a cab to Marylebone High Street and have myself dropped opposite Daunt's bookshop, but in Smiley's day Messrs Francis Edwards, founded 1910, where he whiled away many a happy lunch hour. I plunge into a maze of cobbled alleys and mews cottages that once comprised the Circus's outstation for Covert Operations – or in the parlance, simply *Marylebone*.

Unlike the Stables, which was only ever a safe house dedicated to a single operation, *Marylebone* with its three front doors was a Service to itself: its own desk officers, cyphers, cypher clerks, couriers, and its own grey army of Occasionals, never known to one another and drawn from all walks of life, who had only to hear the call to down tools and rally to the cause.

So was it remotely conceivable that Covert still had its being here? In my fugue, I chose to believe it was. And does George Smiley still skulk behind its shuttered windows? In my fugue I must have persuaded myself that he did. Of the nine doorbells only one worked. You had to be one of the faithful to know which. I press it. No response. I press the other two buttons in the same doorway. I move to the next doorway and press all three. A woman's voice screeches at me.

'She's not bloody *here*, Sammy! She's buggered off with Wally and the kid. You ring again, I'll call the Law, I swear I will.'

Her advice sobers me. The next thing I know, I am seated in the quiet of Devonshire Street, drinking elderflower cordial in a café full of medics in suits, murmuring head to head. I wait for my breathing to come down. As my head clears, so also does my sense of purpose. For the last couple of days and nights, despite every distraction, the image of Christoph, delinquent, criminal, clever son of Alec, brutally interrogating my Catherine on the doorstep of my house in Brittany, has remained with me. Never until that morning had I heard the ring of fear in Catherine's voice. Not fear for herself: fear for me. *He was not agreeable, Pierre . . . farouche . . . big like a boxer . . . he asked, do you stay in a hotel in London . . . what is the address?*

I say *my* Catherine because ever since the death of her father I have regarded her as my ward, and to hell with Bunny's insinuations to the contrary. I watched her grow from infancy. She watched my women come and go until none remained. When she appointed herself the village bad-girl in defiance of her more beautiful sister, and slept with every man-jack she could lay her hands on, I paid no attention to the pompous representations of the village priest, who probably fancied her for himself. I am uneasy with children, but when Isabelle was born I was as happy for Catherine as she was. I never told her what I did for a living. She never told me who the father was. In all the village, I was the only one who didn't know or care. If she wishes it, one day the farmstead will be hers, and Isabelle will trot along beside her, and perhaps there will be a younger man for Catherine, and perhaps little Isabelle will be willing to look him in the eye.

Are we also lovers, with all those years between us? Gradually, it seems we are. The arrangement was brokered by Isabelle, who one summer's evening padded across the courtyard with her bedding and, never a glance at me, installed herself beneath the landing window on the floor outside my bedroom. My bed is large; the spare room is dark and cold; mother and child could not be separated. It is my memory that Catherine and I slept innocently side by side for weeks on end before turning towards each other. But perhaps we didn't wait quite as long as I would like to think.

★

Of one thing at least I was sure: I would have no problem recognizing my pursuer. Clearing out Alec's dismal bachelor pad in Holloway after his death, I had stumbled on a pocket-sized photo album with a pressed edelweiss slipped under the cellophane cover. I was on the point of tossing it away when I realized I was holding in my hand a photographic record of Christoph's life from cradle to matriculation. The German subtitles in white ink under each snapshot had been added, I assumed, by his mother. What had impressed me was how the same locked expression that I remembered from the football match in Düsseldorf had stuck with him all the way to the thick-set, scowling, Alec-lookalike in a Sunday suit, clutching a scroll of parchment as if he was about to jam it in your face.

And what does Christoph know of *me*, meanwhile? That I am in London, burying a friend. That I am being a Good Samaritan. I have no known address, I am not a club man. Not even a researcher of Christoph's vaunted quality will find me listed at the Travellers or the National Liberal Club. Not in Stasi records, or anywhere else. My last known abode in the United Kingdom was a two-room flat in Acton that I had inhabited under the name of Peterson. When I gave my landlord notice, I left no forwarding address. So where, after Brittany, might severe,

108

persistent, impolite, criminal Christoph, son of Alec, strong like a boxer, come looking for me? What would be the one place, the *only* place, where, if he is really lucky, he might, given a fair wind, just possibly run me to earth?

Answer – or the only answer that made any sense to me – my old Service's Lubyanka by the Thames: not the old, hard-to-find Circus of his father, but its gruesome successor, the bastion I was about to reconnoitre.

★

Vauxhall Bridge teems with homebound commuters. The river beneath it is fast-flowing and jam-packed with traffic. I am not a member of a Bulgarian tour group but an Antipodean tourist who is doing the sights of London: cowboy hat, khaki waistcoat with multiple pockets. For my first pass I wore a flat cap and tartan scarf, for my second an Arsenal supporter's woolly hat with pom-pom. Net cost for the entire wardrobe at Waterloo station's flea market, fourteen pounds. At Sarratt we called them silhouette changes.

To every watcher there are distractions to beware of, I used to warn my young trainees: things your eye won't let go, like the pretty girl bravely sunbathing on the balcony, or the street preacher dressed as Jesus Christ. For me, this evening, it's a handkerchief-sized rectangle of lush green lawn entirely enclosed by spikes that my eyes refuse to let go. What is it? An outdoor punishment cell for Circus miscreants? A secret pleasure-garden for senior officers only? But how do they get in? Worse still, how do they get out?

On a tiny pebble beach at the foot of the bastion's outer ramparts, an Asian family in coloured silks picnics amid Canada geese. A yellow amphibious craft lumbers up the ramp beside them and stammers to a halt. Nobody emerges. The time is coming up to five-thirty. I am remembering Circus working hours: ten-till-whenever for the anointed, nine-thirty to five-thirty for the unwashed. A discreet exodus of junior staff is about to begin. I'm counting up likely exit points, which will be dispersed in order to be inconspicuous. When the bastion was first occupied by its present tenants there were tales of secret tunnels under the river all the way to Whitehall. Well, the Circus has dug a tunnel or two in its time, most of them under other people's territory, so why not a couple under your own?

When I first presented myself to Bunny, I had been passed through a man-door dwarfed by a pair of crash-proof iron gates with an art deco motif, but my guess was the man-door was visitors only. Of the three other exits I have spotted, the one that best suits my intuition is a pair of grey-painted doors set at the top of an inconspicuous flight of stone steps on the river side, giving access to the flow of pedestrians on the footpath. As I round the corner, the grey doors part and half-a-dozen men and women emerge, average age twenty-five to thirty. An expression of determined anonymity joins them. The doors close, I suspect electronically. They reopen. A second group descends.

I am Christoph's quarry, and his pursuer. I'm assuming he's been doing what I've been doing this last half-hour: familiarizing himself with the target building, picking likely exits, biding his moment. I'm acting on the assumption that Christoph is driven by the same sound operational instincts as his father, that he has thought his way through the probable actions of his quarry and laid his plans accordingly. If, as Catherine says, I have gone to London to bury a friend – and why should he doubt it? – then it's a racing certainty that I will also have dropped in on my former employers to chew over the irksome historical lawsuit that Christoph and his newfound friend Karen Gold are bringing against the Service and its named officers, of whom I am one.

Another batch of men and women is descending the steps.

As they reach the footpath, I tag along behind them. A grey-haired woman grants me a polite smile. She thinks she should recognize me. Pedestrians on the public footpath mingle with us. A sign says *To Battersea Park*. We approach an archway. I glance upwards and see the hatted figure of a large man in three-quarter-length dark overcoat, standing on the bridge, scanning passers-by below. The spot he has chosen, by chance or design, gives him a grandstand view of three of the bastion's exits. Having profited from the same vantage point myself, I can confirm its tactical value. Owing to the downward turn of his head, and of his hat, which is a black Homburg with high crown and shallow brim, his face is in shadow. But his boxer's bulk is not in doubt: broad shouldered, wide backed and a good three inches taller than I would have expected of Alec's son; but then I never met his mother.

We're through the archway. Dark coat and black Homburg has left the bridge and joined the procession. For all his bulk, he's a quick mover. So was Alec. He's twenty yards behind me, Homburg bobbing from side to side. He's trying to keep sight of someone or something ahead of him, and I'm inclined to think it's me. Does he *want* me to spot him? Or am I being excessively surveillance-conscious, another sin I used to rail against?

Joggers, cyclists and boats whisk past. To my left, apartment blocks. At their base, glitzy pavement restaurants, cafés, fast-food stalls. I am using reflections. I am slowing him down. I am remembering my own pontifications to new entrants: it's you who sets the pace, not the person following you. Be idle. Be indecisive. Never run when you can saunter. The river hums with pleasure boats, ferry boats, skiffs, rowing boats, barges. On the bank, buskers make human statues, kids wave bubbles, fly toy drones. If you're not Christoph, you're a Circus watcher. But the Circus's watchers, even in our worst days, were never this bad.

At St George's Wharf I peel away to my right and make a show of examining the timetable. You will identify your pursuer by giving him choices. Will he hop on to the bus after you, or will he say, to hell with the bus and walk on? If he walks on, maybe he's leaving you to someone else. But the Homburg and black overcoat is not leaving me to someone else. He wants me for himself, and he's hovering at a sausage stand, scrutinizing me in the fancy mirror behind the mustard and ketchup bottles.

At the ticket machine for ferries heading east, a queue is forming. I join it, wait my turn, buy myself a ticket to Tower Bridge, single. My pursuer has decided not to buy himself a sausage. The ferry pulls alongside, the pier rocks, we let the passengers off first. My pursuer has crossed the path and is bending over the ticket machine. He gesticulates irritably. Help me, someone. A Rasta in baggy cap shows him how it's done. Cash, not credit card, and the face still in shadow under the Homburg. We are boarding. The top deck is packed with sightseers. The crowd is your friend. Use it well. I use the crowd on the top deck and find myself a space of railing while I wait for my pursuer to do the same. Does he realize I'm conscious to him? Are we into mutual awareness? Has he, as my Sarratt students would have said, clocked me clocking him? If he has, abort.

Except I won't abort. The boat turns. A shaft of sunlight picks him out, but the face remains in shadow, even if in the left margin of my line of sight I see him casting one stealthy glance after another at me, as if he's afraid I'll make a dash for it or chuck myself overboard.

Can you really be Christoph, son of Alec? Or are you some lawyer's bailiff, sent to slap a writ on me? But if that's who you are, why stalk me? Why not barge up to me here and now, confront me? The boat swings again, and again the sunlight finds him. His head lifts. For the first time I see his face in profile. I have a feeling that I ought to be amazed and delighted, but I am neither. I feel no rush of kinship. I am aware only of a sense of impending reckoning: Christoph, son of Alec, with the same unblinking stare that I remember from the football stadium at Düsseldorf, and the same jutting Irish jaw.

*

If Christoph was reading my intentions, I was also reading his. He hadn't identified himself to me because he was waiting to *house* me, as the watchers have it: to find out where I'm staying and, having done so, choose his time and place. My response must be to deny him the operational intelligence he was after and dictate my own terms, which should be a crowded spot with plenty of innocent bystanders. But Catherine's warnings, added to my apprehensions, force me to consider the possibility of a violent man seeking redress for my perceived sins against his late father.

It was with this contingency in mind that I recalled how as a small boy I had been marched round the Tower of London by my French mother, to her loud and embarrassing exclamations of horror at everything she saw. And I remembered in particular the great stairway on Tower Bridge. It was this stairway that now spoke to me, not for its iconic attractions, but for my self-preservation. Sarratt nursery did not teach self-defence. It taught a variety of ways of killing, some silently, others less so, but self-defence did not feature large on the menu. What I knew for certain was, if it did come to a fight, I needed my opponent's weight above me, and all the help that gravity could provide. He was a prison-trained brawler with forty pounds of bone and muscle on me. I needed to use his weight against him, and I could think of no better place than a steep stairway, with my aged self standing a few steps beneath him to speed him on his

113

way. I had already taken a couple of useless precautions: trans-ferred any small change I had to my right-hand jacket pocket for use as short-range grapeshot, and threaded the middle finger of my left hand round my key-ring as an improvised knuckle-duster. Nobody ever lost a fight by preparing for it, did they, son? No, staff, they never did.

We were queuing to disembark. Christoph was twelve feet behind me, his reflection in the glass door expressionless. Grey hair, Catherine had said. Now I saw why: a mass of it, bulging in all directions from beneath the Homburg, grey, wiry and untamed like Alec's, the central mass of it plaited into a pigtail that hung down the back of his black overcoat. Why had Catherine not mentioned the pigtail? Maybe he tucked it inside his coat. Maybe pigtails weren't uppermost in her mind. In labori-ous crocodile we filed up a ramp. Tower Bridge was down. A green light beckoned pedestrians to cross. Reaching the opening to the great stairway, I turned and looked directly back at him. I was saying to him: if you want to talk, we do it here, with people passing by. He too had stopped, but all I could see in his face and eyes was the football spectator's relentless stare. I took a dozen quick steps down the stairway, which was empty save for a couple of down-and-outs. I needed a midway point. I needed him to have a long way to fall once he'd gone past me, because I didn't want him coming back.

The stairway filled up. Two giggling girls scampered past, hand in hand. A couple of monks in saffron were engaged in earnest philosophical discussion with a beggar. Christoph was standing at the top of the staircase, a hatted silhouette in an overcoat. Step by step, with studied care, he began to descend the staircase, arms half raised from his sides, feet wide, the wrest-ler's stalk. You're too slow, I urged him, come on down at me, I need your momentum. But he had drawn to a halt a couple of stairs above me, and for the first time I heard his adult voice, which was German American, and high-pitched, which some-how shocked me.

'Hi, Peter. Hi, Pierre. It's me. Christoph. Alec's little boy, remember? Aren't you pleased to see me? Don't you want to shake my hand?'

Releasing the small change in my pocket, I reached up my right hand to him. He grasped it, and kept it long enough for me to feel his strength, despite the slithery dampness of the palm.

'What can I do for you, Christoph?' I said, and for answer got one of Alec's caustic laughs and that extra bit of Irish he put into his voice when he was camping himself up:

'Well, boyo, you can buy me a bloody drink for a start!'

★

The restaurant was on the first floor of a self-styled Olde Towne House with fake worm-eaten beams and a slanted view of the Tower through mitred windows. The waitresses wore bonnets and pinafores, and we could have a table if we agreed to eat a full meal. Christoph sat with his huge body slumped in his chair, and his Homburg hat pulled down over his eyes. The waitress brought beer, which was what he'd asked for. He took a sip, pulled a face, set it aside. Fingernails black and chipped. Rings on every finger of his left hand. On his right hand, just the two middle ones that count. The face Alec's, but with pouchy dis-content where pain lines should have been. The same pugnacious jaw. In the brown eyes, when they bothered with you, the same flashes of buccaneering charm.

'So what are you doing with yourself these days, Christoph?' I asked him. He thought for a while.

'These days?'

'Yes.'

'Well, I guess the short answer is: *this,*' he replied, giving me the big smile.

'*This* being what exactly? I don't think I've got the whole story.'

But he shook his head as if to say it didn't matter, and only sat up straight when the waitress brought our steak and chips.

'Nice place you've got over there in Brittany,' he remarked, eating. 'How many hectares?'

'Fifty odd. Why?'

'Your own?'

'What are we talking about, Christoph? Why did you come looking for me?'

He took another mouthful, tipped his head and smiled at me to say I'd made a good point.

'Why I came looking for you? Thirty years now, I've been a fortune hunter. Travelled the whole world. I did diamonds. I did gold. I did dope. I did guns a little. I did jail. Too much. Did I find my fortune? Did I fuck. Then I come home to little old Europe, and I find you. My goldmine. My dad's best friend. His best comrade. And what did you do to your best comrade? You got him killed. That's money, man. That's *real* money.'

'I didn't get your father killed.'

'Read the files, man. Read the Stasi files. They're dynamite. You and George Smiley killed my father. Smiley was the ringleader. You were like his number-one gofer. You set my dad up, and you killed him. Directly or indirectly, that's what you did. And you dragged Miss Elizabeth Gold into the game. It's all in the fucking files, man! This great wicked plot you dreamed up that backfired on you and killed everybody. You *lied* to my dad! You and your big George. You lied to my daddy and you sent him to his death. *Deliberately.* Ask the lawyers. You know what? Patriotism is *dead,* man. Patriotism is for *babies.* If this case goes international, patriotism as a justification will *not* fly. Patriotism in mitigation is officially *fucked.* Same as elites. Same as you guys,' he added and, about to take a refreshing pull of beer, changed his mind and rummaged in the pocket of his black coat, which he had continued to wear despite the heat. From a battered tin box he poured a dab of white powder on to his wrist and, closing one nostril with his spare hand, snorted it in full view of any customer who cared to watch, and several did.

'So what are you doing here?' I said.

'Saving your fucking life, man,' he replied and, reaching out with both hands, grasped my wrist in a gesture of true fealty.

'So here's the deal. Your dream ticket. Okay? My personal offer to you. The best offer you'll ever get in your life. You're my friend, okay?'

'If you say so.'

I had prised myself free of him, but he was still gazing dotingly at me.

'You have no other friend. There is no other deal on the table. This is a one-time offer. Without prejudice. Non-negotiable.' He picks up his tankard, drains it and signals to the waitress for another. 'One million euros. To me personally. No third parties involved. One million euros on the day the lawyers drop the lawsuit, and you never hear from me again. No lawyers, no human rights, no bullshit. You just bought the whole package. Why are you looking at me? You got a problem?'

'No problem. Just that it seems cheap at the price. I had rather understood your lawyers have already refused that amount and more.'

'You're not listening. I am offering you cut price. That's what I'm saying. I am offering you cut price, one payment only, to me, one million euros.'

'And Liz Gold's daughter Karen – she's happy, I take it?'

'Karen? Listen, I know that girl. All I have to do, I go to her, I sing to her, the way I do, I talk about my soul, weep a bit maybe, I tell her I can't go through with this thing after all, it's all too painful to me, my dad's memory, let the dead sleep. I got all the words. Karen's sensitive. Trust me.'

And when I don't exhibit the necessary signs of trust:

'Listen. I invented that fucking girl. She owes me. I did the work, I paid the people, I got the files. I went to her, I gave her the good news, told her where to find her mother's grave. We go to the lawyers. *Her* lawyers. *Pro bono*, the worst. Where does she get them from? Like Amnesty. Some civil rights organization. The *pro bono* lawyers go to your Government, preach them a sermon. Your Government denies all responsibility, makes a back-door, your-ears-only, we-never-said-this, *without prejudice* offer of one million pounds *sterling*. One *million*! And that's a base price, it's negotiable. Personally I would not touch sterling today, but that's a side issue. What do Karen's lawyers do? Preach another sermon. We don't *want* a million pounds, they say. We're high-minded people, we want you to eat shit. And if you don't eat shit, we will take you to court, and if necessary all the way to Strasbourg and the European Court of Fucking Human Rights. Your Government says okay, *two* million, but her *pro bonos* still won't play. They are like Karen. They are holy. They are pure.'

A metallic crash causes every head in the restaurant to turn. Christoph's unwashed left hand with all its rings has landed palm down on the table in front of me. He is craning forward. His face raining sweat. A door marked Staff Only opens, a startled head appears and, at the sight of Christoph, vanishes.

'You gonna want my bank details – okay, *man*? Here they are. And you tell this to your Government, *man:* one million euros on the day we withdraw, or we throw the fucking book at you.'

He lifted his hand to reveal a folded piece of lined paper, and watched me thread it into my wallet.

'Who's Tulip?' he demands in the same threatening tone.

'I'm sorry?'

'Codename for Doris Gamp. Stasi woman, had a kid.'

He had not announced his departure. I was still insisting that Gamp–Tulip was not a name to me. A brave waitress was scurrying over with the bill, but he was halfway down the stairs. By the time I reached the street all I saw of him was his huge shadow in the back of a departing cab, and his white hand flapping lazy goodbyes out of the window.

I know I walked back to Dolphin Square. Somewhere along the way I must have remembered the piece of lined paper with his account number and chucked it into a litterbin, but I would be hard pressed to tell you which one.

8

The benign weather of yesterday had been driven off by a lateral rain that raked the streets of Pimlico like gunfire. Arriving late for my tryst at the Stables, I found Bunny standing alone on the doorstep under an umbrella.

'We rather wondered whether you'd done a runner,' he said, doing his shy-boy smile.

'And if I had?'

'Let's just say you wouldn't have got very far.' Still smiling, he handed me a brown envelope marked On Her Majesty's Service in red. 'Congratulations. You are courteously requested to appear before our masters. The All-Party parliamentary committee of inquiry wants a word with you. Date to be announced.'

'And a word with you too, I imagine.'

'Marginally. But we're not the stars, are we?'

A black Peugeot draws up. He climbs into the back. The Peugeot drives away.

'Got our reading boots on, Pete?' Pepsi asks. She is already installed on her throne in the library. 'Looks like we're in for a heavy day.'

She is referring to the thick buff folder that lies waiting for me on the trestle table: my unpublished masterpiece, forty pages of it.

*

'I am proposing that you draft an official report on the affair, Peter,' Smiley is saying to me.

It's three in the morning. We're sitting head to head in the front parlour of a council house on an estate in the New Forest.

'I see you as the ideal person for the job,' he continues, in the same deliberately impersonal tone. 'A definitive report, please, overlong, rich in irrelevant detail and sparing us the one piece of information that only you and I and four other people in the world, God willing, may ever know. Something that will satisfy the prurient appetites of Joint Steering, and act as an obfuscation for the Head Office post-mortem – I use the word figuratively – that is sure to be called for. To be drafted for my sole approval in the first instance, please. My eyes only. Will you do that? Are you able? With Ilse sitting at your elbow, naturally.'

Ilse, star linguist of Covert: prim, punctilious Ilse who has German, Czech, Serbo-Croat and Polish at her beautiful finger-tips; who lives with her mother in Hampstead and plays the flute on Saturday evenings. Ilse will sit at my elbow, correct my transcriptions of German recordings. We will smile together at my little errors, discuss a choice of word or phrase together, send out for our sandwiches together. We shall lean over the tape recorder together, accidentally butt heads, apologize together. And punctually at half past five, Ilse will go back home to her mother and her flute in Hampstead.

★

DEFECTION AND EXFILTRATION OF SUB-SOURCE TULIP.
Draft report assembled by P. Guillam, Asst to H/Covert
Marylebone, to Bill Haydon H/Joint Steering and Oliver Lacon
HM Treasury. For approval by H/Covert.

FIRST INDICATIONS that sub-source Tulip might be at risk of exposure occurred in the course of a routine treff between Mayflower and his controller Leamas (PAUL) in West Berlin safe house K2 (Fasanenstrasse) on 16 January at approx 0730 hours.

Using his Friedrich Leibach identity, Mayflower had cycled[1] across the sector border into West Berlin with the 'morning cavalry' of East Berlin workmen. A lavish 'English breakfast', including fried egg, bacon and baked beans, cooked by Leamas, has become traditional fare for these treffs, which take place at irregular intervals depending on operational need and Mayflower's professional commitments. As usual, proceedings opened with a routine debriefing and random items of network news:

Sub-source DAFFODIL has had a recurrence of illness, but insists on continuing to play his part, receiving and forwarding 'rare books, brochures and personal mail'.

Sub-source VIOLET's report on the Soviet military build-up on the Czech border was well received by Whitehall customers. Violet to be granted the bonus she is demanding.

Sub-source PETAL has a new boyfriend. He is a twenty-

---

1 Following Mayflower's recruitment by this Service, it was decided to reduce his visible trips to West Berlin to a minimum. Berlin Station therefore supplied him with the identity of Friedrich Leibach, construction worker resident in Lichtenberg, East Berlin, where by his own devices Mayflower obtained the use of a garden shed for his pushbike and worker's clothing.

two-year-old Red Army corporal of signals, a cypher specialist from Minsk, recently attached to her unit. He is an obsessive stamp collector and Petal has told him that her ageing aunt (fictitious) has a collection of pre-Revolutionary Russian stamps that she is tired of, and may be willing to part with at a price. She intends that the price, negotiated in bed, will be a codebook. On advice from Leamas, Mayflower has assured her that London will supply an appropriate stamp collection.

Only now does the conversation turn to sub-source Tulip. Verbatim:

Leamas: And on the Doris front? Is she up or down?

Mayflower: Paul, my friend, I don't know and I can't diagnose. With Doris, each day will be different.

Leamas: You're her lifeline, Karl.

Mayflower: She has decided that her husband Mr Quinz is taking too much interest in her.

Leamas: High bloody time. In what way?

Mayflower: He suspects her. She doesn't know what of. Asks her all the time where she's going, who she meets. Where she's been. Watches her while she cooks, dresses, goes about her life.

Leamas: Maybe Doris has got herself a jealous husband finally.

Mayflower: She refutes it. She says Quinz is jealous only of himself, his shining career and his ego. But with Doris, who knows?

Leamas: How about life in the office?

Mayflower: She says Rapp dare not suspect her because his disciplinary transgressions do not allow him to. She says that if she were suspected by I.S., she would already be sitting in a cage in the detention house down the road.

Leamas: I.S.?

Mayflower: The Stasi's internal security section. She walks past their door every morning on her way to Rapp's suite.

At midday of the same day, as a matter of routine, Leamas instructed de Jong to revisit existing contingency plans for the exfiltration of sub-source Tulip. De Jong confirmed that escape papers and resources for an eastward exfiltration via Prague were current. Having waited for the evening shift of workmen, Mayflower cycled back into East Berlin.

Pepsi is being a fidget, repeatedly coming down from her throne to prowl the room for no reason, or stand behind me to peer over my shoulder. I am imagining Tulip in the same state of restlessness, now at home in Hohenschönhausen, now in her office next to Emmanuel Rapp's in Stasi House Number 3 in the Magdalenenstrasse.

THE SECOND INTIMATION came in the form of a doctor-to-doctor call. With the assistance of the West Berlin police, an emergency contact system had been put in place. If Mayflower called the Klinikum (West Berlin) from the Charité (East Berlin) and demanded to speak to his notional colleague Dr Fleischmann, the call would be immediately re-routed to Berlin Station. At 0920 hours on 21 Jan., the following re-routed conversation between Mayflower and Leamas took place under medical cover.

Verbatim:
Mayflower (calling from the Charité, East Berlin)*:* Dr Fleischmann?
Leamas: Speaking.
Mayflower: This is Dr Riemeck. You have a patient. Frau Lisa Sommer.[2]

2 Cover name for Tulip.

Leamas: What about her?

Mayflower: Last night Frau Sommer reported herself to my Casualty unit suffering from delusions. We sedated her but she discharged herself during the night.

Leamas: Delusions of what?

Mayflower: She fantasizes that her husband suspects her of betraying State secrets to Fascist anti-Party elements.

Leamas: Thanks. Noted. Unfortunately I am required in theatre.

Mayflower: Understood.

Two hours intervene during which Mayflower uncached his *Theatre*³ equipment, tuned it to the recommended specifications, and finally obtained a weak signal. Sound quality patchy throughout the ensuing conversation. Substance:

Early that same morning Tulip had made an unprecedented crisis call to Mayflower in his surgery, consisting of an agreed series of pinpoint taps on the mouthpiece of a third-party telephone (in this case a callbox). In return Mayflower had signalled his assent: two taps, pause, three taps.

The emergency rendezvous [rv] was a spinney outside Köpenick: fortuitously the same spinney that he had previously chosen to cache his *Theatre* equipment. Both parties arrived by bicycle within minutes of each other. Tulip's initial mood, according to Mayflower, was 'triumphalist'. Quinz was 'neutralized', he was 'good as dead'. Mayflower should rejoice with her. God had been at her side. Then the following narrative:

---

3 *Theatre* is a prototype American short-range high-frequency communications system, purpose-built for covert East–West communications within Berlin city area. Leamas has described the system in a DO letter to H/technical dept as 'unwieldy, bloody fiddly, over-produced and typical Yank'. It has since been abandoned.

Returning home from work late last night, Quinz had grabbed the Zenit camera hanging from its strap behind the front door, opened its back, muttered something, snapped it shut and returned it to its hook. He had then demanded to inspect the contents of Tulip's handbag. When she resisted he threw her across the room and searched it anyway. When Gustav ran to his mother's defence, Quinz hit him across the face, causing bleeding from the mouth and nose. Evidently not finding what he was looking for, Quinz then ransacked kitchen cupboards and drawers, frenetically patted the soft furniture, and stormed through Tulip's clothes, and finally Gustav's toy cupboard, all without success.

In Gustav's hearing he then in a loud tone challenged Tulip to explain, in questions counted on his spread fingers: number one, why the family Zenit camera contained no film; number two, why there was only one unused film in the pocket of the camera case, although a week ago there had been two; and number three, why a film that only last Sunday had been sitting in the Zenit with two frames exposed was also missing.

And by way of subsidiary questions *what* had she photographed with the remaining eight frames? *Where* had she taken the film to be developed? *Where* were the results? And *what* had happened to the missing unused film? Or *had* she – his personal conviction – been photographing the classified documents he brought home and selling them to Western spies?

The true facts of the situation, as Tulip well knew, were as follows. Since caching a Minox under the shower stand in the women's toilet of her corridor in House 3, Tulip had on principle kept no Minox either in the fastening of her shoulder bag or at home. If Quinz brought documents of interest home from the GDR Foreign Office, Tulip would wait till he was

126

asleep or engrossed with his male friends and photograph the documents with the family Zenit. On the previous Sunday, she had taken two snaps of Gustav on a swing in the playground. The same evening, while Quinz sat drinking with friends, she had used the remaining frames of the same film to photograph documents from his briefcase. She had then removed the film from the Zenit, buried it in a flowerpot pending her next treff with Mayflower, but had neglected to put a fresh film into the camera, let alone put her finger over the lens and shoot off a couple of frames to represent two misfires of Gustav. Despite all this, Tulip contrived to mount what she considered to be a devastating counter-attack against her husband. She informed Quinz, in case he didn't know, that there were many in the Stasi who remained suspicious of him on account of his odious father and reputed homosexuality; that nobody in the Stasi was taken in by his exaggerated professions of Party loyalty; and yes, she had indeed photographed whatever she could get her hands on from his briefcase, *not* in order to sell to the West or anyone else, but to blackmail him in the event of a custody battle over Gustav, which she considered imminent. Because one thing was for sure, she told him: if it were ever to come out that Lothar Quinz took home classified documents to obsess over during off-duty hours, his dreams of becoming a GDR ambassador abroad would be over.

Return to tape:
Leamas to Mayflower: So how do things stand?
Mayflower to Leamas: She is convinced she has reduced him to silence. He went to work as normal this morning. He was calm, even affectionate.
Leamas: Where is she now?
Mayflower: At home, waiting for Emmanuel Rapp. At midday

precisely he will pick her up in his car and they will drive to Dresden for a full session of the Domestic Security Soviet. He has promised her that this time she will attend the meeting as his assistant. It will be an honour for her. [Fifteen-second pause.]

Leamas: All right. So here's what she does. She phones Rapp's office now. She's been sick as a dog all night, she's got a barking temperature and she's too ill to travel, she's heartbroken. Then she aborts. She knows the procedure. She gets to the rendezvous. She waits.

Leamas then informed Head Office by crash telegram that the requirement for an emergency exfiltration of sub-source Tulip had advanced from amber to red, and that since she was fully conscious to source Mayflower, the entire Mayflower network must be considered at risk. Since the escape plan required the collaboration of both Prague and Paris Stations, the resources of Joint Steering were essential. He also requested immediate permission to undertake the exfiltration 'in person', in the full knowledge that, under standing Circus orders, a serving officer possessing information of high sensitivity who proposes to enter denied territory without diplomatic protection must obtain the advance consent of Head Office in writing – in this case, Joint Steering. Ten minutes later he had his answer: 'Your request refused. Confirm. J.S.' The telegram was otherwise unsigned in accordance with H/JS [Haydon's] policy of collective decision-making. Simultaneously, Signals Intelligence reported a surge on all Stasi wavelengths, while the British Military Mission in Potsdam noted a tightening of security at all crossing points into West Berlin, all along the GDR–West German border. At 1505 GMT, GDR radio announced a nationwide search for an unnamed female *lackey of Fascist imperialism* answering the following description. The description was of Tulip.

Leamas had in the meantime taken steps of his own, in defiance of Joint Steering's instruction. He makes no apology for this, claiming only that he wasn't going to 'sit on his arse and watch Tulip and the entire Mayflower network going up in smoke'. When Joint Steering urged that at least Mayflower himself should immediately be exfiltrated, Leamas's retort was uncompromising: 'He can come out any time he wants, but he won't. He'd rather stand trial like his father.' Less clear is the part played by the Station's recently upgraded Assistant Officer, Stavros de Jong, and Ben Porter, the Station's security guard and driver.

Testimony of Ben Porter (security guard, Berlin Station) to PG, verbatim:
Alec's at his desk on the secure blower to Joint Steering. I'm standing at the door. He puts down the phone and he turns to me and he says, 'Ben,' he says, 'we're on. It's a rolling job. Get the Land Rover out and tell Stas I want him in full drag in the courtyard in five minutes,' he says. At no time did Mr Leamas say to me, 'Ben, I have to inform you we are doing this in direct contravention of Head Office instructions.'

Testimony of Stavros de Jong (probationer attached to H/Covert Berlin) to PG, verbatim:
I asked Head of Covert, 'Alec, are we sure Head Office is behind us on this one?' To which he replied, 'Stas, take my word for it.' So I did.

Their protestations of innocence were mine, not theirs. Since I had no doubt that Smiley had encouraged Leamas to undertake the exfiltration of Tulip himself, I was careful to supply

Porter and de Jong with get-out-of-jail statements in case they were forced to give an account of themselves by Percy Alleline or one of his henchmen.

★

It is three days later. The story is taken up by Alec himself. It is ten o'clock at night and he is being debriefed across a plywood table in the safe room at the British Embassy in Prague where he holed out an hour earlier. He is talking into a tape recorder and on the other side of it sits the Head of Prague Station, one Jerry Ormond, husband to the redoubtable Sally who is also the Station's number two in a his-and-hers Circus partnership. Also on the table, if only in my informed imagination, a bottle of the Scotch whisky, and one glass only – Alec's – which Jerry intermittently replenishes. By the lifeless tone of Alec's voice it is clear that he is exhausted, which as far as Ormond is concerned is all to the good, since his task as debriefer is to take down his subject's story before his memory has had a chance to edit it. In my imagination again, Alec is unshaven and wearing a borrowed dressing gown after the hasty shower he has been allowed to take. The Irish comes through his voice in irregular bursts.

And I, Peter Guillam: where am I? Not in Prague with Alec, though I might just as well have been. I am sitting in an upstairs room of Covert's headquarters in Marylebone, listening to the tape that has been rushed to London by RAF plane, and I am thinking to myself: *it's my turn next.*

> AL: It's eight below on the steps of the Olympic Stadium, ball-breaking easterly blowing fine snow, ice on the roads. I reckon the foul weather's all to the good. Foul weather's escape weather. Land Rover's standing by, Ben's at the

wheel. Stas de Jong comes marching down the steps in full army battledress, squeezes himself into the floor cavity, all six foot three of him, army boots and all. Me and Ben lower the lid on him, I sit up front with Ben. I'm wearing an officer's cap and greatcoat, three pips, East German working clothes underneath. Scruffy shoulder bag under the seat for documents. Rule of mine. Keep your documents separate for the jump. Nine-twenty a.m., we're going through the official Friedrichstrasse crossing point for military personnel, showing our passes to the Vopos through the closed windows, not letting the buggers get their hands on them, which the diplomats tell us is the current way of doing it. Soon as we're through we pick up the usual tail: two Vopos in a Citroën. So it's a normal day. They need to know we're just another British military vehicle asserting our rights under the quadripartite agreement, and that's what we're keen to tell them. We pass through Friedrichshain and I'm hoping to Christ that Tulip has hit the road by now because if she hasn't, she's dead or worse and so's the network. We head north towards Pankow till we reach the Soviet military perimeter, then turn east. Same Citroën on our tail, which is fine by us. We don't need a changing of the guard and fresh eyes on us. I'm leading them a bit of a dance, which is what they expect us to do: the odd sudden turning, backtrack, slow to a crawl, put your foot down. We're turning south into Marzahn. We're still inside Berlin city limits, but it's forest, flat roads and flying snow. We pass the old Nazi radio station which is our first marker. The Citroën's a hundred yards behind us, not enjoying the icy roads. We go into the dip, gathering speed. There's a sharp left coming up and a white factory chimney poking out of the trees which is our second marker: an old sawmill. We make the left turn fast, hold it, skid to a near-halt next to the sawmill. I roll out, plus shoulder bag, minus greatcoat, which is Stas's cue to get out of his box and into the passenger seat and look like me. I'm flat in a ditch with snow all over me so I must have rolled a yard or two. When I take a look, the Land Rover's climbing up the other side of the dip and the Citroën's scrambling after it, trying to catch up.

[A pause, punctuated by the chink of glass and sounds of pouring liquid.]

AL [contd]: Back of the old sawmill there's a disused lorry park and a tin shed full of sawdust. And behind the sawdust there's a brown-and-blue Trabant with a load of steel tubing strapped to the roof. Ninety thousand on the clock and stinks of rat shit, but the tank's full, and there's a couple of spare cans in the back and the tyres have even got a bit of tread to them. Maintained by a trusted patient of Mayflower's who won't even give his name. Only problem is, Trabis hate the cold. It takes me an hour to thaw her out and all the time I'm thinking: Tulip, where are you, have they got you, and are you talking? Because if you're talking, we're all fucked.

JO [Jerry Ormond]: And your identity?

AL: Günther Schmaus. Welder from Saxony. I give good Saxon. My mother was Chemnitz. My dad was County Cork.

JO: And Tulip? When you meet up with her, who will she be?

AL: My own dear wife. Augustina.

JO: And she's where at this minute? All being well?

AL: Rv, north of Dresden. Deep countryside. She'll have tried to bike despite the weather, gone a distance, then ditched her bike because they know she bikes. Then taken the local train, then hiked or bummed a ride to the rv with orders to hunker down for as long as it takes.

132

JO: And the crossing from East Berlin into the GDR? What are you expecting?

AL: It's random. No checkpoints, roving patrols. You're lucky or you're not.

JO: And were you lucky?

AL: Wasn't a big deal. Two police cars. They cut you up, frighten the shit out of you, have you out of the car, shake you down. But if your papers hold, on you go.

JO: And they held. Yes?

AL: I wouldn't fucking be here if they hadn't, would I?

[Change of tape, corrupted passage forty-five seconds. Rejoin. Leamas is describing the drive between East Berlin and Cottbus.]

AL: Best thing about traffic in the GDR, basically there isn't any. A few horses and carts. Cyclists, mopeds, sidecars, the odd clapped-out lorry. A bit of autobahn, then small roads. I'm alternating. If a small road is snowed up, cut back to the autobahn. Steer clear of Wünsdorf whatever you do. There's a bloody great Nazi camp there and the Sovs took it over wholesale: three tank divisions, serious rocketry and a king-sized listening station. We've been spying the shit out of it for months. I make a detour north for safety's sake, not an autobahn, just a straight flat country road. There's heavy snow coming at me, and lines of bare trees chock-a-block with bunches of mistletoe, and me thinking, one day I'll come back and cut down that lot and flog it at Covent Garden market. Then – am I dreaming this? – I'm in the middle of a fucking great Soviet military convoy, and I'm going the wrong way. Lorries packed with troops, T-34 tanks on low-loaders, six or eight artillery pieces, and me in my piebald Trabi dodging between them, trying to get off the fucking road, and them just not bloody looking, rolling straight on. I didn't even have time to take their fucking numbers!

[Laughter, shared by Ormond. Pause. Resumes at a slower pace.]

AL: Four in the afternoon, I'm five kilometres west of Cottbus. I'm looking for an abandoned *Karosserie* works at the roadside. That's the rv. And a baby's mitten jammed on a bit of fencing, which is the safety signal to tell me Tulip's inside. And it was there. The mitten was. Pink. Stuck up there like a fucking flag in the middle of nowhere. And it scares me, don't know why. The mitten does. It's too fucking conspicuous. Maybe it's not Tulip inside the shed, it's the Stasi. Or maybe it's Tulip *and* the Stasi. So I pull up and think about it. And while I'm thinking, the barn door opens and there she is, standing in the doorway with a grinning six-year-old kid on her hand.

[Twenty-second pause.]

AL: I'd never even *met* the bloody woman, Christ's sake! Tulip worked to Mayflower. That was the deal. Knew her from photographs, that's all. So I say, *how d'you do, Doris, my name's Günther and I'm your husband for this journey, and who the fuck's this?* Except that I know too bloody well who *this* is. And she says, it's Gustav my son, and he's coming with me. And I say, like fuck he's coming with you, we are a childless couple, and there's not going to be any hiding him under a bloody blanket when we reach the Czech frontier. So what are we going to do about it? She says in that case she's not coming, and the boy chirps up and says he's not either. So I tell Gustav to get back inside the shed and grab her by the arm and take her round the back and tell her what she knows but doesn't want to hear: there's no ID for him, they'll pull us in and run a check on us, and if we don't get rid of him, you're fucked and so am I, and so is the good Dr Riemeck, because once they've got you and Gustav in their hands, they'll squeeze his name out of you in five minutes. No answer and it's growing dark and the snow's coming on again. So we go back inside the shed, which is big as a bloody aircraft hangar and full of busted machinery, and Gustav, the little bugger, has laid for dinner, if you can believe it: dug out whatever she's got for provisions and set them out on the ground: sausage, bread, a thermos of hot cocoa, boxes to sit on, let's all have a party. So we sit in a ring and have our family picnic and Gustav sings us a patriotic song, and the two of them bed down together under coats and whatever they've got, and I sit smoking in a corner, and as soon as it's half light I shove them in the Trabi and we drive back to the village I passed through the night before, because I'd seen a bus stop there. And by the grace of God there are these two old nellies standing there in black hoods and white skirts, and baskets of cucumbers on their backs, and God bless them they're Sorbs.

JO: Sorbs? What the hell . . .

AL [outburst]: *Sorbs*, for Christ's sake! You've heard of fucking *Sorbs*! Sixty-fucking-thousand of them. Protected species, even in the GDR. Slavic minority, scattered up and down the Spree, been there for centuries, growing bloody cucumbers. Try recruiting one. *Jesus!*

[Ten-second pause. Cools down.]

AL: I pull up, tell Tulip and Gustav to stay put in the car. Don't move. I get out, the first old nellie watches me, the other one doesn't bother. I pull the charm. Does she speak German: that's respect. She speaks German but she'd rather speak Sorbian, she says. Joke. I ask where she's heading. Bus into Lübbenau, then train to the Ostbahnhof in Berlin to flog the cucumbers. They get a better price in Berlin. I pitch her a cock-and-bull story about Gustav: family upset, mother distraught, boy's got to get back to his father in Berlin, and can they take him? She puts the proposition to her pal and they have a debate about it in Sorbian. And I'm thinking, any minute the fucking bus is going to come over the hill and they won't have made up their minds. Then the first one says, we'll take your boy if you buy our cucumbers, and I say, what all of them? And she says, yes, all of them. And I say, if I buy all your cucumbers you won't have any fucking cucumbers to sell in Berlin, so why would you want to go there? They have a good laugh about this in Sorbian. I shove a wad of cash into her hand, so much for the cucumbers, but keep them. And so much for the boy's train fare, and here's some more for his onward journey to Hohenschönhausen. And here's the bus coming, and I'll get the boy. I go back to the car, and tell Gustav to get out, but his mother just sits frozen in the car with her hand across her eyes so he won't budge either. So I *order* him out, bark at him, and he obeys. And I tell him, you march with me to the bus, and these two kind comrades will escort you to the Ostbahnhof. And from the Ostbahnhof you go home to Hohenschönhausen and wait till your father shows up. And that's an order, Comrade. Then he asks me where his mother's going and why he's not going with her, so I say your mother's got important secret work to do in Dresden, and it's your duty as a good soldier for Communism to go back to your father and continue the struggle. And he goes. [Five-second silence.] Well, what the fuck else was he supposed to do? He's a Party kid with a Party father and he's six years old, for fuck's sake!

JO: And Tulip meanwhile?

AL: Sitting in the fucking Trabi staring out of the windscreen in a trance. I get in, drive a kilometre, then stop again and haul her out. There's a helicopter buzzing overhead. Fuck knows what *he* thinks he's doing. Fuck knows where he got a helicopter from. Borrowed it from the Russians? Listen, I tell her. Just fucking listen because we need each other. Sending your kid back to Berlin is not the end of a problem. It's the beginning of a new one. Two hours from now, the entire Stasi will know that Doris Quinz née Gamp was last seen in the vicinity of Cottbus, heading east with her male friend. They'll have a description of the car, the lot. So goodbye to any ideas we had about driving this load of shit into Czecho on false papers, because from now on every Stasi and KGB unit and every frontier post from Kaliningrad to Odessa is going to be on the lookout for a piebald plastic Trabi with a pair of Fascist spies in it. And she takes it on the chin, I'll give her that. No more dramatics, just asks me straight out what the fallback is and I say: one out-of-date smugglers' map that I brought along as an afterthought, which with luck and a prayer might just possibly get us over the border on foot. So she thinks hard about this, and then she asks me – it's like the clincher for her – 'If I come with you, when will I see my son again?' Which suggests to me that she is seriously considering turning herself in for the boy's sake. So I grab her by the shoulders and swear blind into her face that I'll get her boy traded in an agent-swap if it's the last thing I do on earth. And I know as well as you do that there's as much chance of *that* ever happening as . . . [three-second pause] . . . fuck it.

★

Was it purely for reasons of economy that in my later transcript, which I am now reading, I departed from Alec's spoken words at this point, preferring to paraphrase them for greater – shall we say objectivity? From the moment of leaving Gustav in the care of the two Sorbs, Alec clung to minor roads wherever the snow permitted. His problem, he explained, was 'knowing too bloody much' about the perils of the terrain they were crossing. The whole area was awash with Military Intelligence and KGB listening stations, and he knew them all by heart. He spoke of traversing empty, dead-straight minor roads with six inches of virgin snow on them, only the tree-lines to guide him; of his relief at entering forest until Tulip gave a yell of horror. She had spotted the former Nazi hunting lodge where the GDR elite brought visiting dignitaries to shoot deer and wild boar and get drunk. They made a hasty detour, lost their bearings and saw a light burning in a remote farmhouse. Leamas thumped on the door. It was opened by a terrified peasant woman clutching a knife. Having obtained directions from her, he persuaded her to sell him bread, sausage and a bottle of slivovitz, and on his way back to the Trabant tripped over a sagging telephone cable, he assumed for sounding a fire alarm. He cut it anyway.

The day was darkening, the snow thickening, the piebald Trabant was on her last legs: 'clutch shot, heater shot, gearbox shot, smoke belching out of the bonnet'. He reckoned that they were about ten kilometres from Bad Schandau and fifteen from the crossing point on the smugglers' map. Having confirmed their position as best he could by compass, he selected an east-bound timber track and drove until they hit a snowdrift. Huddled together in the Trabi in freezing cold, they ate the bread and *Wurst*, drank the slivovitz, froze and watched the deer go by while Tulip, half asleep with her head on Alec's shoulder, languidly described her hopes and dreams for her new life with Gustav in England.

She would not wish Gustav to go to Eton. She had heard that English boarding schools were run by pederasts like his father. She would prefer a proletarian State school with girls, much sport, not too strict. Gustav would start learning English from the day he arrived. She would see to that. For his birthday she would buy him an English bicycle. She had heard Scotland was beautiful. They would bicycle together in Scotland.

She was still talking in this vein, dozing, when Alec became aware of four silent male figures with Kalashnikovs standing like sentinels round the car. Ordering Tulip to remain where she was, he opened the door and slowly got out while they watched him. None was above seventeen, he reckoned, and they seemed as scared as he was. Seizing the initiative, he demanded to know what they thought they were doing, sneaking up on a courting couple. At first nobody answered. Then the boldest explained that they were poachers, looking for meat. To which Alec replied that, if they kept their mouths shut, he would do the same. They sealed the bond by shaking hands all round, after which the four men silently vanished.

The day dawns clear, no snow. Soon a pale sun is shining. Together, they tip the piebald Trabant down a slope, and chuck snow and branches over it. It's a walk from here on. Tulip has only light leather boots, knee length, no tread. Alec's workman's boots are little better. They set out, grabbing each other's hands as they slide and slip. They are in 'Saxon Switzerland', a wonderland of steep, undulating snowfields and forest. On the hillsides, old houses fallen to ruin or turned into summer orphanages. If the map is to be believed, they are walking parallel to the border. Hand in hand they battle their way up a rise and skirt a frozen pond. They are in a mountain village of small wooden houses.

AL: If the map was right, we were either dead or in Czecho.
[Chink of glass. Sounds of pouring liquid.]

But the story has barely begun: see accompanying Circus telegrams. See also the reason why, having listened to Alec's tape, I am still sitting tensely on the top floor of Covert's HQ in Marylebone in the small hours, waiting any minute to be summoned to Head Office.

*

Sally Ormond, deputy Head of Station Prague, wife to Head of Station Jerry, is the type of upper-class female go-getter the Circus blindly adores: Cheltenham Ladies' College, father in SOE in the war, couple of aunts at Bletchley. Also claims a mysterious kinship-by-marriage with George, which to my mind he bears a little too nobly.

Report by Sally Ormond, DH/Station Prague, to H/Covert [Smiley]. Personal and Private. Priority: CRASH.

Station orders from Covert were to receive, support and securely accommodate one disguised officer, Alec Leamas, and one escaping woman agent travelling on East German papers in an East German registered Trabant, registration supplied, expected to arrive in the early hours of darkness.

The Station was NOT however informed that the operation was being carried out contrary to Joint Steering's instructions. We could only assume that once it was known that Leamas had taken matters into his own hands, HO decided to afford operational support.

Berlin Station (de Jong) had advised us that on entering Czech territory Leamas would signal safe arrival by means of a no-name call to Embassy Visa Section enquiring whether UK visas were valid in Northern Ireland. Prague Station would respond by activating a recorded announcement advising him to call again in office hours. This would be an acknowledgement of message received.

Leamas and Tulip would then proceed by whatever means possible to a point on the road between Prague city and Prague airport, and park in a siding, map reference supplied.

Under the plan put forward by this Station and approved by H/Covert, the couple would abandon the car and a symbolized driver from Prague's GODIVA network would commandeer the Embassy shuttle (CD plates and blackened side windows) which regularly ferries Embassy personnel to and from Prague airport. He would then collect Leamas and Tulip from the agreed rv. The rear of the van would contain formal Western clothing, supplied by this Station. Leamas and Tulip would dress themselves as official dinner guests of HM Ambassador, and on that pretext bluff their way into the Embassy, which is under the permanent watch of Czech security.

At 1040 hours an emergency conference was held in the Embassy safe room, at which Her Excellency the Ambassador [HE] graciously consented to this plan. However, by 1600 hours UK time, having further consulted the Foreign Office, she revised her decision without apology on the grounds that, since the fugitive woman had been in the meantime widely featured on GDR media as a State criminal, the potential for diplomatic repercussions outweighed earlier considerations.

In light of HE's stated position, no Embassy vehicle and no Embassy staff could be deployed in the escape plan. I therefore disconnected Visa Section's automatic reply system in the hope that this would indicate to Leamas that no support was available.

I've replaced my earphones. I'm back with Alec, not in the imperial comfort of our British Embassy in Prague, but stuck at the freezing roadside with Tulip, and no support, no pick-up car and, as Alec would say, no fuck-all. I'm remembering what he's preached ever since I've known him: when you're planning an op, think of every way the Service can fuck you up, then wait for the one way you never thought of, but they have. And I reckon that's exactly what he's thinking now.

AL [verbatim resumed]: When no shuttle showed up, and no joy out of Visa Section, I just thought fuck it, that's London for you, so the only thing is, make it up as you go along. We're a distressed East German couple at the roadside, my wife's sick as a dog, so help us, somebody. I tell Doris to sit on the pavement and look pathetic which suits her just fine, and in due course a lorry full of bricks pulls up and the driver leans out. By the luck of the gods he's a German from Leipzig and he wants to know whether I'm pimping the pretty lady sitting on the pavement. So I say no, sorry mate, she's my wife, and she's ill, and he says okay, get in, and he drives us as far as the hospital in the city centre. I've got a rainy-day UK passport stitched into the lining of my shoulder bag, name of Miller. I unpick it and bung it in my pocket. Then I say to her: you're really seriously ill, Doris. You're pregnant and you're getting more ill by the minute. So do me a favour, bag out your tummy and look as fucking awful as you feel. So they open the doors and in we come. Sorry about that.

JO: Not quite the whole story though, is it? [Liquid pouring.]

AL: Jesus. All right then. We come up your cobble lane out there. We approach your noble gates with Her Majesty's royal crest on them in tasteful gold paint. There's three Czech goons in grey suits hanging around outside, doing nothing very deliberately. Maybe you haven't noticed them. Doris is putting on an act Sarah Bernhardt would have given her eyes for. I wave my UK passport at them: let us in quick. The buggers want to see her passport too. Listen, I tell them in my best English. Just press that fucking button you've got on the wall there, and tell them inside that my wife's having a miscarriage, so get a fucking doctor round. And if she has it here in the street it'll be on your fucking heads. And haven't you got mothers of your own, probably you haven't – or words to that effect, okay? And abracadabra the gates have parted. And we're standing in the Embassy courtyard. And Tulip is clutching her gut and thanking her patron saint for delivering us from evil. And you and your dear lady wife are apologizing profusely for yet another king-sized Head Office fuck-up. So thank you both for the gracious apology, accepted. And if you don't mind, I'll go and get some fucking sleep.

Sally Ormond takes back the story.

Extract from Sally Ormond, DH/Station Prague, personal informal handwritten DO letter to H/Covert [Smiley] by Circus bag. Priority: CRASH.

Well, of course, once we'd got poor Tulip and Alec inside the Embassy compound, that's when the *real* fun started. I honestly think Ambass *and* the FO would have been *far* happier if she had simply been handed back to the GDR authorities and no more said. For starters, Ambass wouldn't have Tulip inside 'her house' *at all*, even if legally it didn't make a jot of difference. She actually insisted that two janitors be moved *into* the main building, just so that poor Tulip could be shoved in the servants' area, which from a strict security point of view works rather better than the main house. But that wasn't *at all* her reason, as she made *totally* clear the moment we were all four of us squashed into the Embassy safe room: Her Excellency, attended by Arthur Lansdowne, her *very* private secretary, plus my dear husband and self. And Alec absolutely not *bien vu* by HE, of which more later, and anyway mopping Tulip's brow in the servants' area.

And P.S. George: a word in your ear if we may.

The Embassy safe room is extremely *stuffy* and a *potential health risk* at all times, as repeatedly reported in vain by self to HO Admin. The Mickey Mouse air-con system is totally kaput. It breathes *in* when it should breathe *out*, but according to Barker (Admin's pest-in-chief), no spare parts have been available for the last two years. And since nobody in the FO has seen fit to send us a new system, anyone using the place just stews and suffocates. Last week poor Jerry nearly *did* suffocate, but of course he's too noble to say. I've suggested about a million times that the safe room be made a Circus responsibility, but that apparently would be an infringement of *FO territorial rights*!!

If you can possibly agitate with Admin unattributably (*NOT* Barker, I suggest!), hugely grateful. Jerry joins me in sending much love and huge fealty as ever, specially to Ann.

S

Text of Immediate Top Secret Telegram from British Ambassador, Prague, personal to Sir Alwyn Withers, H/East European Department, The Foreign Office, copy to Circus (Joint Steering). Minutes of crisis meeting in Embassy safe room, held at 2100 hours. Present: HE Ambassador (Margaret Renford), Arthur Lansdowne, Private Secretary to HE, Jerry Ormond (H/Stn), Sally Ormond (DH/Stn).

Dear Alwyn,

After our secure telephone call of this morning, the following procedure has been agreed between the two of us regarding the onward journey of *our uninvited guest* (OUG):

1. OUG will travel to her next destination on what our Friends assure us will be a valid non-British passport. This will forestall later accusations by Czech authorities that this Embassy is dishing out UK passports to any Tom, Dick and Harry of whatever nationality attempting to evade GDR / Czech justice.

2. OUG will not be assisted, accompanied or transported in any manner by diplomatic or non-diplomatic members of Embassy staff in the course of her departure. No vehicle with British diplomatic number plates will be used for her exfiltration. No false British papers will be issued to her.

3. If OUG at any point claims she has the protection of the British Embassy, it is understood that this will be immediately and robustly denied, locally and in London.

4. OUG's departure from Embassy compound will occur within three working days, or other steps for her removal will be considered, including surrender of OUG to Czech authorities.

My telephone is buzzing and the red light is winking. It's Toby bloody Esterhase, gofer to Percy Alleline and Bill Haydon, yelling at me in his thick Hungarian accent to get my candy arse over to Head Office double-quick. Advising him to watch his language, I jump on my motorbike, which is being held ready for me outside the front door.

Minutes of emergency conference held in Joint Steering's safe room at Cambridge Circus. Presiding: Bill Haydon (H/JS). Present: Colonel Etienne Jabroche (Military Attaché, French Embassy, London, Chief of French Intelligence Liaison), Jules Purdy (JS French desk), Jim Prideaux (JS Balkans desk), George Smiley (H/Covert), Peter Guillam (JACQUES).

Note-taker assigned to meeting: T. Esterhase. Recorded, part transcribed verbatim. Flash copy to H/Stn Prague.

It's five in the morning. The summons has come. I have arrived from Marylebone by motorbike. George has come straight from Treasury. He is unshaven and looks more than usually worried.

'You're entirely free to say *no* at any point, Peter,' he has twice assured me. He has already described the operation as 'needlessly elaborate' but his greater concern, try as he might to conceal it, is that the operational plan is the collective achievement of Joint Steering. We are six at the long plywood table in the Circus safe room.

Jabroche: Bill. My dear friend. My masters in Paris need to be assured that your Monsieur Jacques can hold his own on matters of small farming in France.

Haydon: Tell him, Jacques.

Guillam: I'm not worried about that, Colonel.

Jabroche: Not even in the company of experts?

Guillam: I grew up on a French smallholding in Brittany.

Haydon: Is Brittany French? You amaze me, Jacques.

[Laughter.]

Jabroche: Bill. With your permission.

Switching to French, Colonel Jabroche engages Guillam in an animated discussion on the French farming industry, with particular reference to north-west France.

Jabroche: I am satisfied, Bill. He passes. He even speaks like a Breton, poor man.

[More laughter.]

Haydon: But will it play, Etienne? Can you really get him in?

Jabroche: In, yes. Out, will be up to Monsieur Jacques and his good lady. You are in the nick of time. The list of French delegates closes imminently. We are already holding it open. I suggest we keep the presence of Monsieur Jacques at the conference as brief as possible. We enrol him, he goes on the collective visa, he is delayed by illness, but he is determined to make the closing session. As one of three hundred international delegates, he will not be unduly conspicuous. Do you speak Finnish, Monsieur Jacques?

Guillam: Not a lot, Colonel.

Jabroche: I thought all Bretons did. [Laughter.] And the lady in the case speaks no French?

Guillam: To our knowledge, German and school Russian, but no French.

Jabroche: But she has panache, you say? She is personable. She has élan. She can dress.

Smiley: Jacques, you've seen her.

I had seen her dressed and I had seen her undressed. I select the first:

Guillam: We've only brush-passed. But she's impressive. Good tradecraft, quick thinking. Creative. Spirited.

Haydon: Jesus. *Creativity.* Who the hell needs creativity? Woman needs to do what she's bloody told and shut up, doesn't she? Is it a goer or not? Jacques?

Guillam: I'm up for it if George is.

Haydon: Is he?

Smiley: Given that Joint and the Colonel are providing the necessary field support, we at Covert are prepared to accept the risk.

Haydon: Well, that sounds a bit bloody mealy-mouthed, I must say. It's a goer then. Etienne, I'm assuming you'll supply Monsieur Jacques with his French passport and travel papers. Or do you want us to do that?

Jabroche: Ours are better. [Laughter.] Kindly also remember, Bill, that if things come unstuck, my government will be very shocked to discover that your perfidious English secret service is encouraging its agents to masquerade as French citizens.

Haydon: And we shall deny the accusation vigorously and apologize. [To Prideaux] Jim-boy. A comment? You've been mysteriously silent. Czecho's your patch. Are you happy with us trampling all over it?

Prideaux: Not objecting, if that's what you mean.

Haydon: Anything you want to add or subtract?

Prideaux: Not off-hand.

Haydon: Okay, gents. Thanks all. It's a goer, so let's get down to it. Jacques, our thoughts go with you. Etienne, maybe a private word.

But George doesn't give up his misgivings easily, witness the next serial. The clock is ticking; I am to leave for Prague in six hours.

George,

   We spoke. You asked me to put down my experience of
the Field Dispatch Office at Heathrow, Terminal 3,
presently under Joint Steering's command. In appearance
the FDO is just another seedy airport office at the end of
an unswept corridor. A glazed door is marked 'Freight
Interlink', access is by entryphone. Once inside, the
atmosphere is depressing: a couple of weary couriers
playing cards, a woman barking Spanish into a telephone,
one dresser only working a double shift because her
colleague is off sick, cigarette smoke, full ashtrays and only
one cubicle because they're waiting for new curtains for
the other one.

   The big surprise was the reception party that awaited
my appearance: Alleline, Bland, Esterhase. If Bill H had
been there, I'd have had a full hand. Ostensibly they'd come
to see me off and wish me well. Alleline to the fore as ever,
produced my French passport and conference ID, courtesy
of Jabroche, with great flourish. Esterhase did the same
with my travelling case and props: clothing bought in
Rennes, agricultural handbooks and a history of how
France built the Suez Canal for light reading, etc. Roy
Bland played big brother and slyly asked me if there was
anyone I'd like informed if I was away a few years longer
than expected.

   But the real purpose of their attentions could not have
been clearer. They wanted to know more about Tulip:
where she was coming from, how long she had been
working for us, who had the handling of her? And then the
strangest moment when, having fended off their questions,
I was standing in the cubicle being dressed and Toby E

shoved his head round the curtain saying he had the following personal message for me from Bill: 'Any time you get tired of your Uncle George, think Head of Station Paris.' My reply was non-committal.

Peter

Now meet George in his role as the ultimate operational pedant, bent on closing every loophole in Joint Steering's notoriously slipshod planning:

Signal from H/Covert [Smiley] *to H/Station Prague* [Ormond]
TOP SECRET MAYFLOWER. Priority: CRASH.

A. Finnish passport for sub-source Tulip will arrive tomorrow by bag in name of Venia Lessif, born Helsinki, nutrition expert, married name of spouse: Adrien Lessif. Passport will contain stamped Czech entry visa, date of entry to coincide with Communist French-sponsored conference for *Fields of Peace.*

B. Peter Guillam will arrive Prague airport on Air France flight 412 tomorrow morning at 1040 hours local time, travelling on French national's passport in name of Adrien Lessif, visiting lecturer in Agrarian Economics at Rennes University. Czech entry visa also valid to coincide with conference. Lessif's appearance at conference notionally delayed by illness. Both Lessifs currently appear on Conference List of Participants, one participant (delayed), one spouse.

C. Also by tomorrow's bag, two Air France tickets Prague–Paris Le Bourget, for Adrien and Venia Lessif, departing 0600 hours 28 January. Air France records will confirm that the couple flew to Prague on separate dates (see entry stamps) but will be returning to Paris with fellow academics in the group.

D. Accommodation for Professor and Mme Lessif has been booked at the Hotel Balkan where the French delegation will be housed overnight prior to early morning departure for Paris Le Bourget.

And Sally Ormond in reply, missing no opportunity to sing her own praises:

Extract from second personal letter Sally Ormond to George Smiley, marked Strictly Personal & Private to you, not for the record.

On receipt of your very lucid signal, herewith gratefully acknowledged, Jerry and I decided that I should go and prepare Tulip for her departure from the Embassy and her coming ordeal. I duly crossed the courtyard to the annexe suite where we had housed Tulip: double curtains on street side, camp bed for self in passage outside bedroom door, extra chancery guard posted in downstairs hall in case of unwelcome visitors.

I found her sitting on the bed, and Alec with his arm round her shoulder, but she seemed not to know he was there, just every now and then sobbing in semi-silent hiccups.

Be that as it may, I took firm charge of the situation and, as planned, sent Alec off for fresh air and a boys' walk beside the river with Jerry. My German language being pretty much stuck at Level 2, I couldn't get a lot out of her at first, though I doubt it would have made much difference because she was hardly talking, let alone listening. She whispered 'Gustav' at me several times and I gathered, after a bit of sign language, that Gustav was not her *Mann* but her *Sohn*.

But I did manage to get through to her that she would be leaving the Embassy tomorrow, flying to England but not directly, and that she would be attached to a mixed French tour group of academics and agriculturalists. Her first reaction, very naturally, was how could she possibly if she didn't speak a word of French? And when I said that wasn't going to matter, because she would be Finnish – and nobody speaks Finnish, do they? – her next reaction was: *in these clothes?* – which was my cue to unpack all the brilliant goodies Paris Station had got together for us at no notice at all: gorgeous barley-coloured twinset from Printemps, lovely shoes just her size, dishy nightdress and underclothes, make-up literally to *die* for – Paris Station must have spent a *fortune* – just everything she must have been dreaming of for the last twenty years, even if she didn't know it, and nice labels from Tours to complete the illusion. And a *very* pretty engagement ring I wouldn't have minded myself, *and* a decent gold wedding ring rather than the ersatz bit of tin she was wearing – all to be returned on landing, of course, but I didn't think that needed saying *quite* yet!

And by then she was *into* it. The pro in her had woken up. She looked very carefully at her nice new passport (not actually new) and declared it pretty good. And when I told her that a gallant Frenchman would accompany her and pretend to be her husband for the journey, she said that sounded a sensible arrangement, and what did he look like?

So as ordered I showed her a photograph of Peter G, and she peered at it rather *expressionlessly*, I have to say, given that, as proxy husbands go, you could do a lot worse than PG. Finally she asked, 'Is he French or English?' and I said, 'Both, and you're Finnish and French,' and my dear she *hooted* with laughter!

And quite soon after that Alec and Jerry came back from their walk, and with the ice broken we got down to the serious briefing. She listened carefully and calmly.

By the end of our session, I had the feeling she had really warmed to the whole idea, and in a rather awful way thought it fun. A bit of a danger addict, I thought, and in *that* way only, very like Alec!

Take care, and my love as ever to our gorgeous Ann,

S

*

Make no hasty or inadvertent body movement. Keep your hands and shoulders exactly where they are now, and breathe. Pepsi is back on her throne, but she can't take her eyes off you, and it's not love.

*

Report by Peter Guillam on temporary attachment to Covert Ops, re exfiltration of sub-source TULIP from Prague to Paris Le Bourget, for onward transit by RAF fighter plane to London, Northolt airport, 27 January 1960.

I arrived at Prague airport at 1125 hours local time (flight delayed) in the person of visiting lecturer in Agrarian Economics at the University of Rennes.

I understood that, thanks to French Liaison, my late arrival due to illness had been formally noted at the conference, and my name included on the list of attendees for the benefit of the Czech authorities.

In further verification of my bona fides, I was met by the

Cultural Attaché from the French Embassy, who used his diplomatic credentials to hasten airport processing, which passed off relatively easily with the Attaché acting as my interpreter.

He then drove me in his official car to the French Embassy, where I signed the visitors' book before being delivered, also by French Embassy car, to the conference, where a seat had been reserved for me in the back row.

The conference hall was a gilded, operatic affair, originally built for the Central Council of Railwaymen, and accommodating up to four hundred delegates. Security was cursory. Halfway up the grand staircase, two overworked women who spoke only Czech sat at a desk ticking off the names of delegates from half-a-dozen countries. The conference itself took the form of a seminar conducted by a panel of experts seated on the stage, with choreographed contributions from the floor. No input from myself was required. I was impressed by the deftness of French Liaison, who at short notice had authenticated my presence in the eyes of Czech security, and of the delegates, two of whom were clearly conscious to my role and found time to seek me out and shake my hand.

At 1700 hours, the conference was declared closed, and the French delegates were bussed to the Hotel Balkan, a small, old-fashioned establishment that had been set aside for our exclusive use. On checking in, I was handed a key to bedroom number eight, designated as a 'family room', since I was notionally one half of a married couple. The Balkan has a dining room for residents and, leading from it, a bar with a central table where I placed myself in anticipation of my notional wife's arrival.

My broad understanding was that she would be exfiltrated from the British Embassy by tame ambulance, transported to a safe house in the suburbs and thence to the Hotel Balkan by unexplained means.

I was therefore impressed to see her arrive in a French diplomatic car, on the arm of the same Cultural Attaché who had welcomed me to Prague airport. I wish again to acknowledge here the acumen and tradecraft of French Liaison.

Under the name of Venia Lessif, Tulip had been listed as a delegate's spouse attending the conference *in absentia*. Her good looks and fashionable appearance caused a mild stir among other French delegates in the hotel, and again I was supported by the two male members who, having greeted me with familiarity at the conference, saluted and embraced Tulip as a friend. Tulip in return received their compliments with style, affecting broken German only, which became our lingua franca as a married couple, since my own German is limited.

After dinner taken in the company of the two French delegates, who played their part to perfection, we did not linger in the bar with the rest of the delegates but repaired early to our bedroom, where by tacit agreement our conversation was confined to banalities consistent with our cover, the presence of microphones and even cameras in a hotel for foreigners being virtually certain.

Fortunately, our room was spacious, with several single beds and two hand basins. For much of the night we were obliged to listen to the rowdy chatter of the delegates below and, into the small hours, singing.

It is my impression that neither Tulip nor I slept. At 0400 hours we reassembled and were taken by bus to Prague airport where, miraculously as it now appears to me, we were cleared *en bloc* to the transit lounge and thence by Air France to Le Bourget. I wish once more to offer my unstinted thanks for the support of French Liaison.

How the next entry found its way into my report moment-arily confounds me, until I conclude that I must have added it as some kind of distraction.

Personal and confidential handwritten DO letter to George Smiley from Jerry Ormond, H/Station Prague. NOT for file.

Dear George,

Well, the bird has certainly flown, to massive sighs of relief here as you can imagine, and is by now presumably safely if not happily installed at Chateau Tulip, Somewhere in England. Her flight in both senses seems to have gone reasonably smoothly, despite the fact that JONAH at the last minute needed $500 on top of salary before consenting to drive Tulip to the rv in his ambulance, the little sod. But Tulip isn't who I'm writing to you about, and least of all Jonah. It's Alec.

As you have often said in the past, as professionals bound in secrecy we have a duty of care, and it's for one another. And that means being mutually watchful, and if one of us appears to be cracking under the strain and is not aware of it, then it's our duty to protect him from himself, and by the same token protect the Service too.

Alec is the absolute best fieldman you and I know. He's savvy as hell, dedicated, streetwise, has all the skills. And he has just pulled off one of the neatest and most dicey operations it's been my pleasure to witness, albeit over the heads of Joint Steering, our revered Ambassador and the Mandarins of Whitehall. So when he knocks home three-quarters of a bottle of Scotch at a sitting and then picks a fight with a chancery guard he happens to dislike, we make all the allowances, and then some.

But we walked, Alec and I. Along the river for an hour,

then up to the castle, then back to the Embassy. So a two-hour walk while he was still by his own standards dead sober. And his one theme in all that time was: the Circus is penetrated. Not just by some mail clerk with a mortgage, but at the top of the tree in Joint where it really counts. And it's more than just a bee in his bonnet, it's a whole hive. It's disproportionate, it's not fact based, and frankly it's paranoid. Coupled with his visceral hatred of all things American, it makes for difficult conversation, to say the least, and becomes even more alarming. And under the laws of our profession as defined by no lesser person than yourself, and with all due affection and respect, I am duly reporting my concerns to you.

As ever,

Jerry

P.S. And to Ann, as ever, homage and much love, J

And from Laura a rosette, ordering me to stop.

★

'Nice read?'

'Tolerable, thank you, Bunny.'

'Well, Christ, you wrote it, didn't you? Gave you a bit of a buzz, surely, after all that time?'

He has brought a male friend along with him this late afternoon: a blond, smiling, well-polished youth, not a mark of life on him.

'Peter, this is *Leonard*,' says Bunny ceremoniously, as if I ought to know who Leonard is. 'Leonard will be Counsel for the Service if our little matter ever comes to court, which of course we devoutly hope it won't. He will also be appearing for us at the preliminary meeting of the All-Party Group inquiry next week. At which, as you know, you have already been tapped to appear.' Rictal grin. 'Leonard. Peter.'

We shake hands. Leonard's soft as a child's.

'If Leonard is representing the Service, what's he doing here with me?' I demand.

'A getting-to-know-each-other's-faces,' says Bunny soothingly. 'Leonard's a black-letter lawyer' – and seeing my eyebrows go up – 'which *merely* means that he's versed in every legal wrinkle in the book and some that aren't even in the book. Puts run-of-the-mill lawyers like me in the shade.'

'Oh come,' says Leonard.

'And the reason Laura is *not* here today, Peter, since you don't ask, is that Leonard and I, together, felt it would be rather better for *all* parties, including you, if this was a boys-only discussion.'

'What's that supposed to mean?'

'Good old-fashioned tact, for starters. Respect for your personal privacy. *And* the outside possibility that we might just for once get the truth out of you.' Naughty smile. 'Which would then enable Leonard to take a view about how to proceed generally. Fair comment, Leonard? Or too much?'

'Oh, quite fair, I think,' says Leonard.

'And of course to address in *rather* more detail the issue of whether your personal interests are best represented by having your *own* legal representative,' Bunny goes on. 'In the unhappy event, for instance, that the All-Partygoers simply tiptoe off the stage – which we're told is not by any means unknown – leaving Blind Justice to have her way with you. Us.'

'How about a black belt?' I suggest.

My witticism goes unnoticed. Or perhaps it *is* noticed, if only as evidence that I am particularly on edge today.

'In which case the Circus has a shortlist of eligible

candidates – *acceptable* candidates, let us say – and Leonard, I think you said you were willing to guide Peter's eye if it comes to that, which we dearly hope and pray it won't' – deferring with a collegial smile to Leonard.

'Absolutely, Bunny. The trouble is, there are not *that* many of us who are cleared this far up. I do feel Harry is coming on awfully well, as you know,' says Leonard. 'He's applied for silk and the judges adore him. So personally, not wishing to influence in *any* way – go for Harry. He's a man, and they like a man defending a man. They may not know it, but they do.'

'Who pays for him?' I ask. 'Or her?'

Leonard smiles at his hands. Bunny takes the question:

'Well, I think in the *large*, Peter, much may depend on the *course* of the hearing – and, shall we say, your own personal bearing, your sense of duty, and your loyalty to your old Service.'

But Leonard hasn't heard a word of this, as I can tell by the steadfast way he goes on smiling at his hands.

'So, Peter,' says Bunny, as if coming to the easy part. 'Yes or no.' Squeeze of the eyes. 'Between men. Did you or did you not fuck Tulip?'

'No.'

'Absolutely no?'

'Absolutely.'

'Irrevocably no, here and now in this room, in the presence of a five-star witness?'

'Bunny, forgive me' – Leonard with his hand up in friendly reproach – 'I think you've momentarily forgotten your law. Given my duties to the court, and my obligations to act as counsel for my client, I cannot possibly appear as a witness.'

'All right. Once again, if you please, Peter. *I, Peter Guillam, did not fuck Tulip at the Hotel Balkan in Prague on the night before her exfiltration to the United Kingdom.* True or false?'

'True.'

'Which is a relief for all of us, as I'm sure you can imagine. Particularly as you seem to have fucked everyone else in sight.'

'Immense,' Leonard agrees.

'And even *more* particularly, since Rule One of a Service that hasn't otherwise got many rules dictates that serving officers don't ever, *ever* fuck their joes, as you call them, even out of politeness. Other people's joes when operationally desirable, yes, open season. Just not *ever* their own. You are aware of that rule?'

'I am.'

'And were so aware at the time in question?'

'Yes.'

'And would you agree that, if you *had* fucked her, which we know you didn't, it would constitute not only a monumental breach of Service discipline, but clear evidence of your louche and uncontrollable nature, and your disregard for the sensitivities of a fugitive mother in mortal peril who has just been deprived of her only child? You agree with that statement?'

'I agree with that statement.'

'Leonard, you have a question?'

Leonard plucks at his pretty lower lip with his fingertips, and frowns a creaseless frown.

'You know, Bunny, it sounds awfully rude, but I really *don't* think I *do* have a question,' he confesses, with a startled smile at himself. 'Not after that. I think *pro tem* we've all gone as far as we can *go*. And further.' And to me, confidentially: 'I'll send you that shortlist, Peter. And you never heard me mention Harry. Or maybe better I slip it to Bunny. *Collusion*,' he explains, bestowing another doting smile on me and reaching for his black briefcase, indicating that the lengthy meeting I had been anticipating is over. 'But I do think a man would be good, all the same,' he says to Bunny, not to me, as an aside. 'When it comes to the hard questions, men rather have the edge in these cases. Less puritanical. See you at the All-Party beano, Peter. *Tschüss.*'

★

Did I fuck her? No, I bloody well didn't. I made mute, frenzied love to her in pitch darkness for six life-altering hours, in an explosion of tension and lust between two bodies that had desired each other from birth and had only the night to live.

And I was supposed to *tell* them this? I demand of the orange-tinted darkness as I lie sleepless on my prison cot in Dolphin Square.

I, who was taught from the cradle to deny, deny and deny again – taught by the very Service that is seeking to drag a confession out of me?

★

'You slept well, Pierre? You are happy? You have made a great speech? You are coming home today?'

I must have called her.

'How's Isabelle?' I ask.

'She is beautiful. She misses you.'

'Has he come back? That impolite friend of mine?'

'No, Pierre, your terrorist friend has not come back. You have watched football with him?'

'We don't do that any more.'

9

There was nothing I could see on file – and thank the Lord there wasn't – of the days and nights of eternity that I spent in Brittany after handing Doris over to Joe Hawkesbury, our Paris Head of Station, at Le Bourget airport at seven o'clock on a misty winter's morning. As our plane landed and a voice called out for Professor and Madame Lessif, I was in a state of delirious relief. As we descended the gangway side by side, the sight of Hawkesbury sitting below us in a black Rover car with CD plates and a young woman assistant from his Station in the back seat set my heart plunging.

'And my *Gustav*?' Doris demanded, seizing my arm.

'It'll be all right. It'll happen,' I said, hearing myself parroting Alec's empty assurances.

'When?'

'As soon as they can. They're good people. You'll see. I love you.'

Hawkesbury's girl was holding the back door. Had she heard me? My insane outburst, spoken by someone else inside me? Never mind whether she knew German. Every bloody fool knows *Ich liebe Dich*. I coaxed Doris forward. With a jolt she landed reluctantly on the back seat. The girl hopped in after her and slammed the door. I got into the passenger seat beside Hawkesbury.

'Nice flight?' he enquired, as we raced across the tarmac behind a flashing Jeep.

We entered an aircraft hangar. Ahead of us in the gloom, a twin-engined RAF plane, propellers slowly turning. The girl sprang out. Doris stayed put, whispering German words to herself that I couldn't make out. My own mad words seemed to have made no impression on her. Perhaps she hadn't heard them. Perhaps I hadn't spoken them. The girl tried to jockey her, but she wouldn't budge. I got in beside her and took her hand. She pressed her head into my shoulder while Hawkesbury watched us in the driving mirror.

'*Ich kann nicht,*' she whispered.

'*Du musst,* it'll be all right. *Ganz ehrlich.* Honestly.'

'*Du kommst nicht mit?*' – you're not coming?

'Later. After you've talked to them.'

I got out of the car and offered her my hand. She ignored it and climbed out of her own accord. No, she hasn't heard me. She can't have done. A uniformed aircraftwoman with a clipboard came marching towards us. With Hawkesbury's girl one side and the aircraftwoman the other, Doris let herself be led towards the plane. Reaching the gangway, she stopped, looked upwards and, having steeled herself, began climbing, using both hands. I waited for her to look back. The cabin door closed.

'All done then,' said Hawkesbury briskly, still without turning his head to me. 'So the word from on high is: bravo, you've done a great job, now go home to Brittany, dry out and wait for the great call. Gare Montparnasse suit you?'

'Gare Montparnasse would be fine, thanks.'

And you may be the darling of Joint Steering, brother Hawkesbury, but that didn't prevent Bill Haydon from offering me your job.

★

Even today, I'd be hard put to describe the torrent of conflicting emotions that swirled through me on my return to the farmstead, whether I was driving a tractor, spreading muck in the fields or otherwise striving to make my presence felt as the young master. One minute I was basking in the sensations of a night too momentous to define; the next, I was lost in awe at the monstrous irresponsibility of the compulsive, reckless act I had committed, and the words I had, or hadn't, spoken.

Invoking the silent darkness in which our embraces were fought out, I tried to persuade myself that our lovemaking had been only in the mind, an illusion brought on by the fear that at any minute Czech security might smash down our bedroom door. But one look at the imprint of her fingers on my body told me I was fooling myself.

And no imagining on my part could have delivered the moment when, with the coming of first light, and still not a word between us, she wrapped away one part of her body after another, first standing before me naked and sentinel, as she had stood before me on the Bulgarian beach, then covering herself piece by piece in her French finery until there was nothing left to desire but a sensible workaday skirt and black jacket buttoned to the neck: except that I desired her more desperately than ever.

And how, as she dressed, the light of triumph or desire quieted from her face, and we became by her own choice estranged, first on the bus to Prague airport when she refused my hand, and again on the plane to Paris when, for reasons that eluded me, we were placed in separate rows – until the plane halted and we stood up and started to file out, and our hands found each other again, only to part.

On the laborious railway journey to Lorient – no high-speed trains in those days – an episode had occurred which with hindsight fills me to this day with a sense of the horror to come.

Barely an hour out of Paris, our train came to an abrupt halt, with no explanation offered. Muffled voices from outside were followed by a single unsourced scream, male or female I never knew. Still we waited. Some of us exchanged glances. Others remained determinedly engrossed in their books and newspapers. A uniformed guard appeared in the carriage doorway, a boy of no more than twenty. I remember very well the silence that preceded his prepared speech, which after taking a deep breath he delivered with commendable calm:

'Ladies and gentlemen. I regret to inform you that our progress has been inhibited by human intervention. We shall continue on our way in a few minutes.'

And it was not I, but the studious old gentleman in stiff white collar seated beside me who raised his head and demanded brusquely:

'Intervention of what nature?'

To which the boy could only answer in the voice of a penitent:

'A suicide, monsieur.'

'Of whom?'

'A man, sir. It is believed he was a man.'

Within a few hours of my arrival at Les Deux Eglises, I took myself down to the cove: *my* cove, my place of solace. First the trudge down the matted slope to the edge of my land, then another trudge along the cliff path, and at its base the little patch of sand, and to either side of it low-lying rocks like dozing crocodiles. This was where I'd done my boyhood thinking. This was where I'd brought my women over the years – the loves, half-loves, quarter-loves. But the only woman I craved was Doris. I taunted myself with the thought that we had never conducted a single conversation that wasn't cover. But hadn't I shared every vicarious hour of her life, sleeping and waking, for a whole bloody year? Hadn't I responded to her every impulse, every lurch of purity, lust, revolt and vengeance? Tell me of another woman I had known so long, and so intimately, before I even slept with her.

She had empowered me. She had made me the man I had never been till now. More than one woman over the years had told me – kindly, bluntly, or in outright disenchantment – that I had no aptitude for sex; that I could neither take nor give with abandon; was inept, restrained; that I lacked the true instinctual fire.

But Doris *knew* all that, before we ever embraced. She had known it as we brush-passed, and she knew it as she took me naked into her arms, welcomed me, absolved me, showed me; then formed herself around me until we were old friends, then careful lovers, and finally triumphant rebels, broken free of everything that presumed to control our two lives.

Ich liebe Dich. I meant it. I would always mean it. And when I got back to England, I would say it to her again, and I would tell George that I had said it to her and I would tell him I had served my time and more, and if I had to quit the Service to marry Doris and fight the good fight for Gustav, I would do that too. I would stick to my guns and not even George, with all his velvet arguments, was going to talk me round.

But no sooner had I made this great, irreversible decision than Doris's well-documented promiscuity came to haunt me. Was that her real secret? That she made love to all her men with equal, indiscriminate generosity? I even half persuaded myself that Alec had been there before me: two whole nights spent together, for Christ's sake! All right, the first with Gustav in tow. But what about the second night, crammed into the Trabant, one to one, snuggled up for warmth – her head on his shoulder, his own words! – while she bared her soul to him – and whatever else she bared – whereas I, blind courier, could practically count the words that Doris and I had managed to exchange in our entire lives.

166

But even as I conjured this spectre of imaginary betrayal, I knew I was deluding myself, which made the ignominy more painful. Alec wasn't that man. If Alec, instead of me, had spent the night with Doris in the Hotel Balkan, he would have sat smoking placidly in a corner, just as he had done that night in Cottbus, while Doris held Gustav, not Alec, in her arms.

I was still staring out to sea, reasoning fruitlessly to and fro in these terms, when I realized that I wasn't alone. In my self-absorption I had even failed to notice that I was being followed. Worse, that I had been followed by the least appetizing member of our community, Honoré the poison dwarf, trader in manure, used car tyres and worse. He cut an elfin figure, and a sinister one: squat, broad-shouldered, evil-faced in Breton cap and smock, standing feet astride at the cliff's edge, peering down.

I called up to him. I asked him, with a certain disdain, how I could be of help. What I was really asking him to do was go away and leave me to my thoughts. His answer was to skip down the cliff path, and with not so much as a glance at me, perch himself on a rock near the sea. Dark was gathering. Across the bay, the lights of Lorient were starting to shine. After a while, he raised his head and stared at me, as if in enquiry. Receiving no response, he drew a bottle from the depths of his smock and, having filled two paper beakers from his other pocket, beckoned me to join him, which for civility's sake I duly did.

'Thinking of death?' he asked lightly.

'Not consciously.'

'A woman? Another one?'

I ignored him. I was struck, despite myself, by his mysterious courtliness. Was it new? Or had I not noticed it before? He raised his beaker; I raised mine to him. In Normandy, they would call it Calvados, but to us Bretons it's Lambig. In Honoré's version, it was the stuff they put on horses' hooves to harden them.

'To your sainted father,' he said, talking out to sea. 'The great Resistance hero. Killed a lot of Huns.'

'So they say,' I replied warily.

'Medals too.'

'A couple.'

'They tortured him. Then they killed him. Hero twice over. Bravo,' he said, and drank again, still looking out to sea. 'My father was a hero too,' he went on. '*Big* hero. Mega. Bigger than yours by two metres.'

'What did he do?'

'Collaborated with the Huns. They promised him they'd give Brittany her independence when they won the war. Arsehole believed them. War ended, the heroes of the Resistance strung him up in the town square, what was left of it. Big crowd. Lot of applause. You could hear it all over town.'

Had he heard it too, perhaps? With his hands over his ears, cowering in some kind person's cellar? I had a feeling he might have done.

'So better you buy your horseshit from someone else,' he went on. 'Or maybe they'll hang you too.'

He waited for me to say something but nothing came to me, so he replenished our beakers and we went on looking out to sea.

★

In those days the peasants still played *boules* in the village square and sang Breton songs when they were drunk. Determined to count myself a normal human being, I shared their *cidre* and listened to the Grand Guignol that passed for village gossip: the post office couple who have locked themselves in their upper room and won't emerge because their son has killed himself; the district tax collector whose wife has left him because his father has dementia and is coming down to breakfast fully dressed at two in the morning; the dairy farmer in the next-door village who has gone to prison for sleeping with his daughters. To all of which I did my best to nod my head in the right places while the questions that wouldn't let me go multiplied and deepened.

★

The sheer, unnatural bloody ease of it, for Christ's sake!

Why had everything gone like clockwork when, in any other operation I had ever been involved in, nothing had gone like clockwork even when it had creaked to a successful finish?

A Stasi woman officer on the run in a neighbouring police state seething with informants? Czech Security notorious for their ruthlessness and efficiency? Yet far from being scrutinized, followed, listened to and even interrogated, we are gently ushered towards the exit gates?

And since when, tell me, had French Intelligence been so bloody immaculate? Torn apart by internal rivalries was more what I'd heard. Incompetent and penetrated from top to bottom, and why does *that* ring a bell? Yet suddenly they're grand masters of the art – or are they?

And if those were my suspicions, which they were, and becoming more deafening by the minute, what did I propose to do about them? Confess that to Smiley too before I throw in the towel and resign?

Even now, for all I knew, Doris was cloistered with her debriefers in some rural keep. Was she telling them what ardent love we had made? In matters of the heart, self-restraint was scarcely her strong suit.

And if her debriefers should begin to suspect, as I had, that her escape through East Germany and Czecho had been made unnaturally easy, what conclusions might they draw?

That it was all a put-up job? That she was a plant, a double, part of a high-stakes deception game? And that Peter Guillam, fool of fools, had slept with the enemy? – which was what I myself was beginning to believe by the time Oliver Mendel called me at five in the morning and ordered me in George's name to make my way to the city of Salisbury by the fastest possible route. Not a 'How are you, Peter?' Not a 'Sorry to haul you out of bed at crack of dawn.' Just a 'George says get your backside over here to Camp 4 in double-quick time, son.'

Camp 4: Joint Steering's safe house in the New Forest.

★

Squeezing myself into the last remaining seat of a small plane from Le Touquet, I picture the summary tribunal that awaits me. Doris has confessed to being a double agent. She is using our night of passion as some kind of diversion.

But then the other half of me takes over. She's the same Doris, for pity's sake. You love her. You told her you do, or you think you did, and it's still true either way. So don't rush to judgement just because you're about to be judged yourself!

By the time I landed at Lydd, there was no logic to any of it. By the time my train pulled in to Salisbury station, still none. But at least I'd found time to puzzle over the choice of Camp 4 as a place to take Doris for her debriefing. It was not, by Circus standards, the most secret of its archipelago of safe houses, or the most secure. On paper, it had everything going for it: small estate in the heart of the New Forest, can't be seen from the road, low-lying two-storey building, walled garden, a stream, bit of lake, ten acres of land, part wooded, and the whole lot enclosed by a six-foot-high fence of wire mesh, overgrown and concealed by shrubs.

But for the debriefing of a prized agent, snatched only days ago from the jaws of the Stasi that employed her? A little tarnished surely, a little more visible than George might have wished if Joint hadn't owned the operation.

At Salisbury station a Circus driver named Herbert, known to me from my time in Scalphunters' section, stood holding up a sign reading 'Passenger for Barraclough', one of George's worknames. But when I tried a bit of light conversation, Herbert said he wasn't authorized to talk to me.

We entered the long, pitted drive. Trespassers would be prosecuted. Low-hanging branches of lime and maple brushed the roof of the van. From the shadows loomed the unlikely figure of Fawn, first name unknown, a former unarmed-combat instructor at Sarratt and occasional strongarm man for Covert. But what on earth was *Fawn* doing here, of all people, when Camp 4 boasted its own security guards in the form of that celebrated gay couple beloved of all trainees, Messrs Harper and Lowe? Then I remembered that Smiley had a professional regard for Fawn, and had used him for a number of sticky assignments.

The driver pulled up, Fawn peered in at me, no smile, then with a tilt of his head beckoned us through. The track rose. A pair of solid wooden gates parted and closed behind us. To our right the main house, a fake-Tudor mansion built for a brewer. To our left, the coach house, a couple of Nissen huts and a majestic thatched tithe barn called the Stoop. Three Ford Zephyrs and one black Ford van were parked in the courtyard; and in front of them, the one human being in sight, Oliver Mendel, retired police inspector and longstanding ally of George, holding a walkie-talkie to his ear.

Scramble out of van, haul my rucksack after me. Shout 'Hi, Oliver! I made it!' But Oliver Mendel doesn't move a muscle, he just murmurs into his walkie-talkie while he watches me walk towards him. I again start to greet him, think better of it. Oliver murmurs, 'Will do, George,' and switches off.

'Our friend is somewhat *occupied* at the present time, Peter,' he says gravely. 'We've had a small incident. If you don't mind, you and me will take a stroll round the precincts.'

I have the message. Doris has told all, up to and including *Ich liebe Dich*. Our friend George is *occupied*, meaning he is disgusted, furious, sickened by the chosen disciple who has failed him. He can't bring himself to speak to me, so he has deputed his ever-reliable Inspector Oliver Mendel to give young Peter the dressing-down of a lifetime, and probably his marching orders as well. But why Fawn? And why this feeling of a camp deserted in a hurry?

We have climbed a stretch of lawn and are standing obliquely to each other, which I don't doubt is Mendel's intention. Our eyes are fixed on some uncertain object in the middle distance: a pair of silver birch trees, an old dovecote.

'I have a sad message for you, Peter.'

Here we go.

'I'm very sorry to inform you that sub-source Tulip, the lady you successfully exfiltrated from Czecho, was certified dead this morning.'

★

And since nobody ever quite knows what they said at such a moment, and I am no different, I won't award myself the mandatory cry of pain, horror or disbelief. I know I ceased to see anything clearly, neither the silver birches nor the dovecote. I know it was sunny and warm for the time of year. I know that I wanted to vomit but, true to my inhibited nature, managed not to. I know that I followed Mendel to the derelict summerhouse which lies at the most southern point of the estate, cut off from the main house by a dense coppice of macrocarpa trees. And that when we sat down on the rickety verandah we were looking at an overgrown croquet lawn, because I remember the rusted hoops poking out of the grass.

'Hung by the neck till she was dead, I'm afraid, son,' Mendel was saying, mouthing the words of the death sentence. 'A do-it-yourself job. From the low bough of a tree just the other side of that slope there. By the footbridge. Point 217 on the map. Life extinct certified at 0800 hours by Dr Ashley Meadows.'

Ash Meadows, fashionable Harley Street shrink, improbable friend of George. Circus Occasional with a corner in neurotic defectors.

'Ash is here?'

'With her now.'

I digest this news slowly. Doris is dead. Ash is with her. A doctor stands guard over the dead.

'Did she leave a note or anything? *Tell* anyone what she was going to do?'

'She just hanged herself, son. With a length of spliced nylon climbing rope she appears to have found on the premises. Nine feet in length. Presumed left over from a training course. Somewhat negligently, in my personal view.'

'Has anyone told Alec?' I ask, thinking now of her head resting on his shoulder.

His policeman's voice again. 'George will tell your friend Alec Leamas what Alec needs to know when Alec needs to know it, not before, son. And George will pick his own time to do that. Understood?'

Understood that Alec still believes he delivered Tulip to safety.

'Where is he now? Not Alec. George,' I ask stupidly.

'Just at this moment in time, George is engaged in conversation with a chance Swiss gentleman, as a matter of fact. Caught himself in a snare in the grounds, poor fellow. Not a snare, more a mantrap, placed there by an unscrupulous poacher after a bit of venison, we can only assume. A rusty one, lying in the long

173

grass, we're told. Could have been there for I don't know how long. But the spring wasn't bothered. And those dragon's teeth – they could have cut his foot clean off, I'm told. So he was lucky.' And to my continued silence, in the same conversational tone: 'The Swiss individual concerned is an ornithologist by hobby, which I respect, being in the way of one myself, and he was birdwatching. He didn't intend to intrude on the premises, but he did, which he regrets. Which I would too. What shocks me, between you and me, is Harper and Lowe not coming across it on their rounds of the estate. They're lucky they didn't walk into it themselves is all I can say.'

'Why's George seeing him now?' – and I suppose I meant, *at a time like this.*

'The Swiss gentleman? Well, he's a material witness, isn't he, son? The Swiss gentleman. Like it or not. He was in the grounds – all right, in error, a fellow birdwatcher like myself, these things can happen – but at the relevant time, to his misfortune. George naturally wishes to know if the gentleman saw or heard anything of interest that could shed light. Maybe poor Tulip addressed him in some manner. It's a delicate situation, if you think about it. We're in a highly secret facility, and Tulip is not officially landed in the UK, so the Swiss gentleman stumbled into what we might call a security hornets' nest. That has to be taken into account, regardless.'

I was hearing him but not really listening: 'I need to see her, Oliver,' I said.

To which, unsurprised, he replied: 'Then remain right here, son, while I refer that one upward, and don't move on any account.'

With which he strode into the long grass of the abandoned croquet lawn, once more murmuring into his walkie-talkie. At his gesture, I followed him down to the massive door of the Stoop. He rapped, then stood back. After a delay, the door creaked open, and there stood Ash Meadows himself, a fifty-year-old former rugby player in red braces and check flannel shirt, smoking his habitual pipe.

'Sorry about this, old chap,' he said, standing back for me; so I said I was sorry too.

On a ping-pong table at the centre of the great barn lay the effigy of a slender woman in a zipped-up body bag. She was lying on her back, toes upward.

'Poor girl never knew she was called Tulip till she got here,' Ash was reminiscing in the breezy voice he had evidently developed for speaking in the presence of the dead. 'Soon as she knew she was Tulip, God help anyone who called her anything else. Sure you want to do this?'

He meant: was I ready for him to pull back the zip fastener. I was.

Her face, for the first time since I knew it, expressionless. Her auburn hair plaited and bound with green ribbon, the plait lying beside her head. Eyes closed. I never till now saw her sleep. The neck a slough of blues and greys.

'All done, Peter, old boy?'

He closed the zip anyway.

★

I follow Mendel into the fresh air. Ahead of me, the grass mound rises to a clump of chestnut trees. There's a nice view from the top: the main house, a pine forest, surrounding fields. But I have scarcely started my ascent when Mendel puts a hand across my path.

'We stay down here, if you don't mind, son. No point in being conspicuous,' he says.

And I suppose it's not surprising that I didn't think to question his reason for saying this.

Then there's a period – I can't do the minutes – when we just seem to wander about pointlessly. Mendel tells me about his beekeeping. Then he tells me about this rescue dog Poppy, a Golden Labrador, that his wife is mad about. Poppy, I seem to remember, was a dog not a bitch. I also remember being secretly surprised, because I don't think I knew Oliver Mendel had a wife.

Bit by bit I talk back at him. When he asks me how things are going in Brittany, and how the crops are looking, and how many cows we keep, I give him an accurate and lucid account, which presumably is what he's waiting for, because when we get to the gravel path that leads past the Stoop to the coach house, he steps away from me and says something curt into his walkie-talkie. And when he comes back to me, he's no longer the casual conversationalist, he's all copper once more:

'Now, son. Your attention, please. You're about to meet the other half of the story. You'll see what you see, you won't react in any shape or form, and you will remain entirely silent regarding what you have seen thereafter. That's not my orders. That's George's, personal for you. Furthermore, son, if by any chance you're still blaming yourself for that poor lady's suicide, you can lay off *now*. Got that? That's not George speaking. That's me. Do you speak Swiss at all?'

He was smiling, and to my surprise so was I. The direction of our casual walk took on a chilling purpose. I had momentarily forgotten the Swiss gentleman. I had assumed Mendel was making kindly small talk. Now the mysterious birdwatcher who had trespassed by mistake came rushing back in full force. At the further end of the defile stood Fawn. Behind him rose the stone steps to an olive-green entrance marked DANGER OF DEATH, KEEP OUT.

We climbed. Fawn led the way. We arrived in a hayloft. Mildewed horses' tack hung from old hooks. We passed between bales of rotting hay until we came to the Submarine, a purpose-built isolation cell for instructing trainees in the unlovely arts of resisting and administering harsh interrogation. No refresher course I had attended was complete without a taste of its windowless padded walls, hand-to-foot manacles and head-splitting sound effects. The door was of blackened steel, with a sliding eyehole for seeing in, but never out.

Fawn keeps his distance. Mendel advances to the Submarine, ducks forward, slides back the eyehole, backs away again, nods to me: your turn. And under his breath, in a rush:

'Only she never hanged herself, did she, son? Our birdwatching friend did it for her.'

On my training stints, there had never been furniture inside the Submarine. You either lay on the stone floor or paced it in pitch darkness while the loudspeakers screamed at you until you couldn't take it any more, or the directing staff decided you'd had enough. But these two unlikely occupants of the Submarine have been provided with the luxury of a red-baize card table and two perfectly decent chairs.

In one chair sits George Smiley, looking the way only George looks when he's conducting an interrogation: a bit put out, a bit pained, as if life is one long discomfort for him and no one can make it tolerable except just possibly you.

And across from George in the other chair sits a powerful blond man of my own age with fresh bruises round his eyes, one bare leg bandaged and stuck in front of him, and his hands manacled, palms upward on the table like a beggar's.

And when he turns his head, I see exactly what by now I'm expecting to see: an old scar like a sabre-slash, running the length of his right cheek.

And though I can barely see them for the bruises, I know he has blue eyes, because that's what it said in the criminal record that three years back I had stolen for George Smiley after he'd been bludgeoned nearly to death by the man who is sitting in front of him now.

Interrogating – or negotiating? The prisoner's name – how could I forget it? – is Hans-Dieter Mundt. He is a former member of the East German Steel Mission in Highgate, which enjoyed official but not diplomatic status.

During his London tour, Mundt killed an East London car dealer who knew too much for his liking. When he tried to kill George, it was for the same reason.

And now here's the same Mundt sitting in the Submarine, a KGB-trained Stasi assassin pretending to be a Swiss ornithologist caught in a deer trap, while Doris who wished to be known only as Tulip is lying dead not fifty feet away from him. Mendel is plucking at my arm. It's only a short car ride to wherever we're going, Peter. George will be joining us later.

'What's happened to Harper and Lowe?' I ask him when we're safely in the car, this being the only topic that comes to mind.

'Meadows sent Harper off to hospital to get his face fixed. Lowe's holding his hand. Our ornithologist friend didn't come quietly when he was released from that trap he walked into, put it that way. He required some serious assistance, as you will have observed.'

★

'I have two pieces of paper for you, Peter,' Smiley is saying, and hands me the first of them.

It is two o'clock in the morning. We are alone in the same front room of the same semi-detached police house somewhere on the edge of the New Forest. Our host, an old friend of Mendel's, has lit us a coal fire and brought us a tray of tea and sugar biscuits before retiring upstairs with his wife. We have neither drunk the tea nor touched the biscuits. The first piece of paper is a plain white English postcard, no stamp. There are scratch marks on it as if it's been shoved through something narrow, perhaps under a door. The address side is blank. On the business side, there is an inked, blue-black, hand-printed message in German, capitals only.

I AM A GOOD SWISS FRIEND WHO CAN TAKE YOU TO YOUR GUSTAV. MEET ME AT THE FOOTBRIDGE 0100 HOURS. ALL WILL BE ARRANGED. WE ARE CHRISTIAN PEOPLE. [No signature.]

'Why wait till she got all the way to England?' I manage to ask George after a long delay. 'Why not kill her in Germany?'

'To protect their source, obviously,' Smiley replies in a tone to reproach me for my slow-wittedness. 'The tip-off came from Moscow Centre, who very naturally insisted on discretion. Not a car accident or some equally contrived event. Better a self-inflicted death that will cause the greatest possible dismay in the enemy camp. I see that as entirely logical, don't you? Well, don't you, Peter?'

The anger is in the iron control of his habitually gentle voice, in the rigidity of his normally fluid features. Anger as self-disgust. Anger at the monstrosity of what he has had to do, in defiance of every decent instinct.

'*Shepherded* is Mundt's expression of choice,' he continues, neither waiting for my answer nor expecting one. 'We *shepherd* her to Prague, we *shepherd* her to England, we *shepherd* her to Camp 4. Then we strangle her and hang her up. Never *I*. Always the collective *we*. I told him that he was despicable to me. I like to think it got through.' And as if he has forgotten: 'Oh, and the other piece of paper is for you' – handing me a folded sheet of Basildon Bond stationery with 'Adrien' scrawled large across it, this time in soft pencil. The handwriting neat and painstaking. No needless flourishes. An earnest German schoolgirl writes to her English penfriend.

My darling Adrien, my Jean-François.

You are all the men I love. Please God love you also.

Tulip

'I asked you whether you propose to keep it as a memento or burn it?' Smiley is repeating to my dazed ear in the same voice of frozen anger. 'I suggest the second. Millie McCraig happened on it. It was propped against Tulip's vanity mirror.'

Then without apparent emotion he watches me as I kneel before the fire and lay Doris's letter, still folded, like an offering on the burning coals. And it occurs to me, amid all the turbulent feelings that are wrenching at me, that George Smiley and I are closer than we wish to know in matters of failed love. I dance badly. George, according to his errant wife, refuses to dance at all. And still I have not spoken a word.

'There are certain useful conditions attached to the arrangement I have just made with Herr Mundt,' he goes on relentlessly. 'The tape recording of our conversation, for example. His masters in Moscow and Berlin would not be impressed by it, we agreed. We also agreed that his work for us, capably managed by both sides, will advance him in his distinguished career in the Stasi. He will return to his comrades a conquering hero. The bigwigs in the Directorate will be pleased with him. Moscow Centre will be pleased with him. Emmanuel Rapp's job is going begging. Let him apply for it. He assured me that he would. As his fortunes rise in Berlin and Moscow, and his access rises accordingly, perhaps a day will come when he will be able to tell us who betrayed Tulip and certain others of our agents who have met a premature end. We have much to look forward to, you and I, have we not?'

And still, so far as I remember it, I say nothing, whereas Smiley in closing has something very important to say.

'You, I and only the very fewest are owners of this extremely privileged information, Peter. As far as Joint Steering and the Service at large are concerned, we were greedy, we brought Tulip here too hastily, we paid no regard to her deeper feelings. In consequence she hanged herself. Which is the version that must be trumpeted to Head Office and all out-stations. There must be no exceptions anywhere where Joint holds sway. And that, I am afraid, inevitably includes our friend Alec Leamas.'

*

We cremated her in the name of Tulip Brown, a Russian-born woman of faith who had fled the Communist persecution and settled to a solitary life in England. *Brown*, it was explained to the retired Orthodox priest unearthed by the ladies of Covert who also arranged the tulips on the coffin, was the name she had given herself out of fear of retribution. The priest, an old Occasional, asked no inconvenient questions. We were six: Ash Meadows, Millie McCraig, Jeanette Avon and Ingeborg Lugg from Covert, Alec Leamas and me. George had business elsewhere. The service over, the women departed and we three men went off in search of a pub.

'What the fuck did the stupid bloody woman go and do it for?' Alec complained, head in hands, as we sat over our Scotches. 'All the trouble we went to.' And in the same tone of mock indignation: 'If she'd told me what she was going to do, I'd never have bloody bothered.'

'Me neither,' I said loyally, taking myself to the bar and ordering three more of the same.

'Suicide's a decision certain people have taken early in their lives,' Doc Meadows was pontificating when I returned. 'They may not *know* it, but it's *in* them, Alec. Then one day, something comes along that triggers it. Can be totally trivial, like leaving

181

your wallet on the bus. Can be drastic, like your best pal dying. But the *intention* was always there. And the result's the same.'

We drank. Another silence, broken this time by Alec:

'Maybe all joes are suicides. Some just don't get around to it, poor bastards.' And then: 'Anyway, who's going to tell the boy?'

Boy? Of course. He meant Gustav.

'George says we leave that one to the opposition,' I replied, to which Alec growled, 'Jesus, what a planet,' and went back to his whisky.

10

I have ceased staring at the library wall: Nelson, who has replaced Pepsi, is troubled by my inattention. I dutifully resume reading the report that in my grief and remorse I compiled on Smiley's orders, omitting no detail, however extraneous, in my mission to observe the one secret that none but the fewest would ever share.

SUB-SOURCE TULIP. DEBRIEF AND SUICIDE.
Debrief conducted by Ingeborg Lugg (Covert) and Jeanette Avon
(Covert). In periodic attendance: Dr med. Ashley Meadows,
Covert Occasional.
Drafted and collated by PG and approved by H/Covert
Marylebone for submission to Treasury Oversight Committee.
Advance copy to H/Joint Steering for comment.

Avon and Lugg are Covert's star debriefers, middle-aged, mid-European women of long operational experience.

1. Reception of TULIP and transfer to Camp 4.
On her arrival by RAF plane at Northolt, Tulip underwent no landing formalities, thereby at no point officially entering the UK. Describing himself as 'the appointed representative of a Service that is very proud of you', Dr Meadows made a

brief speech of welcome in the VIP reception room in the transit area, and presented her with a bouquet of English roses which appeared to affect her deeply, for she held them silently to her face throughout the journey.

She was then driven directly by closed van to Camp 4. Avon (workname ANNA), being a qualified nurse with befriending skills, sat with Tulip in the back, providing comfort and conversation. Lugg (workname LOUISA) and Dr Meadows (workname FRANK) sat forward with the driver, it being felt that a bonding between Avon and Tulip was more likely to succeed if the two were left alone in the rear of the vehicle. All three of us are fluent German-speakers, Level 6.

On the drive Tulip alternately dozed and excitedly pointed out features of the landscape that would entertain her son Gustav on his arrival in the UK, which she appeared to consider imminent. She also indicated with enthusiasm paths and areas where she would like to bicycle, also with Gustav. She asked twice after 'Adrien' and, on being told we knew of no Adrien, changed the object of her enquiry to Jean-François. Dr Meadows then informed her that the courier Jean-François had been called away on urgent duty, but would no doubt make himself known in due course.

Accommodation in the guest wing of Camp 4 comprises a master bedroom, living room, kitchenette and sunroom, the latter being a nineteenth-century glass and timber extension overlooking the outdoor (unheated) swimming pool. All spaces, including the sunroom and pool area, are equipped with concealed microphones and special facilities.

Directly behind the swimming pool stands a coppice of coniferous trees from which some, not all, lower branches have been stripped. Fallow deer are commonplace, and frequently to be seen disporting themselves in the swimming pool. Due to the wire perimeter, the deer are effectively a domestic herd confined to the estate, thereby adding to Camp 4's air of cultivated charm and tranquillity.

First, we introduced Tulip to Millie McCraig (ELLA) who, at the request of the H/Covert Ops, had already that day been installed as safe house keeper. At the request of H/Covert, microphones were installed at salient positions, and those still active from previous operations, disconnected.

The safe house keeper's personal quarters at Camp 4 are situated directly behind the guest suite, at the end of a short corridor. An internal telephone connects the two apartments, enabling the guest to summon assistance at any time of night. At McCraig's suggestion, Avon and Lugg occupied bedrooms in the main house, thereby providing Tulip with an all-female environment.

Camp 4's permanent security guards, Harper and Lowe, share quarters in the coach house. Both men are keen gardeners. Harper as a qualified gamekeeper controls the estate's wildlife population. The coach house also contains a spare bedroom, which was commandeered by Dr Meadows.

2. *Debriefing, days 1–5.*
The initial period of debriefing was set at 2–3 weeks extendable, plus follow-up sessions of unspecified length, although this was not revealed to Tulip. Our immediate task was to settle her in, reassure her that she was among friends, speak confidently of her future (with Gustav), which by the end of the first evening we felt we had achieved to our cautious satisfaction. She was informed that Dr Meadows (Frank) was one of several interviewers with special interests, and that there would be others who, like Frank, would come and go during our sessions. She was further informed that the *Herr Direktor* (H/Covert) was absent while attending to urgent matters relating to Dr Riemeck (MAYFLOWER) and other

members of the network, but was greatly looking forward to the honour of shaking her hand on his return.

It being the general rule that debriefings should commence while the subject is still 'hot', our team reassembled in the living room of the main house prompt at 0900 hours next morning. The session continued with intermissions until 2105 hours. Tape recording was monitored by Millie McCraig from her apartment, who also used the opportunity to make a thorough search of Tulip's suite and possessions. Questioning was led by Lugg (Louisa) according to brief, with subsidiaries from Avon (Anna), and interjections from Dr Meadows (Frank) whenever an opportunity was offered to explore Tulip's mind-set and motivation.

Despite attempts to disguise the purpose of Frank's seemingly innocent enquiries, however, Tulip was quick to identify their psychological nature and, on being informed that he was a medical doctor, mocked him for being a disciple of 'that arch-liar and forger Sigmund Freud'. Whipping herself into a fury, she then announced that she had only ever had one doctor in her life and his name was Karl Riemeck; that Frank was an arsehole, and 'if you [Dr Meadows] wish to make yourself useful to me, bring me my son!' Not wishing to be a negative presence, Dr Meadows felt it sensible to return to London but to remain on hand should his services be required.

For the next two days, despite such periodic outbursts, debriefing sessions proceeded efficiently in an atmosphere of relative calm, the tapes of each session being shuttled nightly to Marylebone.

Of primary interest to H/Covert was the flow of Soviet intelligence on British targets, slight though it was, coming into Rapp's office from Moscow. While accepting that very little of such intelligence had featured in the documents Tulip had succeeded in photographing, were there perhaps matters she had read or overheard in respect of Moscow's live sources in the United Kingdom that she had either forgotten or considered unworthy of report? Was there any hint, any boasting, for instance, of highly placed live sources inside the British political or intelligence establishment? Of British codes and cyphers penetrated?

Despite putting such questions to Tulip in many different guises, and it must be said to her increasing irritation, we are not able to point to any positive outcome. The value of Tulip's product should nevertheless in our assessment be rated high to very high, bearing in mind that her reporting has been severely hampered by operational conditions. For as long as she was operative, she reported only to Mayflower, never to Berlin Station direct. Questions of potential sensitivity had not been conveyed to her on the grounds that, if divulged under interrogation, they would reveal weaknesses in our own intelligence armour. These could now be put without restraint: for example, enquiries regarding the reliability of other potential or active sub-sources; identity of foreign diplomats and politicians under Stasi control; the possible explanation of covert pay-streams revealed in documents that she had photographed on Rapp's desk, but not otherwise handled; the location and appearance of secret signals installations she had visited while in Rapp's company, their layout, their entry procedures, the size, shape and direction of their antennae, and any evidence of Soviet or other non-German presence on the site; and broadly any other intelligence which until now had effectively gone to waste due to the scarcity of time available for treffs with Mayflower, the scattershot nature of their conversations and the limitations imposed by clandestine methods of communication.

While frequently expressing frustration and venting it in

abusive language, Tulip also appeared to relish being the centre of attention, even bantering flirtatiously when allowed with Camp 4's two security guards, Harper, the younger one, being particularly favoured. With the coming of each evening, however, her mood swiftly changed to one of guilty despair, its prime object being her son Gustav, but also her sister Lotte, whose life she claimed to have ruined by her defection.

Safe house keeper Millie McCraig sat up with her intermittently through the night. Having discovered a mutual Christian faith, the two frequently prayed together, Tulip's saint of choice being St Nicholas, a miniature icon of whom had accompanied her throughout her exfiltration. Their shared interest in cycling provided further common ground. At Tulip's urging, McCraig (Ella) obtained a catalogue of children's bicycles. Excited to discover that McCraig was Scottish, Tulip immediately demanded a map of the Scottish Highlands so that the two of them could discuss cycling routes together. An Ordnance Survey map was delivered from Head Office next day. However, her mood remained uneven, and tantrums were frequent. The sedatives and sleeping pills that McCraig provided at her request appeared to be of little avail.

At any point in our debriefing sessions, Tulip would demand to know on what date Gustav would be exchanged, and even whether he had been exchanged already. In reply, she was assured according to brief that the matter was being negotiated at the highest level by the *Herr Direktor* and could not be resolved overnight.

3. *TULIP's recreational needs.*
From the moment of her arrival in the UK, Tulip made clear her need for physical exercise. The RAF fighter plane had been cramped, the drive to Camp 4 had made her feel like a prisoner, confinement of any sort was unbearable to her, etc.

Since the Camp 4 paths are not suitable for cycling, she would run. Having obtained her shoe size, Harper went into Salisbury for a pair of plimsolls and for the next three mornings Tulip and Avon (Anna), a keen exercise person, jogged the perimeter paths together before breakfast, Tulip taking with her a light shoulder bag for any fossil or rare stone that might interest Gustav. Borrowing the Russian jargon, she called it her 'perhaps bag'. The estate also offers a small gymnasium which, when other means failed, provided Tulip with temporary relief from her evident stress. Regardless of the hour, Millie McCraig never failed to accompany her to the gymnasium.

Tulip's normal practice was to stand ready-dressed at the French window of her living room at 0600 hours and wait for Avon to appear. However on this particular morning, Tulip was not standing at her window. Avon therefore entered the guest suite from the garden side, calling out her name, rattling the bathroom door and, on receiving no response, opening it in vain. Avon then enquired of McCraig over the interconnecting phone where Tulip was to be found, but McCraig was unable to enlighten her. By now seriously concerned, Avon then set off at a fast pace along the perimeter path. As a precaution, McCraig meanwhile alerted Harper and Lowe that our guest had 'gone runabout', and the two security guards at once began quartering the estate.

4. *Discovery of TULIP. Personal Statement by J. Avon.*
Entered from the eastern side, the circuit path of the estate rises steeply for some twenty yards, and plateaus out for about a quarter of a mile before turning north and descending into a marshy dell crossed by a wooden footbridge leading in turn to an ascending wooden staircase of nine steps, the upper steps being partly overshadowed by a spreading chestnut tree.

On turning north and beginning my descent to the dell, I

caught sight of Tulip hanging by the neck from a low branch of the chestnut, eyes open and hands to her sides. It is my memory that the clearance between her feet and the nearest wooden step was no more than twelve inches. The noose around her neck was so thin that at first sight she appeared to be floating in thin air.

I am a woman of 42. I must emphasize that I have recorded these impressions as they remain in my mind today. I am Service-trained and have experience of operational emergency. It is therefore humbling to confess that my only impulse on seeing Tulip hanging from a tree was to run back to the house as fast as possible and summon help rather than attempt to cut her down and resuscitate her. I deeply regret this lapse of operational composure, although I am now assured categorically that Tulip had been dead for at least six hours when I found her, which is a major relief to me. Plus the fact that I had no knife, and the rope was out of my reach.

Supplementary report by Millie McCraig, safe house keeper, Camp 4, career officer Grade 2, on the care, maintenance and suicide of sub-source TULIP. Copy to George Smiley H/Covert (only).

Millie as I knew her then: bride of the Service, devout daughter of a minister of the Free Presbyterian Church. Climbs the Cairngorms, rides to hounds and has a history of dangerous places. Lost her brother to the war, her father to cancer, and her heart, according to rumour, to a married older man who loved honour more. There were tongues that said the man in the case was George, though nothing I ever saw between them led me to believe it. But woe betide any of us young bloods who tried to lay a finger on her, for Millie would have none of us.

1. Disappearance of TULIP.

Having been informed by Jeanette Avon at 0610 hours that Tulip had set out for a morning run on her own, I immediately requested security (Harper and Lowe) to institute a search of the estate, concentrating on the perimeter path, which I understood from Avon to be Tulip's preferred route. As a precaution I then undertook an inspection of the guest suite and established that her tracksuit and running shoes were still in her wardrobe. The French day clothes and underclothes with which she had been issued in Prague, on the other hand, were not. Although she had neither identity papers nor money in her possession, her handbag, which I had earlier established contained nothing beyond personal necessities, was also missing.

The situation being beyond the competence of Covert, and H/Covert being absent on urgent duty in Berlin, I took the executive decision to call the duty officer at Joint Steering and request him to inform police liaison that an escaped mental patient answering Tulip's description was at large in the vicinity, that she was non-violent, spoke no English and was undergoing psychiatric treatment. If found, she should be returned to this Institute.

I then called Dr Meadows at his consulting rooms in Harley Street and left word with his secretary that he should please return asap to Camp 4, to be told that, having received word from HO, he was already on his way.

2. Discovery of an unauthorized intruder at Camp 4.

I had scarcely completed these calls when I received word from Harper over the Camp 4 internal intercommunication system advising me that, in the course of his search for Tulip, he had discovered, at a wooded point close to the eastern perimeter, an injured person, male, apparently an intruder, who having made his way through a freshly cut hole at a point close to the bypass, had stepped on, and activated, an ancient snare, partly overgrown, and presumably left there by a poacher in the days before the Circus acquired the premises.

The said snare, an illegal and antiquated device, consisted of rusted dragon's teeth, still sprung. The intruder, according to Harper, had caught his left leg in the mechanism and, by thrashing about, entangled himself further. He spoke good English, but with a foreign accent, and insisted that, on seeing the hole in the fence, he had climbed through it in order to perform a natural function. He also explained that he was a passionate birdwatcher.

With the arrival of Lowe, the two men between them had released the intruder, whereupon he had punched Lowe in the stomach, then head-butted Harper in the face. After a further struggle, the two men had pacified the intruder and delivered him to the Stoop, which lay conveniently close. He was now confined in the holding cell (Submarine), with a temporary dressing to his left leg. In accordance with standing security procedure, Harper had reported the incident, providing as full a description as possible of the intruder directly to HO Internal Security and to H/Covert, now on his way back from Berlin. On my enquiring of Harper whether he or Lowe had meanwhile sighted the missing Tulip, he replied that the intruder had temporarily diverted them from their search, which they would immediately resume.

3. News of TULIP's death.
It was approximately at this point of time that Jeanette Avon appeared at the porch of the main house in a distraught condition to announce that she had seen Tulip hanging by the neck from a tree, presumably dead, at point 217 on the estate

map. I immediately passed this information to Harper and Lowe and, having confirmed that their intruder was immobilized, instructed them to proceed with all speed to point 217 and apply necessary assistance.

I then sounded a Red Alert requiring all resident support staff to assemble immediately in the main house. This included the two cooks, one driver, one maintenance man, two cleaners and two laundrymen: see list at Appendix A. I informed them that a dead body had been found on the estate, and they should all remain in the main house until further notice. I did not consider it necessary to inform them that an unauthorized intruder had also been found.

Fortunately at this juncture Dr Meadows appeared, having driven himself at high speed in his Bentley car. He and I at once set out along the eastern perimeter path in the direction of point 217. We arrived to find Tulip cut down and clearly dead, lying on the ground with a ligature in place around her neck, and Harper and Lowe standing watch over her. Harper, bleeding from the face having been head-butted by the intruder, was minded to summon the police, Lowe an ambulance. In the event, I advised that neither should be summoned without the approval of H/Covert who was on his way to Camp 4. Dr Meadows, after a preliminary examination of the body, was of a similar opinion.

I accordingly instructed Harper and Lowe to return to the Stoop, contact nobody, await further orders and on no account attempt to engage their prisoner in conversation. Once they had departed the scene, Dr Meadows confided to me that Tulip had been dead for several hours before discovery.

While Dr Meadows continued his examination of the dead woman, I took note of her attire, which consisted of her French twinset, pleated skirt and court shoes. The pockets of the twinset jacket were empty except for two used paper tissues.

Tulip had been complaining of a slight cold. Her 'perhaps bag' was stuffed with her remaining French underclothes.

Our instructions, which by now were being relayed non-stop from Head Office over the Camp 4 intercom, were to transfer the body immediately to the Stoop. I therefore summoned Harper and Lowe to act as stretcher party. This was promptly done, despite the fact that Harper by now was bleeding profusely from his wound.

Together with Dr Meadows, I returned to the main house. To her credit, Avon had collected herself and was distributing tea and biscuits to the staff, and generally enlivening them. The Head Office crisis party under H/Covert was now expected to arrive by mid-afternoon. Meantime all but Harper and Lowe were to remain in the main house while Dr Meadows cleaned Harper's facial contusions and attended the injured intruder now incarcerated in the Submarine.

A discussion meanwhile took place among those confined to the main house. Jeanette Avon insisted on counting herself the person most responsible for Tulip's suicide, but I took it upon myself to contradict this suggestion. Tulip was clinically depressed, her sense of guilt and longing for Gustav were unbearable, she had destroyed the life of her sister Lotte. Suicide was probably in her mind by the time she arrived in Prague, and certainly by the time she reached Camp 4. She had made her choices and paid the ultimate price.

And now enter George, bearing false messages:

4. Arrival of H/Covert [Smiley] *and Inspector Mendel.*
H/Covert (Smiley) arrived at 1555 hours accompanied by Inspector (retd) Oliver Mendel, a Covert Occasional. Dr Meadows and I immediately escorted them to the Stoop.

I then returned to the main house, where Ingeborg Lugg and Jeanette Avon together continued to soothe the agitations of the assembled staff. It was another two hours before Mr Smiley returned from the Stoop accompanied by Inspector Mendel. Calling the staff together, Mr Smiley offered his personal condolences, together with the assurance that sub-source Tulip had only herself to blame for her death, and nobody in Camp 4 had cause to reproach themselves.

Evening was now coming on. With the shuttle bus waiting in the forecourt and many of the team anxious to get home to Salisbury, H/Covert took a moment to put their minds at rest regarding the discovery of a 'mystery intruder' of whom some might have heard. With Inspector Mendel smiling reassurance beside him, he confessed that he was about to 'blab' to the team a secret they would never normally share, but in the circumstances he had decided that they deserved nothing less than full disclosure.

The mystery intruder was no mystery, he explained. He was a valued member of an elite and little-known section of our sister service, MI5, tasked to penetrate by lawful and unlawful means the defences of our country's most sensitive and secret facilities. As it happened, he was also a personal and professional friend of Inspector Mendel here. Laughter. It was in the nature of such live exercises that the facility targeted should not be informed, and the fact that the exercise had been scheduled for the same day that Tulip had elected to do away with herself was no more than 'the act of a malign Providence', to use Smiley's words. The same Providence had guided the intruder's feet into the deer trap. Laughter. Harper and Lowe had acquitted themselves nobly. Both had had the situation explained to them and ruefully accepted it, even if they felt, understandably, that 'our friend had somewhat overdone his violent reaction' – H/Covert, to more laughter.

And for our further disinformation:

H/Covert further confided to the gathering that the intruder, who was in fact no foreigner but an honest-to-God, all British native of Clapham, was already on his way to Casualty in Salisbury where he would receive a tetanus injection and have his injuries attended to. Inspector Mendel would be visiting his old friend shortly, and taking him a bottle of whisky with the compliments of Camp 4. Applause.

★

It's the Bunny and Laura show again. No Leonard. Bunny leads. Laura listens sceptically.

'So you compiled your report. In tedious detail, if I may say so. You took all available evidence, and then some. You sent an advance copy to Joint Steering. You then *stole the same copy back* from Circus archives. Does that about sum it up?'

'No, it doesn't.'

'Then why is your report lodged here in the Stables, among a whole lot of papers that you *did* steal?'

'Because it never went out on submission.'

'To anyone?'

'To anyone.'

'None of it? Not even a shortened form?'

'The Treasury Committee decided not to meet.'

'You're talking about the so-called committee of the Three Wise Men, I take it? Of whom the Circus lived in supposed dread?'

'It was chaired by Oliver Lacon. Lacon concluded after much soul-searching that a report served no useful purpose. Even in shortened form.'

'On the grounds?'

'That an inquiry into the suicide of a woman who had not landed in the United Kingdom was not a valid use of taxpayers' money.'

'Was Lacon by any conceivable chance prompted in this decision by George Smiley?'

'How should I know?'

'Easily, I'd have thought. If it was your arse among others that Smiley was protecting, if – for instance, taking a purely hypothetical case at random – we assume Tulip hanged herself on your account. Was there perhaps a particular element or episode of the report that Smiley considered too disturbing for Treasury's tender ears?'

'For Joint's tender ears, conceivably. Not Treasury's. Joint was already much too deep into the Mayflower operation for George's comfort. He may have thought an inquiry would open the door even wider. And advised Lacon accordingly. That's only my guess.'

'You don't think by any chance that the real reason the inquiry was binned was that Tulip wasn't the cooperative defector she is painted to be – not least by your arse-kissing report – and paid the price?'

'What *price*? What on earth are you talking about?'

'She was a woman of great determination. We know that. She was also, when she wished to be, a harridan. And she wanted her child back. I'm suggesting she refused to cooperate with the interrogation team until her son was returned to her, and her interrogators took a dim view of that, and their report – your report – was a fudge, cobbled together on Smiley's orders. And Camp 4, since scrapped, boasted as we know a special confinement cell for people like her. It was dubbed the Submarine. It was used for what these days we are pleased to call enhanced interrogation, and it was the preserve of a couple of rather perverted security guards not known for their gentle ways. I'm suggesting she had the benefit of their attentions. You look shocked. Have I touched a nerve?'

It took me a moment to get there:

'Tulip wasn't *interrogated*, for Christ's sake! She was in the process of being debriefed, humanely and decently, by professional people who liked her and were grateful to her, and understood a defector's tantrums!'

'So laugh this one off,' Bunny suggests. 'We have another *letter before action*, and another potential litigant if the case comes to law. One Gustav Quinz, son of Doris, apparently but not certainly at the instigation of Christoph Leamas, has added his name to those who are intent on suing the shit out of this Service. We, this Service, largely in the person of yourself, seduced his dear mother, blackmailed her into spying for us, smuggled her out of the country against her will, tortured her to hell and back, thereby causing her to hang herself from the nearest tree. True? Not true?'

I thought he had finished, but he hadn't.

'And since these allegations, being dignified by the passage of time, cannot be suppressed by the draconian legislation that has been available to us in more recent cases of the same nature, there's a good chance that the All-Party Group, and/or any subsequent litigation, will be used to pry into matters of considerably more relevance to us today. You seem amused.'

Amused. Perhaps I was. Gustav, I was thinking. Well done you. You've decided to collect your due after all, even if you've come to the wrong address for it.

*

I have ridden across France and Germany at breakneck speed through driving rain. I am standing at Alec's graveside. The same rain sweeps the little cemetery in East Berlin. I am wearing my motorcycle leathers, but out of respect for Alec I have removed my helmet and the rain is pouring down my bare face as we silently exchange banalities. The elderly sacristan or whatever he is ushers me into his cabin and shows me the condolence book with Christoph's name among the mourners.

And perhaps that was the *point d'appui*, the spur: first to Christoph, then to the carrot-haired Gustav with the buckwheat grin who had sung his patriotic songs to me, and then to Alec: the same boy who from the day of his mother's death I had secretly, if only notionally, taken into my care, picturing him first in some gruesome East German borstal for children of the disgraced, then tossed out into an uncaring world.

Secretly too, I had from time to time brazenly transgressed standing Circus regulations, tracking him through the archives under a pretext and vowing to myself – or, you may say, fantasizing – that one day, if ever the world turned an inch or two on its axis, I would seek him out and, for love of Tulip, provide him with a leg-up in some undefined way that circumstance would determine.

The rain was still pelting down as I got on my bike and headed, not westward to France, but southward to Weimar. The last possible address I had for Gustav was ten years old: a hamlet west of the city, a house registered in the name of his father, Lothar. After two hours' ride I was standing on the doorstep of a dismal, Soviet-style slab house built ten yards from the village church as an act of Socialist aggression. The slabs were parting. Some of the windows were papered over from inside. Spray-paint swastikas adorned the crumbling porch. Quinz's apartment was 8D. I pressed the bell to no avail. A door opened, a suspicious old woman looked me up and down.

'*Quinz?*' she repeated, in distaste. '*Der Lothar? Längst tot.*' – long dead.

And Gustav? I asked. The son?

'You mean the *waiter*?' she asked, in contempt.

The hotel was called the Elephant and overlooked Weimar's historic main square. It wasn't new. As a matter of fact it had been Hitler's favourite hotel: the old woman had told me that too. But it had been dramatically refurbished, and its façade glistened like a beacon of Western prosperity shoved in the face of its poorer, beautiful neighbours. At the reception desk, a girl in a new black suit mistook my enquiry: we have no Herr Quinz staying in the house. Then she blushed and said, 'Oh, you mean Gustav,' and told me that staff were forbidden to receive visits and I must wait till Herr Quinz came off duty.

When would that be? At six o'clock. And best to wait where, please? At the delivery entrance, where else?

The rain had not relented, the day was darkening. I stood at the delivery entrance as directed. A gaunt unsmiling man who somehow looked older than his age emerged from a basement staircase, pulling on an old army raincoat with a hood. A bicycle was chained to the railing. He stooped to it, and set to work undoing the padlock.

'Herr Quinz?' I said. '*Gustav?*'

His head rose until he stood his full height under the faltering light of an overhead street lamp. His shoulders were set in a premature stoop. The once red hair was sparse and turning grey.

'What do you want?'

'I was a friend of your mother's,' I said. 'You may remember me. We met on a beach in Bulgaria – long ago. You sang me a song.' And I gave him my workname, the same name I'd given him on the beach while his mother stood naked behind him.

'You were a *friend* of my mother?' he repeated, getting used to the idea.

'That's what I said.'

'French?'

'That's right.'

'She died.'

'I heard that. I'm very sorry. I wondered if there was anything I could do for you. I happened to have your address. I was in Weimar. It seemed an opportunity. Maybe we could have a drink together. Talk about it.'

He stared at me. 'Did you sleep with my mother?'

'We were friends.'

'Then you slept with her,' he said, as a matter of historical fact, his voice neither rising nor falling. 'My mother was a whore. She betrayed the homeland. She betrayed the revolution. She betrayed the Party. She betrayed my father. She sold herself to the English and she hanged herself. She was an enemy of the people,' he explained.

And, mounting his bicycle, he rode away.

II

'I think the very *first* thing we should do, heart,' Tabitha is saying in her perennially diffident voice – 'you don't mind if I call you heart, do you? I call all my best clients heart. It reminds them that I've got one, just as they have, even if mine's necessarily on hold. So the *first* thing we do is make a hit-list of all the disgraceful things the other side are saying about us, then we'll knock them down one by one. Just so long as you're sitting comfortably. Are you? Good. You are hearing me, aren't you? I never know whether those things work. Are they the National Health ones?'

'French.'

Tabitha, so far as I remembered from my childhood reading of Beatrix Potter, was the harassed mother of three disobedient children. I was wryly amused therefore to note that outwardly at least the woman of the same name who sat before me shared many of her characteristics: motherly, sweet-faced, forty-something, plump, a little breathless, and heroically tired. She was also, I had been given to understand, my defence lawyer. Leonard had supplied Bunny with the promised shortlist of names, names that Bunny admired *hugely* – would fight for you like absolute *rottweilers*, Peter – and two he was a *teensy* bit doubtful about, not sufficiently road-tested to his mind but don't quote him, and *one* – *entirely* off the record, Peter, and you *must* protect me on this – that he wouldn't touch with a bargepole: doesn't know when to stop, and not the *haziest* idea of how the courts work, and the judges absolutely detest her. That was Tabitha.

I said she sounded just right for me and asked to see her in her chambers. Bunny said her chambers weren't rated secure and offered me his headquarters in the bastion. I told him I didn't rate his headquarters secure. So here we are back in the library, with the full-length figures of Hans-Dieter Mundt and his arch-rival Josef Fiedler scowling down on us.

★

In time present, only one sleepless night has passed since we cremated Tulip, but the world that Tabitha is trying to come to grips with has taken an historic step backwards.

The Berlin Wall has gone up.

Every agent and sub-agent of the Mayflower network has gone missing, been arrested, executed or all three.

Karl Riemeck, the heroic doctor of Köpenick, the network's accidental founder and its inspiration, has himself been merci-lessly shot down while attempting to escape to West Berlin on his workman's bicycle.

To Tabitha, these are facts of history. For those of us who endured them, they are a time of despair, bewilderment and frustration.

Is our agent Windfall for us or against us? From our redoubt in the Stables, we the indoctrinated few had followed with awe his mercurial rise through the Stasi's ranks to his present pos-ition as head of its special operations wing.

We had received, processed and disseminated, under the gen-eric title Windfall, highest-quality intelligence on a raft of economic, political and strategic targets, to muted cries of delight from Whitehall customers.

Yet for all Mundt's undoubted power – or maybe because of

it – he had been unable to halt or even abate the relentless cull of Covert's agents and sub-agents, as conducted by his rival Josef Fiedler.

In this grisly duel for the favour of Moscow Centre and command of the Stasi, Hans-Dieter Mundt, alias source Windfall, claimed he had no option but to present himself as even more fervent than Fiedler in the business of cleansing the utopian German Democratic Republic of spies, saboteurs and other lackeys of bourgeois imperialism.

As one faithful agent after another fell to the competing fury of Mundt or his arch-rival, so the morale of the Windfall team sank to a new depth.

And no one was more affected than Smiley himself, locked night after night in the Middle Room, with only the occasional visit from Control to lower his spirits still further.

★

'Why can't I read the plaintiffs' statements for myself?' I ask Tabitha. 'The letters-before-action or whatever they are?'

'Because your former Service in its wisdom has applied to slap a Top Secret classification on all correspondence on the grounds of national security, and you're not cleared. They won't get away with it in a month of Sundays, but it will gum up the works and make way for a temporary reporting restriction, which is what they're after. Meanwhile, I've scrounged what scraps I can for you. Go?'

'Where have Bunny and Laura disappeared to?'

'I'm afraid they think they've got all they need. And Leonard has accepted their brief. I've had a first peek in the other side's locker. Unfortunately, poor Doris Gamp seems to have had the hots for you from the day she set eyes on you, and she couldn't wait to tell her sister Lotte all about you. And by the time Lotte had poured her heart out to the Stasi interrogators, there wasn't much left of you at all. Did you *really* scamper naked on the beach with her in the Bulgarian moonlight?'

'No.'

'Good. And there's a night of love and laughter you supposedly spent together in a Prague hotel, where nature again took her course.'

'It didn't.'

'Good. Now to the two other deaths: Alec Leamas and Elizabeth Gold, our Berliners. Elizabeth first, as formulated against you by her daughter Karen. It's alleged that you personally contacted her – *either* on your own initiative *or* at the instigation of George Smiley and other conspirators unnamed – that you then *inveigled, seduced or otherwise obtained* her to become *human fodder* – the other side's beastly expressions, not mine – in an *abortive, grandiose and ill-conceived attempt* – who comes up with that stuff, I *can't* imagine – to undermine the Stasi leadership. Did you?'

'No.'

'Good. You begin to see the picture? You're a professional Lothario hired by the British Secret Service, and you roped in susceptible girls as unwitting accomplices in hare-brained operations that fell apart at the seams. True?'

'Untrue.'

'Of course it is. You also pimped Elizabeth Gold for your colleague Alec Leamas. Did you?'

'No.'

'Good. You also, because you do a lot of it, *bedded* Elizabeth Gold. Or if you didn't, you warmed her up for Alec. Did you do either of those things?'

'No.'

'I never for a moment thought you did. And the supposed end effect of your evil machinations: Elizabeth Gold is shot dead at the Berlin Wall, her lover Alec Leamas tries to save her skin, or simply decides to die with her. Either way he gets shot for his pains, and it's all your fault. Time for a cup of tea, or bomb on? Bomb on. Now to *Christoph Leamas's* allegation, which is meatier because his father Alec is the victim of all that goes before. Alec – by the time you inveigled him, lured, bribed, conned, et cetera, into becoming the luckless plaything of your compulsively manipulative nature – was a broken man, in no fit state to cross the road on his own, let alone front a fiendishly intricate deception operation, to wit: *pretend* to defect to the Stasi while actually remaining under your evil influence. True?'

'No.'

'Of course it isn't. So what I suggest is, with your permission, take a big pull of that water, cast your beady eye over what I turned up in the wee hours of this morning when I was *finally* allowed a very limited look at a *tiny* part of your dear Service's historical archive. Question one, does this episode mark the beginning of your friend Alec's decline? And question two, if it does, is it *real* decline or is it *simulated* decline? In other words, are we looking at stage one of Alec making himself insufferable to his own Service and hugely attractive to Moscow Centre's or the Stasi's talent-spotters?'

★

Circus telegram from H/Station Berlin [McFadyen] to H/Joint Steering, copy to H/Covert Ops, H/Personnel Most Urgent, 10 July 1960.
Subject: Immediate transfer of Alec Leamas from Berlin Station on disciplinary grounds.

At 0100 hours this morning, the following episode occurred at the Altes Fass nightclub in West Berlin between DH/Berlin

Station Alec Leamas and Cy Aflon, DH/CIA Station Berlin. The facts are not disputed by either party. The two men have a long-running enmity, for which, as previously stated, I regard Leamas as exclusively to blame.

Leamas entered the nightclub alone and headed for the *Damengalerie*, a bar set aside for single women in search of custom. He had been drinking but was not in his own judgement drunk.

Aflon was seated with two female colleagues from his Station, watching the cabaret and enjoying a quiet drink.

Catching sight of Aflon and his party, Leamas changed direction, walked over to their table and, leaning forward, addressed Aflon in low tones with the following words:

Leamas: You ever try to buy one of my sources again, I'll break your fucking neck.

Aflon: Whoa, Alec. Whoa. Not in front of the ladies, if you don't mind.

Leamas: Two thousand dollars a month for first bite of anything he gets before he sells it to us second hand. And you call that fighting a fucking war? Maybe he gets a French kiss from these nice ladies thrown in?

As Aflon rose to his feet in protest at this flagrant insult, Leamas struck him across the face with his right elbow, causing him to fall to the ground, then kicked him in the groin. West Berlin police were called, who summoned the US military police. Aflon was delivered to the US military hospital where he is presently recovering. Fortunately, no fractures or life-threatening injuries are as yet reported.

I have submitted my abject apologies to Aflon personally and to his H/Station, Milton Berger. This is the most recent of a series of regrettable incidents involving Leamas.

While I acknowledge that recent losses to the Mayflower network have placed the Station and Leamas personally under considerable strain, this in no way justifies the damage he has done to our relations with our most important ally. Leamas's anti-Americanism has long been apparent. It has now become totally unacceptable. Either he goes or I do.

And after Control's green scrawl, Smiley's lapidary reply: *I have already ordered Alec back to London.*

★

'So, Peter,' Tabitha is saying. 'Simulated? *Not* simulated? Are we looking at the official beginning of his downhill slide?'

And when, in genuine doubt, I prevaricate, she offers her own answer:

'Control certainly thought it was the beginning' – indicating the handwritten green scrawl at the bottom of the page. 'Look at his footnote to your Uncle George. *A very promising start*, signed C. You can't get clearer than that, can you, even in *your* murky world?'

No, Tabitha, you can't. And murky it is, no question.

★

It's a funeral. It's a wake. It's a thieves' conference held in desperation at dead of night in this very room, with Josef Fiedler and Hans-Dieter Mundt staring down on us with the same lugubrious intensity. We are the six Windfalls, as Connie Sachs, our latest recruit, has dubbed us: Control, Smiley, Jim Prideaux, Connie, myself and Millie our near-silent partner. Jim Prideaux is just returned from yet another undercover run, this time to Budapest, where he has brought off a rare treff with our most precious asset Windfall. Connie Sachs, in her early twenties already the unchallenged wunderkind of research into Soviet and Satellite intelligence agencies, has recently flounced out of Joint Steering in a huff, straight into George's waiting arms. She is a brisk, chubby little body, bluestocking, born into the clover, and impatient of lesser minds like mine.

Stately, remote, raven-haired Millie McCraig moves among us like a ministering nurse in a field hospital, handing out coffee and Scotch to the needy. Control wants his usual foul green tea, takes one peck at it, leaves the rest. Jim Prideaux chain-smokes his usual foul Russian cigarettes.

And George? Looks so withdrawn, so unapproachable, has an air of introspection so forbidding, that it would take a brave man to interrupt his reverie.

When Control speaks, he trails his tobacco-stained fingertips across his lips as if he is checking them for sores. He is silvery, dapper, ageless and reportedly friendless. He has a wife somewhere but, according to the gossip, she thinks her husband's in the Coal Board. When he stands, his stooped shoulders come as a surprise. You wait for them to straighten, but they never do. He has been in the job since the mists of time, but I have spoken to him precisely twice and heard him lecture once, and that was on my pass-out day at Sarratt. The voice is knife-thin like the man – nasal, monotonous and irritable as a spoilt child's. And it doesn't warm naturally to questions, not even his own.

'So do we or do we not *believe*,' he demands through his fluttering fingertips, 'that we're still getting the best material out of Herr bloody Mundt? Is it second pickings? Is it chicken-feed? Is it smoke? And is he leading us up the garden path? George?'

With Control, nobody uses cover names, house rule. Doesn't care for them. Says they glorify too much. Better to call a spade a bloody shovel than a holy relic.

'Mundt's product seems to be as good as it ever was, Control,' Smiley replies.

'Pity he didn't tip us off about the bloody Wall then. Or did he forget? Jim?'

Jim Prideaux, after reluctantly taking the cigarette from his lips: 'Mundt says Moscow cut him out of the loop. They told Fiedler. They didn't tell Mundt. And Fiedler kept it to himself.'

'The swine killed Riemeck, didn't he? That wasn't friendly. What made him do that?'

'He says he just happened to get there an hour or two ahead of Fiedler,' Prideaux replies in his habitually gruff monotone. And again we wait for Control, who in return lets us wait for him.

'So we don't believe the opposition has turned Mundt back on us,' Control drones on irritably. 'He's still ours. Well, he bloody well should be. We can toss him to the wolves any time we feel like it. He's power mad. He wants to be Moscow Centre's golden boy. Well, *we* want him to be Moscow's golden boy. And *our* golden boy too. So our interests are mutual. But Herr Josef bloody Fiedler is blocking his way. And *our* way. Fiedler suspects Mundt is ours, and he is. So Fiedler's out to expose him and claim the credit. That about the sum of it, George?'

'It would seem to be, Control.'

'*Seems* to be. Everything *seems*. Nothing *is*. I thought we dealt in facts in this job. Yes or no: Herr Josef Fiedler – a saintly man, we are told, by Stasi standards, a true believer in the cause and a Jew to boot – thinks that his esteemed colleague Hans-Dieter Mundt, unreformed Nazi, is the running dog of British Intelligence. And he's not all wrong, is he?'

George glances at Jim Prideaux. Jim rubs his jaw and glares at the worn carpet. Control again:

'So do we believe Herr Mundt? Another question. Or is he talking up a storm, same as a lot of other agents we know? Is he spinning you along, Jim? You agent-runners are a soft lot where your joes are concerned. Even a Class A shit like Mundt gets the benefit of the doubt.'

But Jim Prideaux, as Control well knows, is about as soft as flint.

'Mundt's got people inside Fiedler's camp. He's told me who they are. He's listened to them. He knows Fiedler's out to get him. Fiedler has as good as told him so to his face. Fiedler has his own friends in Moscow Centre too. Mundt thinks they could make a move pretty soon.'

Again we wait for Control, who decides after all that he needs to take a sip of cold green tea; and needs us to watch him do it too.

'Which begs the question, *doesn't it*, George?' he complains wearily. 'If Josef Fiedler was out of the way – means to be discussed – might Moscow love Mundt more? And if they *do* love him more, might we finally discover who the bugger is who is betraying our agents to Moscow Centre?' – and receiving no answer from the company: 'How about you, Guillam? Does youth have an answer to that question? I am being relative.'

'I'm afraid it doesn't, sir.'

'Pity. George and I think we may have found an answer, you see. But George can't stomach it. Well, I can. I've arranged to see your friend Alec Leamas tomorrow. Test the water with him. See what he feels about it all, now he's lost his network to the Mundt–Fiedler shooting club. A fellow in his position might welcome a chance to finish his career on an up-note. Don't you agree?'

★

Tabitha is provoking me, I suspect deliberately:

'The trouble with you spies, nothing personal, is that none of you know the truth from your elbows. Which does make it awfully hard to defend you. I'll give it my best endeavours, mind you, I always do.' And when I return her sweet smile, but otherwise fail to respond: 'Elizabeth Gold kept a diary, that's the trouble. And Doris Gamp told all to poor Lotte, her sister. Women do these things – gossip with each other, keep diaries, write silly letters. Bunny's lot are making hay with it all. They're comparing you with our modern undercover police informants who go about stealing the hearts of their women victims and giving them babies. I did take a peek at the dates to see if you could have given Elizabeth her Karen, but you're absolutely in the clear, which was a bit of a relief, frankly. And Gustav, thank God, is too old even to have been a twinkle in your eye.'

*

It's a balmy autumn afternoon on Hampstead Heath, and one week after Control's announcement that he would be testing the water with Alec. I'm sitting with George Smiley at an outdoor table in the gardens of Kenwood House. It's a weekday, hardly a soul about. We could just as well have met in the Stables, but George has managed to imply that our conversation is so private that we need the open air. He's wearing a Panama hat that blacks out his eyes, with the result that, just as I'm getting only part of the secret, I'm getting only part of George.

We have done the small talk, or I assume we have. Am I happy in my work? I am, thank you. Have I got over the Tulip thing? I have, thank you. Nice of Oliver Lacon to bury my draft; there was always a danger Joint would make too much of that mystery Swiss intruder at Camp 4. I say I'm glad too, although I sweated blood and tears over it.

'I want you to befriend a *girl* for me, Peter,' Smiley confides, puckering his brow for greater earnestness. Then, realizing I might be misinterpreting this request: 'Oh my goodness, not to accommodate any needs on *my* part, I assure you! Strictly for operational purposes. Might you be willing to do that? In principle? For the good of the cause? Acquire her trust?'

'The cause being Windfall,' I suggest guardedly.

'Yes. Entirely. Solely. For the continued successful outcome of Operation Windfall. Its preservation. As a necessary and urgent adjunct,' he replies, and we sip our apple juice and watch the people come and go in the sunshine. 'Also at the specific request of Control, I may add,' he goes on, either as a further inducement or to pass the buck. 'He actually proposed your name: *that young Guillam fellow.* Singled you out.'

Am I supposed to take this as a compliment – or a veiled warning? George, I suspected, had never much liked Control, and Control didn't like anybody.

'I'm sure there are lots of ways of bumping into her,' he goes on, looking on the bright side. 'She's a member of her local branch of the Communist Party, for one. Sells the *Daily Worker* at weekends. But I don't really see you buying a copy from her, do you?'

'If you mean, do I think I come over as a natural *Daily Worker* reader? – no, I don't think I do.'

'No, no, and you mustn't try. Please don't on any account try to be someone who doesn't add up. Much better your usual genial middle-class self. She runs,' he adds as an afterthought.

'*Runs?*'

'Every morning early, she runs. I find it charming. Don't you? Fitness runs. Wellbeing runs. Round and round the local sports track. Alone. Then off to work in a book store in Fulham. Not a book *shop*, a store. But books, for all that. Dispatching them to wholesalers in bulk. It may sound tedious to us, but she sees it as a cause. We must all have books, the huddled masses especially. And of course she marches too.'

'As well as runs?'

'For Peace, Peter. For peace with a capital P. From Aldermaston to Trafalgar Square, then on to Hyde Park Corner for more of the same. If only Peace were so easy.'

Is he expecting me to smile? I try to.

'But I don't see you assisting her with a banner, either, of course I don't. You're a decent bourgeois fellow, making his way in the world, a species quite unknown to her, and therefore all the more interesting. A good pair of running shoes and your puckish smile, you'll be friends in no time. And if you put on your French persona, you'll be able to make a graceful exit when the time comes. Then it will be all done and dusted. You can forget about her. And she about you. Yes.'

'It might be a help if I knew her name,' I suggest.

He thinks about this too – painfully, problematically: 'Yes, well, they're immigrants. The family are. The parents are first generation, she's second. And they have settled, after some deliberation, on the name of *Gold*,' he concedes, as if I have dragged the name out of him. 'First name *Elizabeth*. Liz to her friends.'

I too take my time. I'm drinking apple juice on a sunny afternoon with a tubby gentleman in a Panama hat. Nobody is hurrying.

'And when I've acquired her trust, as you put it, what do I do then?'

'Why, you come and tell me, of course,' he snaps, as if suddenly all the hesitation in him has been replaced by anger.

★

I am a young French commercial traveller named Marcel Lafontaine, presently based in an Indian-owned boarding house in Hackney, East London, and I have the documents to prove it. It's day five. Each morning at crack of dawn, I take a bus to the memorial park and run. Most mornings there are six or seven of us. We run, we stand panting on the sports hall steps, we check our times, we compare. We exchange a couple of words, divide to the shower rooms, say cheers and see you tomorrow maybe. My companions are vaguely amused by my French name, but disappointed that I have no French accent. I explain that I had an English mother, now dead.

In a cover story, kill off any loose thread before it gets out of hand.

Of our three regular female runners, Liz (we have no surnames) is the tallest, but by no means the fastest. In truth, she's not much of a natural runner at all. She runs as an act of will, or self-discipline, or liberation. She is reserved and apparently unaware that she is beautiful, if in a tomboy sort of way. She's leggy, has dark hair cropped short, a wide brow and big, brown, vulnerable eyes. Yesterday, we traded our first smiles.

'Busy day coming up?' I ask.

'We're out on strike,' she explains breathlessly. 'Got to be up the gates at eight.'

'What gates are they then?'

'Where I work. Management's trying to sack our shop steward. Could go on for weeks.'

Then it's see you, see you, till next time.

And next time is tomorrow which is Saturday so apparently there's no picketing, people need to shop. We do a coffee together in the canteen, she asks me what I do. I explain I'm travelling for this French pharmaceutical company, selling products to local hospitals and GPs. She says that must be really interesting. I say well, not *really*, because what I'd like to be doing is studying medicine, but my dad doesn't want me to do that because the company I represent is our family firm and he wants me to learn it from the ground up and take it over. I show her my business card. My firm bears my fictitious father's name. She studies it with a frown and a smile, but the frown wins:

'You think that's right, do you? Like socially? The son of the family inheriting the family firm just because he's the son?'

And I say no, I don't think it's right, it bothers me. And it bothers my fiancée too, which is why I want to be a doctor like her, because I admire my fiancée as well as love her, I think she's a real blessing to mankind.

And the reason I've given myself a fiancée is because, although I find Liz disturbingly attractive, I'm never going to do another Tulip as long as I live. It's also thanks to my mythical fiancée that Liz and I are able to walk beside the canal and earnestly swap our aspirations, now that she knows I'm lost in love and admiration for a woman doctor in France.

When we have traded our hopes and dreams, we talk parents, and how it is to be part foreign, and she asks me whether I'm Jewish, and I say no.

Over a carafe of red wine at the Greek, she asks me whether I'm a Communist, and instead of saying no again I take the frivolous route and say I just can't make up my mind whether to be a Bolshevik or a Menshevik, and can she please advise?

And after that, we get serious, or she does, and we start talking about the Berlin Wall, which is so present in my mind that it never occurred to me that it might be in hers too.

'My dad says it's a barrier to keep the Fascists out,' she says.

And I say, 'Well, that's a view, I suppose,' which annoys her.

'So what do *you* think it is?' she demands.

'I just don't think the Wall's there to keep people out,' I say. 'I think it's more there to keep people in.'

To which I get the unanswerable reply, again delivered after earnest thought:

'Dad doesn't think like that, you see, Marcel. The Fascists killed his family. That's good enough for Dad.'

★

'Poor Liz's diary simply *gushes* about you, Peter,' Tabitha is saying, with her pitying, sweet smile. 'You're such a gallant French gentleman. Your English is so good she keeps forgetting you're French at all. If only there were more men like you in the world. You're a lost cause as far as the Party's concerned, but you're a humanist, you know the true meaning of love, and with a bit of work you might see the light one day. She doesn't say she'd like to put arsenic in your fiancée's coffee, but she doesn't have to. She also took a photograph of you, in case you've forgotten. This one. She borrowed her father's Polaroid camera specially.'

I'm in my running gear, propped against a bit of railing, which was how she posed me. Then told me to be natural, not to smile.

'And I'm afraid it's in their submission too. Exhibit A, so to speak. You're the wicked Romeo who stole a poor girl's heart away and led her to the slaughter. There's practically a song about you.'

*

'We're friends,' I announce to Smiley, not over an apple juice on sunny Hampstead Heath this time, but back in the Stables to the background putter of the cypher machine upstairs and the Windfall sisters at their manual typewriters.

I tell him the rest of the operational intelligence. She lives with her parents. No brothers or sisters. Doesn't go out. Her parents quarrel. The father dickers between Zionism and Communism. Never misses synagogue or shirks a meeting of the comrades. Mother determinedly secular. Dad wants Liz in the garment trade. Mum wants Liz to do teacher training. But I have a feeling that George knows all this already, for why else would he have chosen her in the first place?

217

'But what does Elizabeth want for *herself*, we wonder?' he muses.

'She wants *out*, George,' I reply more impatiently than I intend.

'*Out* in any stated direction? Or just *out* for its own sake?'

Her best thing would be a library, I say. Maybe a Marxist library. There's one in Highgate she wrote to, but they didn't answer. She's already a volunteer at her local public library, I tell him. And she reads stories in English to immigrant kids who are still learning the language. But George probably knows that too.

'Then we must see what we can do for her, mustn't we? It would be helpful if you could remain alongside her for a little longer before you vanish to French shores. Are you comfortable with that?'

'Not very.'

I don't think George is comfortable with it either.

★

It's five days and two canal walks later. And night again at the Stables.

'You might see if *this* appeals to her,' George suggests, handing me a page ripped from a quarterly journal called *Paranormal Gazette*. 'You happened on it by chance in a doctor's waiting room while you were doing your pharmaceutical rounds. The pay is dismal, but I suspect she won't mind that too much.'

The Bayswater Library for Psychical Research is seeking an assistant librarian. Apply with photograph and handwritten curriculum vitae to Miss Eleanora Crail.

★

'Marcel, I *got* it, Marcel!' Liz is saying, laughing and weeping as she waves the letter at me in the sports club canteen. 'I got it, I

218

got it! Dad says I should be ashamed of myself, it's bourgeois superstition gone mad and sure to be anti-Semitic. Mum says go for it, it's the first step on the ladder. So I've gone for it. Starting first Monday of next month!'

And when she has put down the letter, she jumps up and hugs me and tells me I'm the best pal she's ever had. And not for the first time I wish I hadn't invented that steady girlfriend waiting for me in France. And I think she's wishing it too.

★

It wasn't taking much to annoy me, as Tabitha was beginning to find out.

'So as soon as you'd thrown your magic dust in her eyes, you ran off and told your friend Alec what a dear, nice Communist girl you'd found for him, and all he had to do was get himself a job at the same kooky library, and the two of them would be in bed in no time. Is that how it worked?'

'There was no question of telling Alec anything. I had made contact with Liz Gold as part of Windfall. Alec wasn't Windfall cleared. Whatever happened between Alec and Liz once she'd got the job at the library was nothing to do with me, and I wasn't informed.'

'So your orders from Smiley regarding Alec Leamas in his simulated decline into drink, dissolution and betrayal were *what* exactly?'

'To remain his friend and do whatever came naturally as things developed. Bearing in mind that, as the operation advanced, my actions would be as liable to scrutiny by the opposition as Alec's were.'

'So Control's instruction to Leamas, meanwhile, would have been broadly this, correct me: we know you hate Americans, Alec, so go out there and hate them a bit more. We know you drink like a fish, so double the dose. And we know you like a fight when the drink's on you, so don't feel you've got to hold back, and while you're about it, just generally go to hell in a handcart. Does that about sum it up?'

'Alec was to trail his coat any way he thought best. That's all he told me.'

'All *Control* told you?'

What's she driving at? Who does she belong to, one minute coming within touching distance of the truth, then veering away as if it's about to burn her?

'All Smiley told me.'

*

I'm having a lunchtime drink with Alec in a pub a few minutes' walk from the Circus. Control has given him one last chance to behave himself, and put him in Banking Section on the ground floor, with instructions to pilfer whatever he can get his hands on, although Alec doesn't tell me this, and I'm not sure he knows how much I know. It's half past two and we met at one, and if you're on the ground floor you get an hour for lunch and no excuses.

After a couple of pints, he's into the Scotch, and all he's had for lunch is a bag of crisps sprinkled with Tabasco. He has grumbled loudly about what a shitload of weirdos the Circus is these days, and where are all the good guys from the war, and how the only thing the top floor cares about is kissing the American arse.

And I've listened and not said a lot because I'm not entirely sure how much is real Alec, and how much he's living the part, and I'm not sure he is, which is exactly as it should be. It's only when we're out on the pavement with the traffic rolling by that he grabs my arm. For a moment I think he's going to punch me.

Instead, he flings his arms wide and hugs me to him like the emotional Irish drunk he's pretending to be, while tears roll down his stubbly cheeks.

'I love you, hear me, Pierrot?'

'And I love you, Alec' – dutifully.

And before he shoves me away: 'Tell us. Just for information. What the fuck's Windfall?'

'Just a Covert source we run. Why?'

'Something that ponce Haydon said to me in his cups the other day. Covert's got this great new source out there, and why's nobody cutting Joint in on the action? Know what I told him?'

'What did you tell him?'

'If I was running Covert, I said, and somebody from Joint came up to me and said, who's your big source? – I'd kick him in the balls.'

'And what did Bill say to you?'

'Told me to go fuck myself. You know something else I told him?'

'Not yet.'

'Keep your poofy little hands off George's wife.'

★

It's late at night in the Stables. It always is. The Stables is a house that lives by night, in unpredictable surges. One minute we're all bored stiff with waiting, the next there's a scuffle at the front door and a yell of *Shop!* and in strolls Jim Prideaux with Windfall's latest batch of crown jewels. They've flown in by microdot or carbon; Jim's hand-lifted them from a dead letter box in denied territory; they've been passed to him personally by Windfall in a one-minute treff in a Prague back alley. Suddenly I'm dashing up and down stairs with telegrams, I'm crouching at my desk alerting Whitehall customers by green phone, the Windfall sisters' manual typewriters are rattling away, and Ben's cypher machine is burping through the floorboards. For the next twelve hours we will be breaking up Mundt's raw material, spreading it across a range of fictitious sources – a bit of signals intelligence here, a telephone or microphone intercept there – and only rarely, to keep the mix alive, the odd highly placed and reliable informant, but all of it under the one magic name of Windfall, for indoctrinated readers only. Tonight it's a lull between the storms. For once George is all on his own in the Middle Room.

'I bumped into Alec a couple of days ago,' I begin.

'I thought we had agreed you would allow your relationship with your friend Alec to cool, Peter.'

'There's something about the Windfall operation I don't understand and feel I should,' I say, moving into my prepared speech.

'*Should?* By what authority? My goodness me, Peter.'

'It's just a simple question, George.'

'I didn't know we dealt in simple questions.'

'What's Alec's remit, that's all?'

'To do what he's doing, as you well know. To become one of life's angry failures. A Service reject. To appear resentful, vengeful, seducible, buyable.'

'With what *intent* though, George? To what end?'

His impatience was getting the better of him. He started to answer, drew a breath and started again.

'Your friend Alec Leamas is under orders to parade his well-attested character defects in all their glory. To make sure they catch the eye of the opposition's talent-spotters – with a little help from the traitor or traitors in our midst – and place his considerable fund of secret intelligence on the market, for us then to add a few misleading items of our own.'

'So a standard double-agent disinformation operation.'

'With embellishments, yes. A standard operation.'

'Only he seems to think he's on a mission to kill Mundt.'

'Well, he's quite right, isn't he?' he retorts, with no delay, no alteration to his tone.

He was peering furiously up at me through his rounded spectacles. I had expected we would be sitting down by now, but we were still standing, and I am substantially taller than George. But what struck me was the aridity of his voice, which reminded me of our meeting in the police house just hours after he had struck his devil's pact with Mundt.

'Alec Leamas is a professional, as you are, Peter, and as I am. If Control hasn't invited him to read the fine print of his mission, so much the better for Alec and for us. He can't misstep and he can't betray. If his mission succeeds in ways he has not anticipated, he will not feel deceived. He will feel he has accomplished what was required of him.'

'But Mundt's *ours*, George! He's our joe – he's Windfall!'

'Thank you. Hans-Dieter Mundt is an agent of this Service. And as such he must be protected at all costs from those who correctly suspect him of being what he is, and dream only of putting him against a wall and taking over his job.'

'What about Liz?'

'Elizabeth Gold?' – as if he's forgotten the name, or I have mispronounced it. 'Elizabeth Gold will be invited to do precisely what comes naturally to her: speak the truth and nothing but the truth. Do you now have all the information you require?'

'No.'

'I envy you.'

12

It's another morning, a grey one for a change, and a fine rain is falling over Dolphin Square as I board my bus. As it happens, I arrive early at the Stables, but Tabitha is already sitting waiting for me, very pleased with herself for having acquired a sheaf of Special Branch surveillance reports which she claims landed on her doorstep. She doesn't know whether they're authentic, of course, or whether she could ever make use of them down the line, but I mustn't on any account bubble to anyone that she's got them. All of which tells me she has a friend in Special Branch, and the reports are exactly what they say they are.

'So let's kick off with the first day of live action, this one. No hint of who actually *asked* Special Branch to put its dogs on to Alec. Just, at the request of Box – Box, I gather, being police-speak for the Circus in those days. Yes?'

'Yes.'

'Do you have any idea *who* in Box might have placed the request to Special Branch?'

'Joint, probably.'

'Who particularly in Joint?'

'Could have been any one of them. Bland, Alleline, Esterhase. Even Haydon himself. More likely he delegated it to one of his underlings so that he didn't get his feet wet.'

'And Special Branch to conduct the surveillance, and not

your dear friends in the Security Service? Is that normal procedure?'

'Absolutely.'

'Because?'

'Because the two Services didn't like each other.'

'And our splendid police?'

'Disliked the Security Service for meddling and the Circus because we were a bunch of stuck-up pansies whose mission in life was to break the law.'

She thought about this, then about me, frankly studying me with her sad blue eyes.

'You're very *assured* sometimes. Anyone might think you had superior knowledge. We're going to have to watch out for that. A junior official caught up in the slipstream of historic events is what we're after. Not somebody with a big secret to hide.'

★

Commander Special Branch to Box. Top Secret & Guard.
Subject: OPERATION GALAXY.

Prior to taking up their positions my officers made discreet background enquiries regarding the known activities of subject couple, as per their mode of employment, lifestyle and cohabitation.

Both parties are currently employed full time at the Bayswater Library for Psychical Research, a privately funded institute managed by Miss Eleanora Crail, a single woman aged fifty-eight of eccentric manner and appearance, not previously known to police. Unaware that she was confiding in one of my officers, Miss Crail freely volunteered the following background information regarding the pair.

VENUS, whom she refers to as her 'darling Lizzie', has

been in her full employment as an assistant librarian for the last six months and in the view of Miss Crail is without blemish, being punctual, respectful, intelligent, clean in her habits, a fast and conscientious learner with good handwriting, and is 'well spoken considering her class'. Miss Crail has no objection to her Communist views, of which she makes no secret, 'provided she doesn't bring them into my library'.

MARS, whom she calls her 'nasty Mr L', has been in her full employment as second assistant librarian pending the redesign of the library, and is not in her opinion 'at all satisfactory'. She has twice complained to the Bayswater Labour Exchange regarding his behaviour, without result. She describes him as slovenly, discourteous, overstays his lunch hours, and frequently 'smells of alcoholic beverage'. She resents his habit of affecting a thick Irish accent when rebuked, and she would have dismissed him after one week had not her darling Lizzie (Venus) interceded on his behalf, there being an 'unhealthy' mutual attraction between the two, despite their differences in age and outlook, which in Miss Crail's opinion may already have flowered into full-on intimacy. Why else, after a mere two weeks of acquaintance, would they arrive simultaneously in the morning, plus on more than one occasion she has observed them holding hands, and not just because they are passing books.

Asked casually by my officer what previous employment Mars had claimed, she replied that according to the Employment Exchange he had been 'some kind of insignificant clerk in a banking house' to which she could only say that no wonder the banks were what they were coming to these days.

Surveillance.
For their first day of observation my officers selected the second Friday of the month, this being the day on which the

226

Goldhawk Road Branch of the British Communist Party sponsors its Open Day to all shades of left-wing opinion at the Oddfellows' Hall, Goldhawk Road, Venus having recently transferred her Party affiliations from Cable Street to Goldhawk Road on taking up residence in Bayswater. Regular attendees include members of the Socialist Workers' Party, 'Militant', the Campaign for Nuclear Disarmament, plus two undercover officers from my own Force – one male, one female – thereby providing cover for toilets.

On departing the library at 1730 hours, the target couple paused at the Queen's Arms in Bayswater Street, where Mars drank a large whisky and Venus a Babycham, arriving as anticipated at the Oddfellows' Hall at 1912 hours, the theme of the evening being 'Peace at What Price?' and the hall, which accommodates 508, containing on this occasion an estimated 130 persons of varying skin colours and stations in life. Mars and Venus duly seated themselves side by side at the rear, close to the exit, with Venus, a popular figure among the comrades, receiving smiles and nods.

After a short opening address by R. Palme Dutt, Communist activist and journalist, who then immediately left the hall, lesser speakers took the stand, the last being Bert Arthur Lownes, owner of Lownes the People's Grocer, Bayswater Road, self-styled Trotskyist and well known to the police for incitement to violence, affray, and other acts calculated to cause a breach of the peace in a public place.

Until Lownes took to the microphone, Mars had behaved in a sullen and bored manner, yawning, nodding off and periodically refreshing himself from a flask, contents unknown. The hectoring manner of Lownes, however, roused him from his slumbers, to quote my officer, prompting him unexpectedly to raise his arm in order to catch the eye of the Chairman conducting the meeting, also treasurer of the Goldhawk Road

Branch, Bill Flint, who duly invited Mars to state his name then put his question to the speaker in accordance with Open Day rules. My officers' records of the exchange, taken during and after the meeting, are uniform and read as follows:

Mars [Irish accent. States name]: Librarian. Here's a question for you, Comrade. You're telling us we should lay off arming ourselves to the teeth against the Soviet threat because the Sovs aren't threatening anybody. Am I right there? Get out of the arms race now, and spend the money on beer?

[Laughter.]

Lownes: Well, that's an over-simplification, if ever I heard one, Comrade. But all right. If you want to put it like that. Yes.

Mars: Whereas, according to you, the real enemy we should be worrying about is America. American imperialism. American capitalism. American aggression. Or is that another over-simplification I'm making?

Lownes: What's your question, Comrade?

Mars: Well it's this, you see, Comrade. Should we not be arming ourselves to the teeth against the *American threat*, if they're the boys to be afraid of?

Lownes's reply drowned by laughter, angry jeers and scattered applause. Mars and Venus exit through rear door. On the pavement, they at first appear to engage in a lively altercation. However, their differences are short-lived, and they walk arm in arm to the bus stop, pausing only to embrace.

Addendum.

On comparing notebooks, two of my officers separately recorded the presence of the same well-dressed thirty-year-old man of medium height, wavy fair hair and effeminate appearance who, having left the meeting directly after the pair, followed them to the bus stop and boarded the same bus, thereupon seating himself on the lower deck while the pair favoured the upper deck, enabling Mars to smoke. When the pair alighted, the same individual also alighted, and having seen them as far as their apartment building and waited until a light appeared on the third floor, he repaired forthwith to a phone box. My officers not being under instruction to pursue ancillary targets, no attempt was made to identify or house this individual.

★

'So the grand plan was working. The beasts of the forest were starting to sniff at your tethered goat. As represented by our well-dressed thirty-year-old man of effeminate appearance. Yes?'

'Not my goat. Control's.'

'Not Smiley's?'

'When it came to planting Alec on the opposition, Smiley played second fiddle.'

'Which was the way he wanted it?'

'Presumably.'

I'm detecting a new Tabitha. Or the real one, showing her claws.

'Had you seen this report before?'

'Heard about it. The substance.'

'Here in this house? Together with your Windfall-cleared colleagues?'

'Yes.'

'So, great rejoicing all round. Hurrah, they've taken the bait.'

'Pretty much.'

'You don't sound very sure. You weren't feeling queasy about the operation at all, you personally? Wishing you could get out of it, and not seeing how?'

'We were on course. The op was going to plan. Why should I be feeling queasy?'

She seemed about to question this assertion, then changed her mind.

'I *love* this one,' she said, pushing another report at me.

★

Commander Special Branch to Box. Top Secret & Guard.
Subject: OPERATION GALAXY. REPORT No. 6.
Unprovoked assault on Bert Arthur LOWNES, owner of
LOWNES THE PEOPLE'S GROCER, a business run on
cooperative lines in the Bayswater Road, at 1745 hours, 21 April 1962.

The following information was taken informally from witnesses not called for trial in view of the uncontested nature of the case.

Over the week preceding the incident, it appears that Mars had made a habit of calling in at Lownes's emporium at all odd hours of day in an inebriated state, ostensibly to make a purchase on a personal monthly savings account kept in the name of Venus, to which he had access, but in reality to engage in verbal exchanges with Lownes conducted in a loud and provocative Irish voice. On the day in question, my officer observed Mars loading up a basket with a large quantity of comestibles, including whisky, in the approximate value of £45. On being asked whether the intended purchases were to be paid for in cash, or debited to the Venus account, Mars responded with, I quote, 'Credit, you arsehole, what d'you effing think?' plus words to the effect that being a fully paid-up member of the starving masses, he was entitled to his fair share of the world's riches. Ignoring Lownes's warning that, the Venus account being overdrawn, no further credit was available, he thereupon advanced towards the main exit carrying the heavily laden basket of unpaid-for goods in front of him. At which point the said Lownes advanced from behind the counter and in robust language ordered Mars to give up his basket forthwith and remove himself from the premises. Instead of which, without further argument, Mars delivered a rapid succession of blows to Lownes's stomach and groin area, culminating in an elbow-blow to the right face.

Making no attempt to escape while customers screamed and Mrs Lownes dialled 999, Mars exhibited no remorse, but continued to pour insults on his luckless victim.

As one of my younger officers afterwards remarked, he was highly grateful not to have been present at the scene since he would have felt obligated to cast aside cover and intervene. Moreover, he frankly doubted his ability to confront the assailant single-handed.

In the event, uniformed police quickly attended, and the assailant did not resist arrest.

★

'So my question is: did you personally know in advance that Alec was going to beat up poor Mr Lownes?'

'In principle.'

'What does that mean?'

'They wanted a moment when Alec burned his last bridge. He'd come out of prison, be on his uppers, have no way back.'

'They being Control and Smiley.'

'Yes.'

'But not you. It wasn't your own brilliant idea, cooked up by you and poached by your elders and betters?'

'No.'

'What worries me is that you personally might have put Alec

up to it, you see. Or the other side will suggest you did. Urged your poor broken friend to even greater depths of depravity. But you didn't. Which is a relief. The same with the money Alec filched from Circus's Banking Section. That was six other people telling him to do it, not you?'

'Control, I assume.'

'Good. So Alec was trailing his coat for his superiors, you were his pal, not his evil genius. And Alec was aware of that, presumably. Yes?'

'I assume so. Yes.'

'So did Alec also know that you were Windfall cleared?'

'Of course he bloody didn't! How could he? He didn't know anything *about* Windfall!'

'Yes, well, I was afraid you'd be indignant. I'm going off to do some homework if you don't mind, while you browse through this horror. The English translation is dire. But so, I'm told, is the original text. Makes one long for Special Branch's magic way with words.'

EXTRACTS FROM HITHERTO UNRELEASED STASI
FILES MARKED NOT TO BE RELEASED TILL 2050 AS
EXCERPTED AND TRANSLATED BY ZARA N. POTTER
ASSOCIATES, COURT-APPROVED INTERPRETERS
AND TRANSLATORS AS COMMISSIONED BY MESSRS
SEGROVE, LOVE & BARNABAS, SOLICITORS AT LAW,
LONDON W.C.

As the door closed after her, I was seized by an irrational anger. Where had she gone, damn her? Why did she walk out on me like that? To render a breathless account to her pals in the bastion? Is that the game she's playing? They hand her a bunch of Special Branch reports and say: *try these on him for size*? Is that how it works? But it wasn't how it worked. I knew that. Tabitha was every defendant's good angel. And her soft sad eyes saw a sight further than Bunny's or Laura's. I knew that too.

*

Alec is propped against the grimy window, peering out. I am sitting in the only armchair. We are in an upstairs bedroom of a commercial hotel in Paddington that lets out rooms by the hour. This morning he called me on an unlisted line at Marylebone reserved for joes: 'Meet me at the Duchess, six o'clock.' The Duchess of Albany, Praed Street, one of his old haunts. He is haggard, red-eyed and twitchy. The glass in his drinking hand trembles. Short, grudging sentences, bitten out between pauses.

'There's this girl,' he is saying. 'Bloody Communist. Can't blame her. Not where she comes from. Anyway, who blames who for what any more?'

Wait. Don't ask. He'll tell you what he wants.

'I told Control. Keep her out of it. I don't trust the old bastard. Never know what he's up to. Wonder whether he does himself.' Long contemplation of street below. Continued sympathetic silence from me. 'Anyway, where the fuck's George hiding?' – swinging round on me accusingly. 'I had a treff with Control in Bywater Street the other night. George didn't bloody show up.'

'George is doing a lot of Berlin, just now,' I say untruthfully, and again I wait.

Alec has decided to mimic Control's donnish bray:

'*I want you to get rid of Mundt for me, Alec. Make the world a better place. Are you up for that, old man?* Course I'm bloody up for it. Bastard killed Riemeck, didn't he? Killed half my bloody network. Had a go at George too, a year or two back. Can't have that, can we, Pierrot?'

'No, we can't,' I agree heartily.

233

Did he catch a false note in my voice? He takes a pull of Scotch, and goes on staring at me.

'You don't happen to have *met* her by any chance, Pierrot?'

'Met who?'

'My girl. You know bloody well who I mean.'

'How the hell could I have met her, Alec? What are you bleating about? Jesus, man.'

He turns away at last. 'Someone she'd met, a man. Sounded a bit like you. That's all.'

I shake my head in mystification, shrug, smile. Alec goes back to his contemplations, peering down at the passers-by on the pavement as they scurry through the rain.

★

SUBJECT: FALSE ACCUSATIONS MADE AGAINST COMRADE HANS-DIETER MUNDT BY FASCIST BRITISH INTELLIGENCE AGENTS. FULL, TOTAL AND COMPLETE EXONERATION OF H-D MUNDT BY PEOPLE'S TRIBUNAL. LIQUIDATION OF IMPERIALIST SPIES WHILE ATTEMPTING TO ESCAPE. SUBMITTED TO SED PRAESIDIUM. 28 OCTOBER 1962.

If the Star Chamber that sat in judgement over Hans-Dieter Mundt was a travesty, the official account of it was worse. The prologue might have been written by Mundt himself. Perhaps it was.

The odious and corrupt counter-revolutionary agitator Leamas was a known degenerate, a drunken bourgeois opportunist, liar, womanizer, thug, obsessed by money and a hatred of progress.

The devoted Stasi operatives who had procured the false

testimony of this evil Judas had done so in good faith and could not be blamed for introducing a viper into the heartland of those dedicated to combating the forces of Fascist imperialism.

The trial was a triumph of Socialist justice and a call for ever-greater vigilance against the intrigues of capitalist spies and provocateurs.

The woman who called herself Elizabeth Gold was a political simpleton of pro-Israel sympathies, brainwashed by the British Secret Service, besotted by her older lover and lured wide-eyed into a web of Western intrigue.

Even after the impostor Leamas had made a full confession of his crimes, the woman Gold had treacherously assisted him in his escape, and paid the full price for her duplicity.

And a closing word of congratulation to that fearless guardian of Democratic Socialism who didn't hesitate to shoot her down as she made her escape.

*

'So, Peter. A quick replay of the truly awful kangaroo trial in plain English. Are we up for that?'

'Whatever.'

But her voice was brisk and purposeful, and she had plonked herself down directly in front of me across the table like a People's Commissar.

'Alec arrives in the Star Chamber as Fiedler's prize witness with best-laid plans to dish the dirt on Mundt. Yes? Fiedler tells the court all about the bogus money trail that leads to Mundt's front door. Yes? He makes a whole mouthful of Mundt's time as a pseudo-diplomat in England which, according to Fiedler, was when he was picked up and turned by the forces of reactionary imperialism, alias the Circus. Then we have a list of all the shocking State secrets Mundt has allegedly sold to his

Western masters for his thirty pieces of silver, and it's all going down a storm with the tribunal's judges. Until *what*?'

The sweet smile is long gone.

'Until Liz, I suppose,' I reply grudgingly.

'Until Liz, indeed. Up pops poor Liz and, because she doesn't know any better, she puts the kibosh on everything her beloved Alec has just told the court. Did you know she was going to do that?'

'Of course I didn't! How the devil could I?'

'How could you indeed? And did you notice, by any chance, what actually *sank* Liz – *and* her Alec? It was the moment when she brought up George Smiley's name. Her absolutely innocent admission to the Star Chamber that one *George Smiley*, accompanied by a younger man, had dropped in to see her soon after Alec's mysterious disappearance, and *told* her that her Alec was doing a marvellous job – implicitly for his *country* – and everything was going to be hunkydory. Your George then left his *visiting card* with her to make sure she didn't forget. *Smiley* being anyway a name effortlessly remembered, and by no means unknown to the Stasi. *Such* an inept thing to do, don't you think, for a sly old fox like George?'

I said something to the effect that even George could slip up now and then.

'And were you the younger man who tagged along with him, by any chance?'

'No I wasn't! How could I be? I was *Marcel* – remember?'

'So who was it?'

'Jim, probably. Prideaux. He'd come across.'

'Across?'

'From Joint to Covert.'

'And was also Windfall cleared?'

'I believe so.'

'Only believe?'

'He was cleared.'

'Then tell me this, if you're allowed to. When Alec Leamas was sent off on his mission to shaft Mundt at any price, who did he believe was the *anonymous source* who was providing the Circus with all its lovely Windfall material?'

'No idea. Never discussed it with him. Probably Control did. Don't know.'

'Let me put it another way, if it's simpler. Would it be fair to say, on balance, by inference, by a process of elimination, by certain hints half dropped, that by the time Alec Leamas sets out on his fatal voyage he has taken it into his fuddled head that Josef Fiedler is the vital source he is protecting, which is why the odious Hans-Dieter Mundt has to be eliminated?'

I heard my voice rise and couldn't stop it:

'How the *hell* am *I* supposed to know what *Alec* thought or didn't think? Alec was a *fieldman*. You don't think round corners if you're a fieldman. There's a Cold War on. You've got a job to do. You get on with it!'

Was I talking about Alec? Or myself?

'So help me solve this knotty little conundrum, if you will. You, P. Guillam, were Windfall cleared. Yes? One of the very, very few. Can I go on? I can. Alec was emphatically *not* so cleared. He knew there was an East German super-source, or bunch of sources, with the generic name Windfall. He knew Covert had the running of him, her or them. But he didn't know anything about this place we're sitting in now, or what it was actually up to. True?'

'I suppose so.'

'And it was vital that he should *not* be Windfall cleared, which has been your refrain from the outset.'

'*So?*' – in my dead weary voice.

'Well, if *you* were Windfall cleared, and Alec Leamas *wasn't* Windfall cleared, what did *you* know that *Alec* wasn't allowed to know? Or are we exercising our right to silence? I wouldn't recommend it. Not with the All-Party lot waiting to tear into you. *Or* when you're sitting in front of a tame jury.'

★

This is what Alec went through, I'm thinking: defending a hopeless case and watching it fall apart in his hands, with the difference that nobody's dying except of old age. I'm clinging for dear life to a great untenable lie I promised I'd never betray, and it's sinking under my weight. But Tabitha has no mercy:

'So our *feelings*. Can we talk about *them* for a change? So much more illuminating than facts, I always think. What did *you* feel, you yourself, when you heard that poor Liz suddenly stood up and trashed all Alec's marvellous hard work? Trashed poor Fiedler too, while she was about it?'

'I *didn't* hear.'

'I'm sorry?'

'Nobody picked up the phone and said, *heard the latest about the trial?* First thing we got was an East German newsflash. Traitor unmasked. That was Fiedler down the drain. Senior security official totally exonerated. That was Mundt in the clover. Then we got the prisoners' dramatic escape, and a nationwide hunt for them. And then we got—'

'The shootings at the Wall, presumably?'

'George was there. George saw it. I didn't.'

'And your *feelings* again? As you sat here, in this very room, or stood here, paced, or whatever you did, and the awful news came trickling through in bits and pieces? Now hear *this*, now hear *that*? On and on?'

'What d'you think I bloody did? Whistled up the champagne?' Pause, while I collect myself. 'I thought, Jesus God, that poor girl. Caught up in it all. Refugee family. Head over heels in love

238

with Alec. Meant no harm to anyone. What a bloody awful thing to have to do.'

'*Have* to? You mean she *intended* to appear before the tribunal? She *intended* to save the Nazi and kill the Jew? That doesn't sound like Liz at all. Whoever would have told her to do a thing like that?'

'Nobody bloody told her!'

'The poor girl didn't even know why she was at the trial. She'd been invited to a comrades' jamboree in the sunny GDR, and all of a sudden she's testifying against her lover in a kangaroo court. How did you *feel* when you heard that? You personally. Then to hear they'd both been mown down at the Wall. Shot while escaping, allegedly. Anguish, it must have been. Utter, surely?'

'Course it was.'

'For all of you?'

'All.'

'Control too?'

'Not an expert on Control's feelings, I'm afraid.'

That sad smile of hers. It's come back.

'And your Uncle George?'

'What about him?'

'Just how did he take it?'

'I don't know.'

'Why not?' – sharply.

'He disappeared. Took himself down to Cornwall alone.'

'Why?'

'To walk, I assume. It's where he goes.'

'For how long?'

'A few days. Maybe a week.'

'And when he came back. Was he an altered man?'

'George doesn't alter. He just gets his composure back.'

'And he did?'

'He didn't talk about it.'

She thought about this, seemed reluctant to let the subject go.

'And no little smidgeon of triumph *anywhere*?' she resumed after further thought. 'On the *other* front? The *operational* front – no sense anywhere of – well, that was the collateral damage, it's tragic and it's awful, but mission accomplished nonetheless. Nothing of *that* kind, so far as we're aware?'

Nothing has changed. Not her gentle voice, not her creamy smile. Her manner, if anything, even kindlier than before.

'What I'm asking you is: when *did* you know, in your own mind, that Mundt's triumphant vindication was *not* the fuck-up it was made out to be, but a grand-scale intelligence coup in disguise? And that Liz Gold was the necessary catalyst that made it all happen? It's about your defence, you see. Your intent, your foreknowledge, your complicity. You could stand or fall by any one of them.'

A silence for the dead. Broken by Tabitha in a voice of casual enquiry.

'You know what I dreamed last night?'

'Why the hell should I?'

'I was doing my due diligence, wading through that endless draft report that Smiley made you write and decided not to circulate. And I got to wondering about that peculiar Swiss ornithologist who turned out to be an undercover member of the Circus's domestic security arm. And then I asked myself *why* didn't Smiley want your report circulated? So I did some more due diligence, and nosed around wherever I was allowed to nose, and for the life of me I couldn't turn up a single thing about anybody testing the defences of Camp 4 over that period. And absolutely *nothing* about an overzealous undercover operator who punched out Camp 4's security guards. So it didn't exactly take an epiphany to stitch together the rest. No death certificate for Tulip. Well, we know the poor girl hadn't landed officially, but not many doctors like putting their names to a bogus death certificate, even Circus doctors.'

I glowered into the distance, and tried to pretend I thought she was mad.

'So my reading is: Mundt was sent over to murder Tulip. He murdered her, but the good Lord wasn't on his side and he got caught. George put the hard word on him. Spy for us or else. He does. Cornucopia of lovely intelligence, suddenly at risk. Fiedler looks like rumbling him. Enter Control with his revolting plan. George may not have cared for it but, as ever with George, duty called. Nobody reckoned on Liz and Alec getting shot. That would have been Mundt's big idea: shoot the messengers and get a better night's sleep. Not even Control could have spotted that one on the horizon. Your George went straight into retirement, vowing never to spy again. Which we love him for, although it didn't last. He still had to come back and catch Bill Haydon, which he did wonderfully well, bless him. And you were for him all the way, which we can only applaud.'

Nothing came to mind, so I said nothing.

'And to twist the knife in what was already a very large wound, no sooner had the Star Chamber done its business than Hans-Dieter was summoned to a power conference in Moscow, never to be seen again. So goodbye to any last hopes that he might get his nose under the wire at Centre, and tell us who the Circus traitor was. Presumably Bill Haydon had got there ahead of him. Can we talk a little more about *you*?'

I couldn't stop her, so why try?

'If I was allowed to argue that Windfall was *not* the cock-up of all time but a fiendishly clever operation that was wildly productive of top-grade intelligence and only went off the rails at the last minute, I have very little doubt that the All-Partygoers would roll over and put their paws in the air. Liz and Alec? Tragic, yes, but in the circumstances, acceptable losses in the cause of the greater good. Am I winning? I'm not. Oh dear. Only suggesting. Because I don't think I can defend you any other way. In fact I'm quite sure I can't.'

She had started to pack her things together: spectacles, cardigan, paper tissues, Special Branch reports, Stasi reports.

'You spoke, heart?'

Did I? Neither of us is sure. She's called a halt to her packing. She's holding her briefcase open on her lap, waiting for me to speak. Eternity ring on second finger. Odd I haven't noticed it till now. Wonder who the husband is. Probably dead.

'Look here.'

'Still looking, heart.'

'Accepting for one moment your absurd hypothesis—'

'That the fiendishly clever operation worked—?'

'Accepting it, *theoretically*, which I absolutely do not – are you seriously telling me that – in the impossible event that documentary proof to that effect should ever come to light—'

'Which we know it won't, but if it ever did, it would have to be cast iron—'

'Are you telling me that in such an improbable eventuality, the charges – the accusations – litigation – the whole bang shooting-match against whomever – me, George, if he can be found, even the Service – would go away?'

'You find me the evidence, I'll find you the judge. The vultures are gathering as we speak. If you don't show up for the hearing, the All-Partygoers will fear the worst, and act accordingly. I asked Bunny for your passport. The brute won't part with it. But he will extend your stay at Dolphin Square on the same miserly terms. All to be discussed. Will same time tomorrow morning suit you?'

'Could we make it ten?'

'I'll be on the dot,' she replied, and I said I would too.

13

When the truth catches up with you, don't be a hero, run. But I took care to walk, slowly, into Dolphin Square and up to the safe flat I knew I would never sleep in again. Draw curtains, sigh resignedly for the television set, close bedroom door. Extract French passport from dead letter box behind fire precautions notice. There is a calming ritual to escape. Don clean set of clothes. Shove razor in raincoat pocket, leave the rest in place. Make my way down to grill room, order light meal, settle to my boring book like a man reconciled to a solitary evening. Chat up Hungarian waitress in case she has reporting responsibility. Actually I live in France, I tell her, but I'm over here to talk business with a bunch of English lawyers, can she imagine anything worse, ha ha? Pay bill. Saunter into courtyard with retired ladies in white hats and croquet skirts, seated in pairs along garden benches, enjoy the unseasonable sunshine. Prepare to join exodus to Embankment, never to return.

Except that I do neither of these last two things, because by now I have spotted Christoph, son of Alec, in his long black coat and Homburg hat, lounging twenty yards away on a bench all to himself, with one arm thrown affectionately along the back of it, and one large leg slung over the other for leisure, and his right hand buried, ostentatiously to my eye, in his overcoat pocket. He is staring straight at me and he is smiling, which is not something I have seen him do before, whether as a child watching a football match or as a man eating steak and chips. And perhaps the smile is new to him too, because it comes with a peculiar whiteness in the face, intensified by the blackness of his hat, and there is a flicker to his smile like a faulty light bulb that doesn't know whether it's on or off.

And I am as much at a loss as he appears to be. A tiredness has come over me which I suspect is fear. Ignore him? Give him a cheery wave and continue with my planned escape? He will come after me. He will raise a hue and cry. He's got a plan too, but what is it?

The sickly-pale smile continues to flicker. There is something about his lower jaw, an irritation he seems unable to control. And has he actually *broken* his right arm? Is that why it's jammed so awkwardly in his coat pocket? He makes no effort to get up. I set out towards him, closely observed by the seated ladies in white hats. In the whole courtyard, we are the only two males and Christoph cuts an eccentric, not to say gargantuan figure, occupying a whole stage to himself. What is my business with him? they are wondering. So am I. I come to a halt in front of him. Nothing of him moves. He could be one of those bronze statues of great men you see seated in public places: a Churchill, a Roosevelt. The same moist complexion, the same unconvincing smile.

The statue comes slowly to life in a way that other statues don't. He uncrosses his legs, then with his right shoulder high and his right hand still jammed in his overcoat pocket, shuffles his big body until there is space on the bench for me at his left side. And yes, he is sickly pale, and agitated around the jaw, now smiling, now grimacing, and his gaze is feverish.

'Who told you where to find me, Christoph?' I ask him as cheerfully as I may, because by now I am grappling with the far-fetched notion that Bunny or Laura, or even Tabitha, has put him on to me, with the aim of negotiating some other kind of underhand deal between the Service and its litigants.

'I remembered' – the smile widening with dreamy pride – 'I'm a memory genius, okay? The brain of fucking Germany. So we have our nice meal and you tell me to go fuck myself. Okay, you didn't tell me. I go away. I sit down with my friends. I smoke a little, I snort a little, I listen. Who do I hear? Want a guess?'

I shake my head. I'm smiling too.

'My daddy. I hear my daddy. His voice. On one of our little walks together round the prison courtyard. I'm doing time, he's trying to play catch-up, be the ever-faithful father he never was. So he's talking about himself, entertaining me, telling me about the years we didn't spend together, like pretending we did. What it was like to be a spook. How special you all were, how dedicated. Such naughty boys you were. And you know what? He's talking about *Hood House*. The house of hoods. This joke you all had. How the Circus owned these crappy safe flats in a place called Hood House. We're all hoods, so that's where they put us.' The smile becomes a scowl of indignation. 'You know your shit Service has even got you *registered* here under your own name, for fuck's sake? P. Guillam. How's *that* for security? Did you *know* that?' he demanded.

No. I didn't know. Neither was I marvelling, as I should have done, that in more than half a century, the Service hadn't thought to change its habits.

'So why don't you tell me what you've come for?' I asked him, unsettled by his smile, which he seemed unable to shake off.

'To kill you, Pierrot,' he explained, with no lift or variation to his voice. 'To shoot your fucking head off. Bingo. You're dead.'

'Here?' I asked. 'In front of all these people? How?'

With a Walther P38 semi-automatic pistol: the one he has drawn from the right-hand pocket of his overcoat and is now brandishing in plain sight; and only after plenty of time for me to admire it does he restore it to his overcoat pocket while keeping his hand on it and, in the best tradition of gangster movies, pointing the barrel at me through the folds of his coat. What the ladies in white hats make of this display, if anything at all, I shall never know. Perhaps we're a film unit. Perhaps we're just silly grown-up boys, playing a game with a toy gun.

'Good gracious me,' I exclaim – a term I had never consciously used in my life until now – 'wherever did you get *that* from?'

The question annoyed him, extinguishing the smile.

'You think I don't know wise guys in this fucking town? People who will lend me a gun like *that*?' he demanded, flicking the thumb and forefinger of his free hand in my face.

Prompted by the word *lend*, I peered instinctively round for the rightful owner, since I was not imagining a long-term loan: which was how my eye came to settle on a Volvo saloon repaired in various colours and parked on a double yellow line directly opposite the archway on the Embankment side; and its one bald male driver with both hands on the wheel, staring hard ahead of him through the windscreen.

'Do you have a particular reason for killing me, Christoph?' I asked him, maintaining as best I could the same note of casual enquiry. 'I've told the powers that be of your offer, if that's what you're worried about,' I threw in mendaciously. 'They're thinking about it. Her Majesty's bean-counters don't cough up a million euros overnight, naturally.'

'I was the best thing in his lousy rotten life. He told me that.'

Spoken in a low tone, forced from between rigid teeth.

'I never doubted that he loved you,' I said.

'You killed him. You lied to my dad and you killed him. Your friend, my dad.'

'Christoph, that's not true. Your dad and Liz Gold weren't killed by me or anyone else in the Circus. They were killed by Hans-Dieter Mundt of the Stasi.'

'You're all sick. All you spies. You're not the cure, you're the fucking disease. Jerk-off artists, playing jerk-off games, thinking you're the biggest fucking wise guys in the universe. You're nothings, hear me? You live in the fucking dark because you can't handle the fucking daylight. Him too. He told me that.'

'He did? When?'

'In prison, where the fuck d'you think? My first prison. Kids' prison. Pervs, cokeheads and me. *Somebody to see you, Christoph. Says he's your best pal.* They cuff me and take me to him. It's my dad. Hear this, he says. You're a lost cause and there's fuck all that I or anybody else can do for you any more. But Alec Leamas loves his son, so don't fucking forget it. You speak?'

'No.'

'Stand the fuck up. Walk. That way. Through the archway. Like the rest of the people. You fuck with me, I kill you.'

I stand up. I walk towards the archway. He follows me, his right hand still in his pocket and the gun pointed at me through the cloth. There are things you're supposed to do in these cases, like wheel round and catch him with your elbow before he has time to fire. We rehearsed it with water pistols at Sarratt, and more often than not the water squirted past you on to the gym mat. But this isn't a water pistol, and it isn't Sarratt. Christoph's walking four feet behind me, which is where the well-taught gunman should be.

We have passed through the archway. The bald man sitting in the multi-coloured Volvo still has his hands on the steering wheel and although we're walking straight towards him he pays us no attention, he's too busy staring ahead. Does Christoph intend to take me for the proverbial ride before he puts me out of my misery? If he does, my best chance of breaking free will come when he tries to get me into the Volvo. I'd done that once long ago: broken a man's hand for him with the car door when he was trying to get me to climb into the back seat.

Other cars are passing in both directions, and we have to wait for a gap in the traffic before we cross the road, and I'm wondering whether I'll get a chance to grapple with him and in the worst case shove him at an oncoming car. We've reached the opposite pavement and I'm still wondering. We've also walked past the Volvo without a sign or word passing between Christoph and its bald driver, so maybe I've got it wrong and they're nothing to do with each other, and whoever lent Christoph the Walther is sitting in Hackney or somewhere, playing a game of cards with his fellow wise guys.

We are standing on the Embankment and there's a brick parapet about five feet high and I'm standing facing it, with the river in front of me and the lights of Lambeth on the other bank because it's dusk already, still mild for the time of day, a nice breeze coming up and quite big boats gliding by, and I have my hands on the parapet and my back to him and I'm hoping that he'll come close enough for me to try the water-pistol trick, but I can't feel his presence, and he's not talking.

Keeping my hands wide where he can see them, I turn slowly round and he's standing six feet away from me, still with his hand in his pocket. He's breathing in gulps and his big pale face is moist and luminous in the half-light. People pass us by, but they don't pass between us. Something about us tells them to step around us. More accurately it's something about Christoph's bulk, overcoat and Homburg hat. Is he brandishing the gun again, or is it in his pocket? Is he still adopting his gangster posture? It occurs to me, late in the day, that the man who dresses like that wants to be feared; and the man who wants to be feared is afraid himself, and perhaps this is what gives me the bravado to challenge him.

'Come on, Christoph, do it,' I say, as a middle-aged couple

scurry past. 'Shoot me, if that's what you've come for. What's another year to a man of my age? I'll settle for a good clean death any time. Shoot me. Then spend the rest of your life congratulating yourself while you rot in jail. You've seen old men die in prison. Be another.'

By now the muscles in my back are squirming and there's a pulse beating in my ears and I couldn't have told you whether it came from a passing barge or was something going on inside my own head. My mouth had gone dry from all the speaking and my gaze must have misted over, because it took me a while to acknowledge that Christoph was beside me, slouched over the parapet, retching and sobbing in gulps of pain and anger.

I put an arm across his back and eased his right hand free of his pocket. When it came out with no gun in it, I drew out the gun for him and slung it as far as I could into the river, but heard nothing in reply. He had his arms on the parapet and had sunk his head into them. I fished around in his other pocket, on the off-chance that he had provided himself with a spare magazine to embolden him, and sure enough he had. I had just thrown that into the river too when the bald man from the multi-coloured Volvo, who by contrast with Christoph was very small and looked half starved, seized him by the waist from behind and hauled at him, to no effect.

Between us we prised him away from the parapet and between us we manhandled him as far as the Volvo. As we did so, he began to howl. I made to open the passenger door, but my companion-in-arms had already opened the back door. Between us we bundled him in and slammed the door after him, damping but not silencing the howls. The Volvo drove away. I stood alone on the pavement. Slowly the traffic and the sounds returned. I was alive. I hailed a cab and asked the driver to take me to the British Museum.

★

First the cobbled alley. Then the private car park that stank of rotting rubbish. Then the six kissing gates: ours was the end one on the right. If Christoph's howls were still ringing in my head, I refused to hear them. The fastener on the gate squeaked. I heard that all right. It always had done, however many times we oiled it. If we knew Control was coming we'd leave the gate open so we wouldn't have to listen to the old devil's sour comment about being heralded by the clashing of cymbals. Slabs of York stone. Mendel and I had laid them. And sowed grass between. Our birdhouse. No bird turned away. Three steps to the kitchen door, and Millie McCraig's motionless shadow looking down on me through the window, holding her hand up, forbidding me to enter.

We stand in an improvised garden shed, built against the wall to shelter her dustbins and the remnants of her ladies' upright bicycle, exiled from the house by Laura, draped in a tarpaulin and stripped of its wheels for security. We are speaking in murmurs. Perhaps we always did. The classified cat watches from the kitchen window.

'I don't know what they've put where, Peter,' she confides. 'I don't trust my telephone. Well, I never did. I don't trust my walls either. I don't know what they've got these days, nor where they put it.'

'You heard what Tabitha said to me about evidence?'

'Part, I did. Enough.'

'Have you still got everything we gave you? The original statements, correspondence, whatever else George asked you to hide away?'

'Microdotted by myself. Cached. I have too.'

'Where?'

'In my garden. In my birdhouse. In their cassettes. In oilskins. In that' – *that* being the remnants of her bicycle. 'They don't know where to *look* these days, Peter. They've no proper *training*,' she adds indignantly.

'Including George's interview with Windfall at Camp 4? The recruitment interview? The deal?'

'I do. As part of my classic collection of gramophone records. Transferred for me by Oliver Mendel. I listen to them now and then. For George's voice. I still love it. Are you married at all, Peter?'

'Just the farm and the animals. Who have you got, Millie?'

'I've my memories. And my Maker. The new lot have given me till Monday to get out. I'll not keep them waiting.'

'Where will you go?'

'I'll die. Same as you. I've a sister in Aberdeen. I'll not let you have them, Peter, if that's what you've come for.'

'Not for the greater good?'

'There's no greater good without George's say-so. There never was.'

'Where is he?'

'I don't know. And I'd not tell you if I did. Alive, for sure. The cards I get on my birthday and at Christmas. He never forgets. Always to my sister, never here, security. Same as always.'

'If I had to find him, who would I go to? There's someone, Millie. You know who it is.'

'Maybe Jim. If he'll tell you.'

'Can I call him? What's his number?'

'Jim's not a telephone man. Not any more.'

'But he's in the same place?'

'So I believe.'

Without another word she grasps my shoulders in her fierce, spindly hands and grants me one stern kiss of her sealed lips.

★

251

I got as far as Reading that night, and lay up in a hostel near the railway station where no one bothered with names. If I hadn't by now been reported missing from Dolphin Square, the first person to notice my absence would be Tabitha at ten next morning, not nine. If there was going to be a hue and cry, I didn't see it breaking before midday. I breakfasted at leisure, bought a ticket to Exeter and stood in the corridor of an overcrowded train as far as Taunton. By way of the car park, I headed for the outskirts of town and hung around waiting for the dusk to fall.

I hadn't clapped eyes on Jim Prideaux since Control had sent him on the abortive mission to Czecho that had cost him a bullet in the back and the unsleeping attention of a Czech torture team. By birth, we were both mongrels: Jim part Czech and part Norman, where I'm Breton. But there the comparison stopped. The Slav in Jim ran deep. As a boy, he had run messages and cut German throats for Czech Resistance. Cambridge may have educated him, but it never tamed him. When he joined the Circus, even Sarratt's close-combat instructors learned to be wary of him.

A cab dropped me at the main gates. A muddy green sign read NOW OPEN FOR GIRLS. A pitted drive wound towards a dilapidated stately home surrounded by low prefabricated buildings. Picking my way between potholes, I passed a playing field, a tumbledown cricket pavilion, a couple of labourers' cottages and a group of shaggy ponies grazing in a paddock. Two boys on bicycles rode by, the larger with a violin on his back, the smaller a cello. I waved them down.

'I'm looking for Mr Prideaux,' I said. They peered blankly at each other. 'A member of your staff here, I'm told. Teaches languages. Or used to.'

The larger boy shook his head and started to ride on.

'You don't mean *Jim*, do you?' the younger one said. 'Old bloke

252

with a limp. Lives in a caravan in the Dip. Does French Extra and Junior Rugby.'

'What's the Dip?'

'Keep left past School House, down the track till you see an old Alvis. We're late actually.'

I keep left. Behind tall windows, small boys and girls crouch at desks under white neon lights. Reaching the other side of the building, I passed through an avenue of temporary classrooms. A track descended towards a clump of pine trees. In front of them, under a tarpaulin, the outlines of a vintage car; and beside it a caravan with one light burning in the curtained window. Strains of Mahler issued from it. I knocked on the door and a gruff voice responded in fury.

'Go away, boy! *Fous-moi la paix!* Look it up.'

I went round to the curtained window and, with a pen from my pocket, reached up and tapped out my pinpoint, then gave him time to put away his gun, if that's what he was doing, because with Jim you never knew.

★

A bottle of slivovitz on the table, half drunk. Jim has produced a second glass and switched off his record player. By the paraffin lamp his craggy face is crooked with pain and age, his uneven back propped against the meagre upholstery. The tortured are a class apart. You can imagine – just – where they've been, but never what they've brought back.

'Bloody school collapsed,' he barks, with a burst of hectic laughter. 'Thursgood, fellow's name was. Headmaster. Perfectly good wife. Couple of kids. Turned out to be a bloody pansy,' he declared, with exaggerated derision. 'Did a moonlight flit with the school chef. Took the fees with him. New Zealand or somewhere. Not enough in the kitty to pay the staff till the end of the week. Never thought he had it in him. *Well'* – chuckling, as he tops up our glasses – 'what to *do*, eh? Can't leave the kids in the lurch, middle of a school year. Exams coming up. First Eleven fixtures. School prizes. I had my pension, plus a bit of extra for getting myself knocked about. Couple of parents chipped in. George knew a banker. Well, after that, school's not going to sling me out, is it?' He drank, eyeing me over his glass. 'Not going to pack me off to Czecho on another wild goose chase, are you? Not now they're cosying up to Moscow again.'

'I need to talk to George,' I said.

For a while nothing happened. From the darkening world outside, just the rustle of trees and the moan of cattle. And in front of me, Jim's lopsided body hoisted motionless against the wall of the little caravan, and his Slav gaze glowering at me from under ragged black brows.

'Been bloody good to me over the years, old George has. Welfaring a clapped-out joe, not everybody's taste. Not sure he needs you, frankly. Have to ask him.'

'How would you do that?'

'Not a natural player of the spying game, George. Don't know how he got himself into it. Took it all on his own shoulders. Can't do that in our trade. Can't feel all the other chaps' pain as well as your own. Not if you want to carry on. That bloody wife of his had a lot to answer for, my view. Hell she think she was up to?' he demanded, and once again fell silent, grimacing, daring me to answer his question.

But Jim had never cared much for women, and there was no answer I could offer him that didn't include the name of his nemesis and former lover Bill Haydon, who had recruited him to the Circus, betrayed him to his masters and slept with Smiley's wife for cover along the way.

'Got himself all cut up about *Karla*, of all people,' he was